## About the Author

I am Paul Tuley. Having served nine years in the army, I have travelled and enjoyed it immensely.

I have worked as a security guard on the Thames flood barriers, followed by another lifetime in warehousing.

Now, I write a little, hoping to entertain someone, somewhere, with these female-based fantasies

# Adhiambo and the Luo Lake Goddess

Paul Tuley

# Adhiambo and the Luo Lake Goddess

Olympia Publishers
*London*

**www.olympiapublishers.com**
OLYMPIA PAPERBACK EDITION

Copyright © Paul Tuley 2020

The right of Paul Tuley to be identified as author of
this work has been asserted in accordance with sections 77 and 78
of the Copyright, Designs and Patents Act 1988.

**All Rights Reserved**

No reproduction, copy or transmission of this publication
may be made without written permission.
No paragraph of this publication may be reproduced,
copied or transmitted save with the written permission of the
publisher, or in accordance with the provisions
of the Copyright Act 1956 (as amended).

Any person who commits any unauthorised act in relation to
this publication may be liable to criminal
prosecution and civil claims for damage.

A CIP catalogue record for this title is
available from the British Library.

ISBN: 978-1-78830-571-6

This is a work of fiction.
Names, characters, places and incidents originate from the writer's
imagination. Any resemblance to actual persons, living or dead, is
purely coincidental.

First Published in 2020

Olympia Publishers
Tallis House
2 Tallis Street
London
EC4Y 0AB

Printed in Great Britain

# Dedication

Intonix Media, Nairobi, Kenya, for taking the cover photos in Lamu City.

Belinda Adhiambo and Betina Awuor Ogwayo for being the cover women.

# INTRODUCTION

Fathers,
do not shackle your daughters,
so that they can only see the sun,
through the dirty window.
Do not despise
debase your daughter!
Give her liberty,
free her from the confines,
of her chains.

Open the door —
so that she can run
to the sun.
Feel its warmth,
inherit its wisdom.

As your daughter sits
beneath the stars,
her teacher shares her knowledge
and experiences with her.
So shall your daughter gain,
her wisdom, intellect, knowledge .
Your daughter will be able
to count the stars,

She sits with the elders.
Making a life of her own
Then share it
With her own daughter.
All because her father
opened the door,
to let the sun come in.

Ever since Anjella had known him, she was very fearful of his fractious outlook on life; of his presence and his outward-glaring bluster. She never wanted to get close to him, definitely did not want to be in his social circle. She knew he was a thug, bully, ireful, a disrespectful boy with a violent temper. Uncontrollable, due to him being fatherless, his mother worked all hours to provide for him, but still he showed her no motherly love, only disdain. Most of the time when they were at school he was odious, always hanging around with his gang of jerks and sidekicks. None of them ever learnt anything of any use, not one of them knew that they lived in the capital of Kenya. How bad is that! He and his coolies just hung around the back streets of Nairobi, knowingly mixing with the mobsters, miscreants of the Light of Africa, a terrorist outfit that had sprung up as a foil against Western influence and education. They did not have any goal or aspirations, nor conception of what they actually wanted to succeed in, masquerading as a cult with some sort of religious influence. Anjella liked the company of her two dear friends, Suzie Wokabi and Jeanette Oromo, a tight knit trio, never far from each other. Almost all the time where you found one, the other two would be. Always discussing their thoughts, ideas and dreams. What did they hope to do when they left school? Anjella was hoping to become a doctor. Suzie wanted to get into the beauty business, Jeanette wanted to be able to communicate with people and, with as many as possible.

The young Michael grew up ignorant of most things, spending nearly all his spare time with the social outcasts, out of work dragon chasers and vagrants. He spent hardly any time at school. He could get his hand on any sort of weapon he desired, was shown how to make IEDs[1], along with EODs[2], both large and small. He knew who to see in case he ever needed forged documents. Michael was and has been indoctrinated, not only by his Kenyan counterparts, but also other willing insurgents from Ethiopia, Somalia, Uganda, Tanzania, Sudan and South Sudan. Now at the age of eighteen, having dropped out of any formal education three years earlier, he finally though he was a man of the world, that everyone looked up to him, especially Anjella. She was two years younger than Michael, yet she still didn't want to see him or be with him, requiring him to keep his distance from her, so she could study, wanting to make a life for herself.

    He thought respect was guaranteed, not realising that in the real world, respect had to be earned. He thought that, because he could do just as he wanted, there would be no consequences, that he would be able to escape everything that came his way. He had already made an explosive device, crossed the border into Uganda, and planted it in the first official building that he came across, in the dead of night. Then drove back into Kenya, getting his head down, sleeping the rest of the night away. On rising the following morning, he laughed, joking with his buddies at the carnage and devastation he had caused, after watching the outcome that was shown on the television, with a journalist reporting the facts on site. On receiving so much enthused congratulations from his fellow usurpers, he went round to Anjella's home. She was studying in her bedroom and did not want to answer the door, so Michael Ironi forced his way in. he just marched

---

[1] Improvised explosive device
[2] Explosive ordnance disposal

into her bedroom, telling her what he had just achieved. Then he jumped onto her bed, squatting over her.

"Do you respect me now, Anjella?"

"No, Michael. I have never respected you, never will. You are just a thug and a lout."

Then she pushed him off her. Tumbling off her bed onto the floor, he looked quite silly and submissive just lying there. Then he saw red, he had always thought that this young lady had been for him, waiting for him to mature. Now he knew that it had all been in his mind, that she did not feel the same way as he did. He picked himself off the floor and, without a second thought, he threw her down onto her bed. Forcing himself on to her. Getting this sixteen-year-old girl, to perform felatio on him, he then indulged in cunnilingus on Anjella. Then he took her doggy style, with full vigorous penetration, fornicating, ejaculating into her chaste, virgin body. Taking all her self-worth, self-esteem and self-respect from her, all in a single flourish. Mr Michael Ironi thought there and then that he was the man. He had finally had the girl of his dreams; but now he regretted it so much, his selfish impulse, his desire to impregnate the young, provocative Anjella, was not quite what he expected. Between the sobs and the heavy-duty tears streaming down her cheeks, she now stood up, facing her rapist. She told him there and then shouting at him, as he backed away from her:

"YOU ARE A VILE, IRRESPONSIBLE, INEPT, INANE PIG. YOU ONLY THINK OF YOURSELF, BUT IF I FALL PREGNANT, I WILL BE GOING TO THE POLICE TO REPORT YOU. NOT ONLY FOR RAPING ME, BUT ALSO AS THE UGANDAN BOMBER, YOU DEPRAVED WASTER."

"What will it take for you not to report me. to the Nairobi authorities, Anjella?"

Now he cowered away from her, he was unsure of what to do. He had always fancied Anjella, even when they were at school. He knew she was very intelligent, having had plans to go to university. Michael had always been under the false impression that she had been tied to him. He thought she had been besotted with his larger-than-life attitude.

"It will take your oath that you will always look after me and our child, no matter whether it is a daughter or son. No matter where this crazy world you live in takes you. I want my child and myself to be safe and out of harm's way. Regardless of the danger you put yourself in. You are the father, from this moment in time, or you will have no life at all. Especially as you have just ruined my future, you have brought it down, crashing around me in a million pieces."

"OK, Anjella, we will be partners. You will look after the two of you. I will make sure that the three of us have somewhere to live. That we have money to survive, that will be on my back."

"In that case your secret will be safe with me. No one will ever know or glean the information from me."

Michael takes a signet ring from his finger that his father had given him a lifetime ago. Now placing it on Anjella's thumb, he looked deep into her sparkling brown eyes,

"This now ties us together Anjella. Until one of us departs this sinister world."

"OK, Michael, until death separates us, we are as one."

Now Michael is more involved with the Light of Africa, ransacking and robbing three branches of the Kenyan Co-operative Bank. Creeping out at the dead of night, the crack of dawn or at the time of the deepest twilight, he bombed two of the local police stations and a subsidised Western school, along with an electrical substation. Then he would sneak back home, at just the strangest times of day he could imagine. Then the fractious blaggard was venturing off to Tanzania, Uganda, Ethiopia and Somalia, being deployed as an insurgent bomber, because of his prowess at creating his own devices. He was essentially there to disrupt all the governments in and around his home country of Kenya. He was also away to South Sudan, showing some of their soldiers of the Light of Africa, how to make IEDs as well as EODs. Anjella confided in her two girlfriends Suzie and Jeanette, that she did not feel very well. They both cuddled her, trying to make her feel better, when neither of them were ever going to be able to.

The young petrified Anjella could feel something was not right, with her immature, ravaged body. So she had to get her father, Ramon to take her to the Nairobi Women's Hospital and Medical School, seeing as how Michael was not there to assist her in any way possible. A young scared girl under the age of seventeen, all alone — not what she wanted! So her father drove her to the hospital. They took her immediately to the Gynaecology and Oncology Unit, straight into the operating theatre, to give birth to her first child. She now knew it was breached, they told her it was "flexed breached", with the umbilical cord wrapped around the baby's neck, so that caused further complications. Anjella was so young, they decided to perform a caesarean section. The gynaecologist had already explained that the infant's body was the wrong way round. So it would come out bottom first, instead of head first. The delivery was very painful, exhausting, slow and very deliberate: even with the use of painkillers. The specialist hoped he could give life to the new baby, as well as keeping alive, the over-young mother as well. So that the mother and baby would spend a lifetime together. With some temperance, lots of patience, care and tenderness, with all the attending nurses talking to her, after a long four hours, both the mother and daughter came out the battle together. With all the temperance they could muster, the team with their combined experience, knowledge and tenderness showing that they all loved their job. Anjella drifted in and out of a strange existence for a long excruciating four hours or more. But finally both mother and daughter came out of it, surviving together. Both felt extremely weak and weary but with a bond no one was ever going to sever, or break. They were entwined forever within each other's lives. Always protecting each other, any way they could, from this day forward. They would need to, especially from the husband and father they had both inherited. The pain was made more bearable by the constant appearance of Anjella's two dear friends, the beautiful Suzie Wokabi and the delightful Jeanette Oromo, always at her side giving her all the assistance she needed.

He came waltzing in, back from the Sudan, thinking he was going to claim his home as his own.

"Anjella, Anjella, where are you? Answer me! Where are you hiding?"

It was Tristina who answered him, shouting at him in disgust:

"I SEE THE HERO IS HOME! WANTS SOME ATTENTION DOES HE? HAVE YOU MADE ENOUGH BOMBS TO BLOW UP EAST AFRICA WHILE MY SIXTEEN-YEAR-OLD DAUGHTER HAS A BREECHED

DELIVERY THAT NEARLY KILLED HER, GIVING BIRTH TO MY GRANDDAUGHTER?"

"Damnation, I forgot she was so close to her delivery date. It was not an easy birth then?"

"NO, NOT FOR A SIXTEEN-YEAR-OLD GIRL, WITH NO ONE TO CARE FOR HER, OR BOTHER TO BE THERE FOR HER. JUST A HERO THAT CAUSES DEATH, DESTRUCTION AND FAMINE."

Tristina begrudgingly puts a plate of food in front of him, "Which hospital did she go to?"

The mother-in-law completely ignores him as she gets on with the weekly wash. Not answering him, nor intending to help the smug, self-satisfied waster in any way at all.

"I asked you a question, old lady."

"I chose to ignore it. If you are that interested, go and check all the hospitals and find them. Can you even remember my daughter's name?"

Michael finishes his meal. Knowing when he is not wanted, he goes out, driving around all the local hospitals, looking for Anjella. Finally, he finds her at the Nairobi Women's Hospital, going in and up to the front desk.

"I am looking for Anjella Ogwayo."

"She is in ICU."

"Can I see her?"

"Hold on, sir, who are you?"

"I am Michael Ironi, her partner, father of her child."

"Let me find out for you."

The attending nurse at reception phones the appropriate department, to find out how the patient is.

"Can the father come up and see mother and child?"

He strains but cannot hear the answer, but she is smiling at him as she replaces the phone.

"Yes, sir, you can visit, straight down the hall to the end. Turn right, there you will find ICU."

"OK."

He strides down following the directions, going as quickly as he can, getting to the unit. He is stopped by the matron.

"Who are you, sir?"

"I am Anjella Ogwayo's partner and father to her baby,"

"OK, sir, quietly please, she is asleep. Third bed on the left."

Michael treads very softly, making his way to her room. Finding her father at her side, he looks up failing to be impressed.

"So, Michael, here you are at last. You missed their big fight to survive, luckily they both made it, mother and daughter fighting to be together. She is a little jewel, beautiful, captivating. She has your sense of survival, but she has Anjella's eyes, elegance, beauty and eloquence."

"When did she give birth Mr Ogwayo?"

"Early hours of yesterday evening. It took them four hours, to deliver the baby. Now they just need rest, quiet and support. So that they can both recover from the battle they put up, to survive. Anjella needs to recover from the labour pains she endured."

"How long do you and Mrs Ogwayo plan on staying?"

"Until Anjella and the baby no longer need us in attendance. The doctor told us about six to eight weeks."

"Why is that?"

"We know we cannot trust you to stay with her and the child. Your occupation seems to be far more important than your daughter's and so-called partner's problems. The dressings on Anjella, will need changing daily. She cannot do anything for herself for at least six weeks. She and the baby will need feeding, Anjella can breastfeed her daughter. Are you going to do the laundry, the shopping, cooking, along with all the other running around? Not you, that is for sure, Michael."

"In that case you and Tristina can stay there and welcome. I will find somewhere else to stay, out of the way, until they can fend for themselves. Then I will return, claiming my place back, with my daughter, alongside her mother."

"That is fine by me. I just need to make sure my daughter and granddaughter both make it out of here in one piece. As soon as they are both well enough to get up, that Anjella is capable of looking after her daughter properly, then we shall both leave, you can come back. Then carry on from where you left off, with each other."

Michael sneers at the old man, not overly beholden to him at all. They have never liked each other, but try to get along, for Anjella's sake. Mr Ironi storms out of the IC unit, disturbing everyone within it. Anjella turns and winces, then falls back into her original comfortable position. She mutters just loudly enough to her dear father.

"Is Belinda here, Dad, Is she safe, does she need feeding?"

"She is right beside you Anjella. I will not let anyone take her from your side. She is fast asleep my princess, you rest. I will be here for you both, if you need me. Your baby will not move, until her mum is ready to pick her up and feed her."

Anjella smiles as she falls back into a groggy, drug-induced sleep, all for her own good, aiding a swifter recovery for both Anjella and her baby. Now she is out for the count, deep in slumber, taking a well-earned rest so that she can completely recover from the unexpected, dangerous ordeal, all stemming from the day she had a wastrel in her bedroom, without her parents knowing. She had never told them that she was raped on that fateful day. Mrs and Mr Ogwayo, thinking that their daughter is paying the ultimate price for being a silly young girl, infatuated with the infamy of being tied into the life of a young terrorist. But Mr Ogwayo promised his wife that there would be no reprisals or recriminations, no splitting the family because of one simple mistake. The only things that mattered, above all else, were the lives of their daughter and, the blessed new life of their granddaughter. So Ramon sits there, biting his tongue, biding his time, just hoping that they still have a beautiful young daughter, along with an even more astounding granddaughter, at the end of it all. Gradually he fell asleep in the chair they provided for him. Staying at her bedside, he resolved that he would leave the hospital with two precious beings under his wing, both alive and in good health. So that his wife, Nanny Ogwayo could fuss and be broody over the two of them, for as long as she cared to.

Once the change of shifts had concluded, Mr Ogwayo awakes, a little stiff with a slight chill in his old bones. He gets up, walks around, getting his blood flowing, slowly easing the cold and stiffness from his body. He has been here for three days now, helping as much as he is able, at Anjella's bedside assisting her when she needs to manoeuvre her daughter into the correct position for feeding. He makes sure they both get as much contact as possible, so that mother and daughter can make the bonds they need, as quickly as possible.

"Mr Ogwayo, the gynaecologist is just coming through, to visit Anjella and her daughter. Could you give us about fifteen minutes, please."

"Of course, Sister, I need a coffee and to phone the wife."

"Thank you, very much."

Ramon leaves to get himself a strong black coffee, just as the surgeon goes into Anjella's unit. The old man is talking to his wife.

"I might find out today. The specialist has just this minute, gone in to see her and baby. I will call you back as soon as I know. Loving you Tristina."

Ramon prowls up and down the hallway, waiting for the doctor to re-emerge from the IC unit. When he finally sees him walk out, talking to the sister, just before he leaves, Ramon walks back up to the unit, catching the sister by tapping her on the shoulder, she turns around smiling at him,

"Sister please did he tell you anything, about Anjella and her daughter?"

"Yes Mr Ogwayo. He is very happy with their recovery. If you want to take her home, you can. But she must not do anything for eight weeks, she will need to be attended to, for all of that time, she is so young and frail. The baby daughter will need lots of attention as well."

"Yes, me and the wife will both be there for them both. So they can both rest, for as long as they need to."

"That is good. We have also shown Anjella how to express her milk, so she can carry on feeding her daughter. So that will help her get better, with drinking mother's milk. Also, in her bag we have put extra wound dressings, that will need to be changed every day. If there is anything you are unsure about, please bring her back to us. She will also need a course of antibiotics, which are these, for the next three months. To stop any infection."

"We will pay close attention to both our daughter and granddaughter, if something seems wrong, I will bring her back."

"We are just doing the paperwork for her release, if you would like to sit with Anjella, we will bring it to you, as soon as it is ready to sign."

Ramon goes back to the bed, sitting with Anjella, who is now rather perky, bright eyed, and in the process of feeding her daughter.

"Anjella, you look like a ray of sunshine, baby too. Two pearls from the same oyster."

"Thank you, Dad, you have been amazing staying here with me. Where is Mum?"

"She is at home, getting everything ready for your return. She has fed Michael, but he did not stay."

"Did he come here at all?"

"He did for a short while, but you were asleep, so you missed him."

"Did he stay long?"

"About half an hour, talking to me."

"What did you both talk about?"

"I told him that your mother and myself would be staying with you, until you are properly better. Also, until you are able to look after your daughter, as well."

"What was his response to that?"

"He was not happy in the slightest. I told him he could not look after you, he was the last person we would trust with you and the baby's welfare. He told me, that he would find somewhere else to stay."

"That is good to hear. I would much prefer you and Mum looking after me and Belinda. Michael thinks so much more of his job than ever bothering to look out for me and his new daughter."

"He is just a thug, a mobster after all. He is not worried about life, his only interest is death, disruption, degrading people who have done him no harm at all."

"I never have liked Michael, even at school when he bothered to attend, he was a bully, blaggard and a coward."

"Then why did you let him into your bedroom, have sex with him Anjella, when we were not there? We thought we had taught you different from that."

"Have you seen the size of the man, compared to me Dad, a sixteen-year-old virgin?"

"I know he is a brute, an evil demeaning, implacable beast, he always will be."

"Do you want to know the truth about your granddaughter, Dad. Can you take it, then perhaps you will understand once and for all?"

"OK, tell me, Anjella, my *mondo*, what happened on that day?"

"I was studying alone for my upcoming exams, when I heard a loud bang. Which as it turned out, was Michael forcing the front door open. He called my name three, four times. I did not answer him, hoping he would leave. But he came, found me in my bedroom with only my dressing gown on. He seemed insatiable, transfixed. He just stood there, at first. I could see he was very excited. That was probably me, improperly dressed, at the time. I was not expecting any visitors. Then he undressed himself in front of me, disclosing just how aroused he was. He then knelt on the bed, pulled me by the hair, forcing me to perform felatio on him. I was already in tears, when he pushed me onto my back, to perform cunnilingus. I shouted at him, telling him to leave the house, before you and Mum returned. But he just ignored me. Instead, he sat on me, his hand across my throat, squeezing it. I had given up trying to force him off me. I managed to scream st him, that he had no right to do this to me. I think that is when he saw red, losing his temper with me. he had one hand squeezing my throat, the other pulling my hair as if he was going to pull it out. He looked into my eyes, telling me I was his submissive, he could do just as he liked with me. Slamming his whole body against mine, three or four times. He ejaculated, leaving himself inside me, until he had finished. I could feel the force generated, because he hurt me. it was still hurting when you and Mum finally came home. I could not tell you what had happened, because I felt degraded and unclean, that it was my fault that it had happened. Does that make you happy now, that you know Belinda was not planned? Was not the final result of some romantic love-making session."

"No, it does not make me happy at all. I am sorry I stirred all these nasty thoughts back up again, for you to live through. But we must never let Belinda know of this. You will have to tell your mother, now that you have told me. I will be with you Anjella, you tell her this evening, when we get home, OK?"

"OK, Dad, but I want you sitting next to me when I do it."

Dad went to Anjella, kissing her, helping he to tuck those dark memories away once again. Then he kissed baby Belinda, knowing she would always have his love as long a she lived. Both Anjella and Ramon signed the release forms. One of the nurses assisted Anjella in getting dressed, then sat her in the wheelchair, sitting Belinda on her lap. The same nurse pushed her out to Ramon's car. Getting them both comfortable, she then thanked all the nursing staff for their patience, care and attention over the past four days. Then Ramon drove her home, back to sanity, sanctuary and security, but most of all the spectacular love of Mum and Grandmother.

"Mum, Mum? We are home."

Tristina comes running out, smiling, wrapping her arms around Anjella and the delightful baby Belinda. Ramon looks up.

"Tristina my love, would you take Belinda, while I bring Anjella in?"

"Of course Ramon, then I can get them both comfortable, while you bring the rest of their belongings in."

Anjella is sat in pride of place, on the three-seat sofa, all smiles at the joy of being home. But also with a little trepidation filling her, knowing now that she is home, she has to tell her mum about the woeful night of the conception, of the jewel that is her granddaughter. But Dad would be here, so everything would be fine between the four of them, just as it was before. No secrets between them, well nearly no secrets. Ramon came in with the small suitcase, putting them to one side as his wife had made a pot of fresh tea, to go with the freshly baked almond cake and *maandazi*[3]. Ramon squeezed the blackcurrants into his cup, pouring the hot tea over them, just as Tristina squeezed the redcurrants into her cup, pouring the tea over her favourite flavour. Anjella just stuck with the vanilla, sipping it cautiously, as it was still hot. Grandmother

---

[3] See glossary

was cooing over her *mondo*, Belinda, not being able to concentrate on anything else at that precise moment in time.

"Anjella, I think now is a good time to tell your mother about the night of the conception of Belinda."

"I do, Dad. This is beautiful just the three of us at home. Mum, do you know on the night I was alone, when you and Dad were both out of the house?"

"Yes Anjella, what of it?"

"You have always thought I let Michael in, so that we could have sex."

"Yes, my dear, but I have never thought any more of it."

"Well, I have told Dad what really happened. So now I need to you the whole story. So are you ready to listen?"

"Yes my precious daughter, I am ready to listen to you. But I get the feeling I am not going to enjoy this, one iota."

Anjella tells her mother the whole sad story, just the same way she had told her father. Not missing a single thing out, both women sat on the sofa, in each other's arms, cradling each other, as the tears rolled from their eyes, in a constant flow. During the sobbing Tristina managed to say:

"So it was worse than I thought, Anjella. It was a complete mistake, thinking that you let him in, then casually had sex. That he actually forced himself upon you, a schoolgirl, all your education wasted, my dear."

"He told me he will be the father, he will look after us. So at least we have that on our side, for however long that commitment lasts, Mum, Dad,"

"We are on your side Anjella. So anything you need, we are both here for you and Belinda, at any time you need us."

"That is what I wanted to hear. So we are still a family unit. I am so sorry for not telling you the truth, in the first place."

"Now we can move on together."

"Yes, Mum, with all our love spent on this gorgeous little girl."

"When Michael comes back into the equation, you will keep in touch, even more so?"

"Yes, we will, Dad. He will not splinter our umbilical cord. Now it is back in place, no one will sever it, no matter who tries and how hard they persevere."

"That went very well, Anjella."

"Far better than I expected. But now you both know, I feel better, a weight off my heart, which has been there for some time."

"We shall share the burden with you my love."

Anjella kisses her mum, with all the love she could muster, then her dad with the same verve. She feels only too happy that Belinda will have all the love, care and comfort she will ever need, just in case her father disappears for good, one of these fine days. Anjella lays back into the familiarity of her home, with the assurance of her parents always at her side, as well as her young daughters. As Anjella drifts off into a passive sleep, surrounded by all those that love her, that she has loved passionately all her life. Belinda starts crying, so Tristina comes to pick her up, ssshhing her, singing a lullaby, humming the words of *Lulu Kilya N'daa*[4] and *Kavuli Tutu*[5], gently in her ear, until she finally falls asleep on her

---

[4] Lulu, Lulu, quiet
[5] Hold my baby for me, dove

grandmother's shoulder. Ramon goes to the bag, getting a bottle of the expressed milk, to give to Tristina. She puts up to the little one's mouth, who latches onto it in an instant.

"How did you know Ramon, you clever old man?"

"After four days at the hospital, if I know nothing else, I know when our granddaughter is hungry."

"Would you check the oven for me? Dinner will be ready shortly."

"OK, my love, what is on the menu?"

"Well Ramon, one of your favourites, *matoke* and goat, followed by coconut and sweet potato pudding."

"It smells divine Tristina. A little different from the hospital canteen."

"I can imagine. I hope Anjella will eat some too."

"I am sure she will, she has never refused your food when it has been offered to her."

"I know. She is a great cook herself, after all she has learnt from me and her old nana."

Belinda burps three or four times as she lays high on Tristina's shoulder, slowly falling asleep once again. Laying her back down once again into her snug little carrycot, she is still a little restless, but slowly she drifts off into a deep slumber, then all is quiet and subdued. Tristina checks on dinner, all four then eat in each other's company, all at peace with the world. Anjella returns to the sofa, slowly fading into a light sleep. Grandma takes her intoxicating granddaughter, changing her nappy and re-fastening her onesie, lying her back down, allowing her to wistfully go back to sleep, once again full of her mothers' milk. Ramon is out in the kitchen, doing the washing-up. Nothing is left to chance, with the frailty of the demure and very young mother and daughter.

Both Anjella and her baby daughter recover from all their earlier exertions and tribulations. Both look extremely healthy, and back to their best. Now they stood on the banks of the voluminous Lake Victoria, accompanied by the whole of the Luo tribe, there to support the inspirational new life there amongst them. Each and every one, is looking forward to the annunciation of its newest member, here at the tribe's ancestral home. Both of Anjella dearest, closest friends Suzie Wokabi and Jeanette Oromowere there, at the front with the family, as both were the godmothers of the young Adhiambo.

The shaman stood at the promontory, on the narrowest point, where Anjella held Belinda in front of him. The whole of the Luo tribe stood with them, covering the whole promontory; with Tristina and Ramon standing either side of the shaman. Anjella stood tall and proud, dressed in an immaculate red floral sleeveless midi wrap dress, with a pair of dusky pink sequined double-strapped stiletto sandals. The precious Belinda is encased in a christening shawl, made of the finest red Maasai, interwoven with fine Kenyan gold. All is embellished and bejewelled with a small tsavorite clasp.

He who would invoke the Goddess of the Lake, the great Lake Victoria, commenced his volatile, explosive invocation. Closing his eyes, casting his mind back into the wilderness that belonged to the Luo. Softly at first, then with great delight, he chants, as he feels the presence of Her, the Deity, their Goddess.

The Goddess ascends, casting the whole lake into a maelstrom. Wearing it like a robe, she, the Deity, circumrotates the peak of Mount Kenya, her voice alone reverberating across the Great Rift Valley, heralding her occupation of her lake. Both the Mount and Rift Valley chant her name, her illustrious name, *Adhiambo*, as it echoes across the plains of Kenya. She then disperses herself into the most wild, awesome, magnificent, resplendent waterfall the Luo tribe have ever cast their eyes upon. The shaman takes the middle finger of Belinda's tiny, right hand, nicking it with his very sharp kukri. Squeezing so softly, allowing a single globule of her virgin blood to form, then spill into the sacred waters of the lake. With this the vast volume of water rises, forming a new shroud for the Luo Lake Goddess to wear. Whereupon the deity of the Luo tribe, leaning forward looking into Belinda's eyes, smiles at her astounding beauty. Then taking her face tenderly, gently into her two hands, she kisses the baby on her lips, anointing her whole body with the goddess's own sacred waters. Lingering she caresses her forehead, then in a whisper, heard by the gathered tribe, she regales a sacred promise to both mother and daughter.

"Belinda, whose true name is now Adhiambo, meaning Born in the Evening. It is the same as your goddess, you will never be alone. You now have my fire, spirit, my love of life. Know her as you all know me, she will never let you die, nor fade into exile or extinction. She has my name, she is and will always be my *Nyamin*. She will never be any man's chattel or serf. I now mark her as mine, she is my very own Nyarkingi."

The Goddess Adhiambo stands before the settled child, taking the *kukuri* from her holy man. Cutting deep into her tiny digit, thus making the waters of her great Lake Victoria flow red; as if it were her pumping vein. She then wraps a fingerlet of water around the hand of the baby, so that both mother and daughter can feel her surge of life as it enters them both. They all three, the immortal, Anjella and Adhiambo all become as one. After what seemed a lifetime, the Luo Lake Goddess kisses them both, then turns to her tribe.

"Remember you and your daughter are mine, I am here for you always. I am now *Nyamin* to both mother and daughter."

Then casting herself above her tribe, so that her whole spirit encased the whole of the Luo, she chanted for all of them to hear, in a loud, delicate, enchanting voice.

*Adhiambo,*
*born in the evening,*
*with the most sensational sunset*
*across my Lake Victoria.*
*As you open your eyes,*
*the brown sparkles, glints, glistens*
*as do mine.*
*A true amber sky,*
*to match your radiant*
*head of hair*
*my young one.*
*The Luo Lake Goddess tells you why.*
*She is of the Luo of the Lake,*
*she is* nyamin *with its goddess,*
*of the same given name.*
*They are as one,*
*it will always be so,*
*ADHIAMBO, ADHIAMBO.*

Then the waters of the beautiful Lake Victoria turn back to the purest aquamarine. Slowly they flow back to its original location. As it did so, the whole of the Great Rift Valley, along with the majesty of Mount Kenya, paid homage as they echoed the name of "Adhiambo, Adhiambo, Born In The Evening." back to the Luo. For they are the keepers of the wilderness, all of its wild treasures, along with its cultures of old.

Michael Ironi appears twice, coming to his daughter to see how she is faring, making sure she is well and adjusting to life. He brings with him a cuddly toy, in the shape of a lioness and her cub. Also, with him he has two new dresses for Anjella, he also restocks the cupboards with food, nappies, ointments, a cot and baby clothes. He chose to stay the first time, being very civil and cordial with his in-laws. Breaking open a bottle of Sauvignon blanc from Kenya's wine growing estate at Gethumbwini Leleshwa, for the two ladies. Enjoying a couple of cold beers with Ramon, he happily wets the baby's head. Then feeling he was getting to comfortable with Tristina and Ramon, after his sixth tusker, he said his goodbyes and left them to it. The second time he came, he did much of the same, restocking on food, other groceries, clothes and other items he felt both Belinda and Anjella might need in his absence. They were both asleep on his arrival, so he took Ramon to one side,

"Ramon I am going to be away for some time, on this particular journey. Keep them both safe, I am not sure when I will make my return. But here is 250,000 shillings, if you need to spend it, then make use of it, OK?"

"Sure, Michael, what do you want me to tell Anjella?"

"Whatever makes her happy. I am going to Somalia this time, I will be back as soon as I can."

"We will take good care of them both. You try and keep safe as well."

"I will Ramon."

Then he was gone, off into the twilight zone. When Anjella awoke Ramon told her that Michael would be gone for some time.

"Dad, he will not be happy until someone shoots him down in cold blood. Let him go, we are better off without him, in our lives anyway."

As she said that to her dad, she thought to herself that the Light of Africa just added to the mayhem, carnage and the desperate struggle which was slowly taking over East Africa. The unholy blitz of all and sundry, in their so-called holy war, attempting to take over these countries to form their own caliphates, the despots wanting to be presidents for life, so that they could bleed the country of all its wealth, leaving the populous with nothing to aim for. Also wanting to glean and scavenge the offerings from other nations, hiding that away in hidden bank accounts, they had not the slightest interest in aiding or assisting their own people or country. They just wanted to be fat and oppressive while keeping their people down in the dirt, while they spend millions on holidays, their wives' wardrobes, palaces and celebrations in their own conceited glory. They would bleed national institutions dry, until they are defunct, less than useless, then blame someone else for their loss and the country's demise. This was the plan of the Light of Africa, to become spoilers, wreckers, extortionists, to eat away at the core of the country, until it fell into disrepair. Then take it over, run it as their own personal piggy bank, just like the regime before. Anjella felt sorry for Kenya, watching it fall apart, not being able to assist it in any way at all.

Somalia was the weakest link, so at the moment all their energies were focused on the destruction and collapse of an unimposing country. So, Michael with the Light of Africa at his beck and call, was off to help it fall apart even quicker, so that they could have their own caliphate. In the hope of ruining and dictating to other cultures and dynasties from there. Michael with three of his acolytes drives off to Mogadishu, driving across country, mostly desert. Scattered in their path lay the bleached bones of cattle, goats and the myriad of human relics of previous wars, decomposing bodies of mothers with babies in their arms, the adult skull with a bullet hole in it, indicating that the baby died alone of starvation, its corpse half eaten by starving vultures. Not so far behind the terrorist vehicle was a flotilla of Somalia military armoured cars were giving chase. With nowhere to hide, they hole up in a deserted village, waiting for the military to catch up with them. They waited entrapped, not sure how they were going to get out of this tight situation. They had between them a small mortar, two RPG7s, three AK47s, with a spare clip for each. Turning to his comrades, Michael told them:

"You three stay here with all the weapons. I am going to get help."

Leaving the three of them there, he takes their vehicle and carries on driving towards Mogadishu, finding the safe house. There he hides for his own safety, waiting for the dead of night to shield his escape bid. It was inclined to unsettle his nerves, being stationary, unable to complete his task. It was really testing his resolve. Now deciding they were no longer relevant to the cause, that they had forfeited their lives, so he could make good his escape, from the oncoming fracas. But they had been Somalis anyway, coming back home, to try and bring the present government down in any way possible. Not to worry though, the Light of Africa, had been paid for their training.

Their life expectancy was far from his personal concern, he was now more involved in trying to figure out an escape route for himself.

He had decided to drive straight through the bustling city, then double back on himself, hopefully disorientating the local police and imposing militia, on his daring journey back home. He was beginning to wonder how Belinda was faring with her mother, along with the guidance of her loving grandparents. Probably better than he was, at this point in his life. The in-laws, his partner and young daughter, not giving Ironi a second thought,I as he had never been part of their lives, since Belinda had been conceived. His only thoughts were for himself, everyone else was always excluded.

The four-wheel-drive Suzuki was tanked up, he had some *canjeero, borana* samosa and a hand full of *macsharo yariis*, in a bag. His personal weapon loaded with one up the spout, with the safety off. He was all ready to make a move that night, after hiding away for almost a week. He decided that once he had left the city, he would not stop for anything regardless. He had a single IED available to him, he would keep that handy just in case of any unforeseen circumstances or problems. It was now 21:30, he would sleep now, wake at 03:30, then leave at first light. So bedding himself down, getting as comfortable as he could, shuteye came easily to Michael. Setting the alarm on his wristwatch, then lying out fully on his back, he slept in the basement of the safe house. The buzzer went, so he rose to the dulcet tones of his timepiece. Making himself a strong black coffee and munching on some *borana samosa, canjeero*, he dipped a *masharo yariis* into his now warm coffee, then scoffing a slice of rice cake. It all put him in the mood to finally abscond from Somalia.

Making sure the city was alive, awake and that there was traffic on the streets, Michael Ironi calmly walks out to his vehicle, climbs in, starting it up, then slowly joining the hubbub of local vehicular movement. Driving through the centre of Mogadishu, then onto the outskirts, back into the main drag once again. Now out onto a minor road, via a small bypass, he avoids as much of the mainstream traffic as he can. Hoping that he would avoid all the warlords, along with the instant threat everyone one of them imposed, he had just made it onto the open stretches of desert roads and tracks, when one lone gunship, with its single heavy calibre weapon, mounted in the rear, approached the Suzuki. He swerved to avoid contact and its immediate threat. But on the return maneouver, Michael made sure that the open window of the gunship was opposite him. As they both approached each other, the Somali militia fired warning rounds at the Suzuki, expecting it to come to a halt. As they drew close enough, Mr Ironi tossed his last IED into the open window of the warlords' wagon. Then speeding away, he depressed the green button on his remote. Looking into his rear-view mirror, watching with disdain and sheer delight as the metal coffin disintegrated, with all its contents, under the forceful impact of the contained explosion.

Then with a happy heart, he continued to drive on his way, passing the same deserted village where he had left his three Somali compatriots a week ago. Just as a matter of interest, he detoured so that he could pass the building where they had made their last stand. He noticed the small mortar, an empty RPG7, the scattered AK47s, all alongside the remains of three freshly picked skeletons. So they did not make it, he thought to himself. Then just drove across the open, unmarked border with Kenya. He returned to the Sarova Panafric, went up to his room. He would go and report to his control officer later in the afternoon. All he wanted to do now, was lay down to sleep for as long as he was able. Michael strolled into Jomo's office, who was having his afternoon Tusker, ice cold and from the bottle.

"Ah Michael, it has been a while. What happened to you, your first failure and it does not sit good with our Somali contacts?"

"We got caught crossing the border, by the Somali military. We had a stand-off at a little deserted village, Baardheere. The three Somalis took on the advancing flotilla, while I took the four-wheel drive, to take the security forces away from the deserted building, where I had left my three comrades. I disrupted their advance, with two EODs. With that they gave up chasing me, returned to the hideaway, killing the three locals. I continued onto our safe house in Mogadishu. Then made my back here, as soon as I possibly could. I had to use my last IED on an encroaching warlord, close to the Kenyan border. So the next time I venture into Somalia, I will have to find a new way in."

"Yes, no doubt you will, Michael. A shame about the three Somalia counterparts, but we got paid for their training, so it is not all bad news."

Jomo reaches into his fridge, drawing out a cold beer

"Here have a Tusker Michael, it will all go smoother on your next job."

They both laugh as they crack the two bottles together, in admiration of the work they were doing achieving between them, taking long, mighty swigs at the chilled beers.

Michael had not shown up, which was par for the course. So Anjella, the darling Adhiambo, Tristina and Ramon, had decided to treat themselves to a family dinner, at one of the local restaurants. Having not used any of the money that Michael had left in Ramon's charge, the father thought that a treat for them all would do them all a power of good in the vain hope of getting both Anjella and Tristina out of the doldrums. They had both been at their daughter's and granddaughter's side now for six months or more. Adhiambo was growing up fast, still breastfeeding, as her mother was still producing milk. Also, she just loved the calming effect it had on her, when her little mondo was suckling on her ultra-sensitive, receptive and delicate nipples.

"Are you sure we can afford this dad?"

"Of course Anjella, otherwise I would not have offered to take us all out."

"So which one are we going to, Mum?"

"You choose Anjella, one close by, so we can walk our granddaughter out and, show her off to everyone in her new pushchair. The fresh air will do her good, in fact it will do us all some good, instead of being stuck indoors all day."

"Do you feel well enough to venture out princess?"

"I feel amazing, Mum, six months rest. You and Dad doing everything for us both, what is not to like? I feel so spoilt, but the good thing is, I have managed to catch up with all my schoolwork. So I feel I am ready to go back. Providing you do not mind looking after our precious Adhiambo?"

"We love having her in our lives, she brightens up the whole day, like a ray of golden sunshine. As long as you can keep expressing your milk, we can keep feeding her from you, Anjella."

"OK, Mum, you are both treasures. Let us go to Fogo Gaucho in Westlands. It is only a short walk away."

"Are we ready then?"

"Yes Ramon."

"Lead the way, Dad, we are right at your side."

Michael is sitting alone in his hotel room, not overly concerned about anything. But he feels he should go and pay a visit to his daughter and partner. He takes a slow walk round to his house, letting himself in.

"Anjella, Tristina, Ramon, anyone home?"

No reply. Well it had been about six months since he last paid them a social call. Perhaps they think he has given up on them entirely. He decides he will return in the morning. On the way back to the hotel, he picks himself a young lady from a nearby brothel. Taking her back with him, with no due finesse or care, not treating her as an attractive, amazing, African woman, he undresses himself. Then he gets her to perform felatio on him, as he sits on his bed. Then he slaps her taut, perfect behind. She disrobes for him, kneeling on the bed in front of him. Then aggressively taking her doggy style, he lunges deep, hard until he can express all his carnal longing and deep-rooted frustration in a single thick torrent. One that smothers her delicious buttocks, thighs and widespread loins. He had paid her for the whole night, but had now lost interest in that idea. So with a sweep of his hand, he majestically dismisses her saying:

"That will be all my lovely, you can go back, I will not need your services any longer."

She in turn feels more feckless than usual, so with an acrimonious retort, she tells him,

"OK, mister, I am gone then."

She gets dressed in her skirt, top and heels, leaving the hotel and heading straight back to the brothel, as her night's work has only just started. The grandparents, granddaughter and Anjella were all savouring the delights of their chosen eatery.

"Anjella?"

"Yes, Dad?"

"When do you plan on going back to school?"

"On Monday, or as soon as I can, as soon as they will let me."

"In that case I will drive you there and wait for you, as I have nothing else planned."

"OK, Dad, that will save me either walking, or catching the bus."

"All I will need to know is that they will be happy to have you back."

"I am sure they will be glad to see me. I know I will be so pleased to get back to my books, get some structure and learning back into my life."

The sun was beginning to fade as they all walked home together. They got indoors locked up first, then Adhiambo became a little unsettled. So Mummy picked her up, loosened the top of her dress, not needing to do anything else as her daughter knew exactly where her nightcap was hidden, also how to retrieve those goodies that were on offer to her. As she suckled away, Tristina made hot chocolate for the three adults. They all sat close, sipping their hot beverages, watching the sparkling *mondo*, drink from her mother. Then without stopping, she took the second teat, until she had emptied her mother.

"She sure can drink, Anjella."

"I know, Mum, she empties me every time I feed her."

"She is going to be a big, stand-up girl when she gets older, that is for sure."

"You are right, Mum, she is going to be able to hold her own with anyone, male or female."

"I just hope she won't be inclined towards her father's way of life, as she grows into a woman."

"I will make sure she does not. Studying will be her forte, her reason to exist. Learning, knowledge, insight, wisdom, asking questions. Then a good job, whether it is here, or somewhere else, I will make sure she has the life she wants. Not one planned for her, by an outsider trying to abuse her."

After Adhiambo has been winded, changed put into her all-in-one night suit, they all go to bed. Anjella is the first one up, happily expressing her milk, ready for Grandma to use during the course of the day. Anjella and her father are just heading for the front door at the same time that Michael opens it and strolls in.

"Good morning one and all."

They all answer him back very cheerfully, as he turns to Anjella.

"Anjella, are you off somewhere?"

"Yes, I am heading off back to school, to finish my studies."

"Oh, I see, so who is going to look after Belinda?"

"I hardly think that is any of your concern, you obnoxious thug. You have shown no interest in your daughter's welfare or safety, since she was born. You are just a fractious, unsalutary ingrate. Now you feign concern, interest in her life, it is too late. You are an inept, vile gangster."

Michael Ironi could not contain himself, to be shown up by a woman, a girl so much younger who was obviously trying to emasculate him. He sees red, but does not see Ramon step into impede him, as Mr Ironi steps forward with a clenched fist, ready to strike out at the beautiful Anjella. Mr Ogwayo carries on with his movement, striking Michael with a straight right, into his unprotected genitals. There in front of Anjella, Tristina and Ramon, Michael crumples to the floor, with all his wind removed from his sails. Ramon looks over to his daughter smiling at her:

"Anjella, come here for a moment, would you?"

"Of course, Papa."

Anjella goes over to where he stands.

"Now listen to me, Anjella. I want you to do something for me, so that you will never be imposed upon or threatened by any man, ever again, or anyone else that attempts to control or possess you."

"I will, Papa, what do you want me to do?"

"First I want you to clench your fist, as tight as you can."

Ramon shows Anjella the way, then showing her the pad formed by the bottom part of her fingers, he tells her:

"Now, strike Michael anywhere you like, then see what he does."

Anjella draws back, then strikes her partner with some rancour, wroth, in the side of his face. He raises his hands trying to prevent the punch.

"I see he raised his hands to his face, Dad."

"Yes. So when that happens, if he has provoked you, or you are not satisfied with his response, then kick him between his legs, as hard as you can. Then he will stop instantly, then you will be in control of the situation."

"I understand, Daddy, then he will be obsequious. I will degrade him, abase him, like he tried to do to me. I will take him off his pedestal."

"You will my dearest daughter. You will be able to do that to anyone who feels that they are stronger, more wilful than you."

With his daughter standing beside him, standing like a Rhodesian Ridgeback over Michael, glaring down at the scum before him, shouting at him, making even his wife and daughter jump as he was normally a very quiet man. He definitely scared his granddaughter, making her cry. Now, even she was wide awake,

"DO NOT EVER STRIKE, OR TRY TO HARM MY DAUGHTER! ARE WE CLEAR ON THAT YOU INEPT, DISSOLUTE ORDURE?"

The antagonist looks up at Ramon, then nods, confirming he understood the statement in its entirety. Then Ramon told him:

"If you still want to see your daughter, she is here with her grandmother."

Tristina comes forward as Michael regains his feet, as well as his footing. She hands the delightful granddaughter over to him. Michael takes his little beauty, along with the bottle, as she sucks contentedly for a short while, then starts to cry uncontrollably.

"What is up with her now? I have not done anything wrong."

The noble grandmother answers, trying to explain the problem to him.

"That is the whole problem, she does not know you, she does not know who or what you are. This is the first time you have bothered to interact, get close and personal with your very own darling daughter. After six months this is your sole contribution towards Adhiambo's life. She needs time to adjust to you, to know you."

"Well it will be hard for her, because it will always be like this, in my line of work. She will just have to get used to seeing me for limited periods of time. Make the most of it, when I do decide to spend my valuable time with her."

"So what you are saying is, that you could not really care less, if your own daughter gets to know you or not?"

"In a nutshell, yes. She will have to work her life around mine, Tristina."

"SHE WILL NOT MICHAEL. IF YOU ARE SO PREDISPOSED WITH YOUR INSENSATE, DELETERIOUS LINE OF WORK, THEN IT IS BETTER THAT ADHIAMBO NEVER GETS INVOLVED WITH YOU, YOUR JOB OR YOUR CIRCLE OF SO-CALLED FRIENDS. SHE WILL BE SAFER WITH MY MOTHER AND FATHER, WHILE I AM BACK AT SCHOOL."

"She will not Anjella. Why do you keep calling her Adhiambo? What does it even mean?"

"Michael, it is her Luo name. The whole of the tribe were there, at Lake Victoria with us, to be part of it. The name means Born in the Evening."

"Where was I then?"

"No idea, probably killing someone with one of your bombs. Also, we are off. Come on Mum, Dad, you will take me to school. Michael can look after his daughter, all day long on his own. See you later, father dear."

"So what do I do, if she starts crying again?"

"Sing her to sleep. I was under the impression you had it all in hand, all under your control that you were in charge. You Michael Ironi the big "I AM," is just as worthless as I thought. You knew what you were doing, you did not want to leave her with my mother, so you look after her. Ah, but what happens if your work phones now, with a crisis on their hands? Do you tell them find someone else, I am busy looking after my daughter, I am unable to help you at the moment!"

"You know I cannot do that."

"So what is more important to you Mr Ironi, your daughter or your job?"

He stood before his partner staring down at her.

"My job, Anjella."

"So Michael, you go and do your pox ridden job. Let me and my parents look after my daughter. Seeing as you do not have the time or the inclination to bond with your stunning little daughter."

Michael hands his daughter back over to her grandma, knowing when he has been beaten verbally and physically, with all the principles she has just thrown at him. He goes over to Anjella, takes notes from his wallet, then hands them over to her.

"This should help with your schooling, along with whatever else you might need for our daughter. Is it all right if I come in the evenings, to get to know her a little better?"

"Of course it is Michael. Once she gets to know you and used to you, your interaction will be so much better for the both of you."

"I can make sure I do that, for the sake of Belinda."

"Michael, I do not want you to stay away. Just make more time for your beautiful daughter. I am sure she will appreciate it, so will you, then the two of you will get to know each other so much better."

"OK, Anjella, what time do you finish school?"

"Four o'clock. Dad will pick me up, so I should be back home, by about quarter to five. Dad?"

"Yes, Anjella, if not a bit earlier."

"In that case, I will come by about five."

"That will be good, you can feed her and see her to bed."

Ramon turns to Michael:

"Can we drop you anywhere, Michael?"

"Yes, please, I am staying at the Sarova Panafric Hotel."

"OK, jump in then, you got yourself a ride. We will see you this evening."

They drop him off at his hotel, as they both carry onto Anjella's school. Ramon goes in with her, they approach the secretary together, to see if Anjella could speak to the principal. The secretary rises and knocks on his door, putting her head around to speak to him.

"Sir, is it possible for Miss Ogwayo and her father, to come and speak with you now?"

"Of course, it is, please send them in."

The secretary turns leaving the door ajar, smiling and beckoning to Anjella and her father.

"Would you both like to go in?"

"Thank you very much, miss."

They both walk into the principal's office.

"Mr Ogwayo, Anjella, so nice to see you both. Well I thought, young lady, that you had given up on us, as well as your studies."

"No, sir, I have a personal problem, which has now been dealt with."

"Would you like to tell me what the problem was? Perhaps the school could help you, in some small way?"

Anjella looks across to her father, who smiles at her and whispers.

"Tell them what you think they need to know, so that the principal knows the outline of the story at least."

"A while ago, I gave birth to an amazing, adorable daughter. It was a breeched birth, so it came with some no small complications; due to my age and size. But we both survived, thankfully."

"Was it planned Anjella?"

"Far from it sir, I was taken advantage of, in my own bedroom, while I was studying."

"Oh, dear, that does sadden me. Not safe in your own home, that is very unsatisfactory. So how can we help you now?"

"I would like to come back to school, if that is at all possible?"

"I do not envisage any problems with that. When would you like to start attending the school again?"

"Today if possible, sir, or as soon as possible."

"Of course, today is a good day, allow me to sort you out now Anjella."

Ramon leans across, kissing his daughter, says goodbye. Then thanks the principal, shakes his hand very warmly. He heads back to Tristina and Adhiambo, while his daughter heads out into her first class of the day, to continue adding to the wisdom and knowledge she already has. The gleaming *mondo* spends hours in the company of her two loving, adoring grandparents as well as her besotted mother. It was a hard slog, hours spent in her books, attached in part to the Nairobi

Hospital for Women and Medicine School. Anjella knew university would be very trying and difficult, not only for her, but for both Tristina and Ramon as well. Adhiambo was now walking, talking, the centre of everyone's attention. Anjella the doctor spent every spare moment she had with both her parents, as well as her luculent, radiant and iridescent pearl that was her daughter.

Michael did not show up for that evening of reconciliation. His control officer, Jumo, had him taking two trainees out to their training camp on the other side of Mount Kenya. He spent eight long weeks with them, showing them both the intricacies of making their own improvised explosive device, as well as about explosive ordnance disposal. How to set land mines followed, along with the art of using remote-control detonations. Finally, he taught how to apply them, to their own homemade IEDs and EODs. After a gruelling two months, they were both proficient and efficient in all aspects of being a local insurgent. Their deliberations had been meticulous, their groundwork had been excellent, so all three of them drove over the border, heading towards Dodoma, the capital of Tanzania. They found a government border post, where the two newbies planted their EOD at precisely 23:45 hours. They elected to use remote control, before retreating the required distance. Michael observed with his infra-red binoculars the three of them were safe. One of his trainees depressed the blow button, counting down from ten. They had also installed a short time-delay sequence, that worked a treat. As it blew on the zero second it rocked the ground, decimating the outpost completely. Scattering debris everywhere and in every direction. All three smiled and shook hands all round, as the two new insurgents completed their first task, with some professionalism. Michael turned to both of them:

"So where would you fellahs like dropping off, before I head back to Nairobi?"

"Just outside the city Michael, we will show you where, when we get there."

He dropped them both off in the suburbs of Dodoma, saying their goodbyes, then drove slowly back over the border to Nairobi, Kenya. Looking at his watch, noticing it was now 07:00 hours, he decided to go and visit Anjella and his little Belinda. He arrived just as they had all sat down to breakfast. Tristina went and got another plate, dishing up a hot meal for Michael.

"Sit, Michael, eat and enjoy, it is good to see you."

Anjella was not so happy, nor in such a forgiving mood as her mother.

"This is a funny five o'clock tonight, to see my daughter to bed, nearly three months after our last meeting. I suppose we are rather lucky that you can fit us in at all, with your rather busy schedule."

Michael did not rise to her contempt this time. He did not say a word, but he sat and enjoyed his breakfast, then put a wad of shillings on the table in front of Anjella. Then just got up and left very quietly. None of them saw him again until Anjella had gained her doctorate at the training school. She had also discovered that her very dear friend Suzie Wokabi had finished at university and had now started her own company, called Suzie Beauty. Now Anjella had a full-time position at the Women's Hospital and Training School.

He had gone to Mombasa with two erstwhile thieves, to rob the main branch of the Kenyan Co-operative Bank. He had constructed two mini IEDs, especially for the job. The first to gain entry into the bank, the second to blow the timing mechanism at the vault face. But the second IED did not react to his remote control. Michael gave it all due respect for a full half-hour. Then approached his own device. He was just about to handle it, his hand approaching the connections, when it bit him hard, with force, alacrity and complete disrespect for its maker. Doing no damage whatsoever to the strong room, but taking off Michael's hand, killing his two henchmen in the process. Barely conscious, but having the savvy to wrap his hand as well as his stump in the remnants of an old shirt. He wasted no time in running away to hide in a deserted outbuilding on the outskirts of the city.

Ramon was just taking a sip of his first choffee[6], when his mobile rang. it was Michael.

"Ramon, would you do me a big favour?"

"Of course, if I am able."

"Come and collect me here in Monbassa, I need you right away."

"OK, Michael, I am on my way, where are you?"

"I am just past Digo Road, on the A109, hiding in an alleyway."

The pain was slowly killing him, along with the loss of blood. Ramon eventually arrives and managed to find him, right up the far end of a deserted building. Tucked away in a very dark corner, Michael was delirious and in the throes of a major cardiac arrest, in and out of an fitful sleep. Drenched in sweat, pale and clammy, on the verge of closing his eyes and saying goodnight for the very last time. Ramon helped him

---

[6] A mixture of coffee and drinking chocolate

clamber into his old jalopy. Then he drove through the city, via the back streets, looking for a hospital. Finally, they come across the Mombasa General with its doors wide open, lit up like a fairy tree. Pulling up with a screech, Ramon struggled to get Michael out as quickly as possible, staggering under the weight of such a big man. Taking him to the entrance then he left him on the floor, to be found by the hospital porters. Then Ramon rushes back to his nondescript old banger, once again keeping to the darkened back streets, until he reaches the freeway. Then driving straight back to Nairobi, He washes the back of his old van out at his home before going to the Hospital for Women and Medicine School, to pick up his daughter after her shift.

Adhiambo had started school, going to her mother's fine educational establishment, which Anjella enjoyed so much — the Kianda School.

"So how was your day, my darling daughter?"

"Still fighting malaria, no closer to a solution, but the battle continues."

"One of these days, it will jump out and bite you on your pretty little nose. Then all your research, development and hard work would have paid off."

"I do hope so, Dad. So how was Adhiambo, did she enjoy her first day at school?"

"She did, she is also very excited, just waiting for you to get home."

"Why is that, Dad?"

"Because she helped Mum make dinner tonight."

"She is a very clever girl then."

"Just like her mum. I am not meant to tell you, so be surprised for your daughter, please."

"I will, Dad, I promise."

They pull into the carport and head indoors. The little treasure that is Adhiambo, runs up to her mummy, hugging her tight around her legs, not letting her go anywhere. Then with due ceremony Anjella picks her up, hugging her tight and close, giving her a nice long kiss. Then the little charm, the enchantress, that is her beloved daughter, looks deep into her mother's wise brown eyes with her own sparkling, wide wild eyes.

"Mummy I helped make dinner with Nana."

"Oh, my you are a clever little girl. What are we having my little chef?"

Adhiambo looks across at her adoring grandmother.

"What is it called again, Nana?"

"It is called *su ku ma*, my precious."

"*Sukuma*, Mum."

Anjella smiles at her daughter as she repeats it parrot fashion.

"*Wi ki.*"

Then Tristina tells the little bundle of joy:

"You can also tell your Mummy, we are having it with *mutura*."

"With *mutura* mummy."

"That is one of my favourites, Grandpappys' as well."

"Do you like it, Gramps?"

"I love it my little pearl, especially if you cooked it for me."

Adhiambo smiles at her granddad as her mother puts her down. She laughs out loud, runs full throttle, throwing herself into her grandfather's open arms, catching her then swinging her around, just like a helicopter. Her little legs fly out as she screams, enjoying the interaction between young and old. But before Ramon gets all dizzy, he stops, hugging her tight and really close to him, telling her:

"You are my little treasure, Adhiambo."

"Is treasure good, Mummy, Nana?"

"Treasure is beyond price, my darling daughter."

"It is the best my sweetheart."

Then the little girl turns to them all to announce:

"Then you are my treasures as well."

Tristina with a tear in her eye speaks:

"Come on, let us all sit down and eat, before it all gets cold."

They all seat themselves, enjoying the goat sausage with mixed vegetables. Very tasty it was, Anjella looking proudly at her daughter, who was sat next to her.

"How was school today, dearest?"

"It was good, Mummy. I loved with all the other girls. We had a great time together."

"That is wonderful, so tomorrow Mummy will take you OK?"

"That will be nice, Mummy."

Ramon looked directly at his daughter, after both Tristina and he had discussed this together beforehand.

"Do you want more time and room with Adhiambo, Anjella?"

"No, Dad, I do not want you and Mum to move out, if that is what you are going to tell me. Adhiambo and I would not have survived without you both there. But if it is an inconvenience for the both of you, I will look for a nanny."

Tristins turns to Anjella.

"Do not be silly. We love it here, with you and our granddaughter. But we did not want to get under your feet, or be in your way. We seem to have been here for so long."

"OK, we can sort this out now, get it straight between all four of us. I love having you both here at our side. You are not in my way. You are my family and we stick by one another. Adhiambo has grown up with two doting mothers, along with a truly wonderful father. Which I might add, Michael never was, or has been, or capable of being. We have not seen him in years. His daughter probably would not recognize him now anyway. So you stay here with me, now I have a great job, we have nothing to worry about."

Tristina kisses Anjella, just as Adhiambo speaks up in front of everyone:

"Are Nana and Gramps leaving us Mum, why?"

"They thought they were in our way, my baby, what do you think?"

With big wet tears streaming down her cheeks and deep heartfelt sobs, she tries to say:

"How will I survive without my grandma and grandpa, they both know me so well. They do not love me any more, what have I done wrong?"

"No, no, my beautiful, now you are older, they just thought they were in the way of the two of us. They thought they were no longer needed here."

"But they are needed, I need them, I love them both so much. My life would not be the same, it would be empty without them in it."

"Now do you see what you have managed to do? My daughter thinks she has done something wrong, that you are now going to disown her and leave her."

Tristina is in tears and fails to control her sobbing, wishing now that they had not started this conversation. But it was too late, the little ears had heard it all. Grandma goes to her beloved granddaughter, picks her up and cuddles her close, smothering her in kisses, then telling her:

"We just thought you and your mum wanted more time together, my precious *mondo*. We can never stop loving you Adhiambo, you are part of us, you are our blood. We will always be here for you."

"Then you, Nana and Gramps, will stay with me?"

"This is where we will stay, you beautiful girl. For as long as you want us to."

Adhiambo hugs her nanny so tight, as they both cry together in each other's arms. Anjella looks at her father and smiles,

"Well, Dad, that seems to have cured that crisis."

"It does, I think we need to be careful what we talk about, when out little girl is about."

They all go into a group hug, all cuddling up tight and close, all feeling each other's warmth. With the little cherub Adhiambo in the middle with her devoted grandma. All three adults squeezing the apple of their eye, so full of love for her tight knit family.

"NOW WE HAVE A CIRCLE OF *AHERI*!"

Adhiambo shouts at the top of her little voice.

Michael is taken directly into surgery, into the intensive care unit operating theatre. His vital signs are on the verge of flat-lining, but with the faintest of pulses found in his neck, they wired him up, going to work immediately. They are not sure where he came from, or where and who brought him in. But he needed their skills now and, having received them in abundance, that is what saved his mortal coil. But his severed hand that he had clutched onto for so long, was of no further use to him, so it was discarded. Having recovered, recuperated and reinstated his vital signs, after a five-hour intense operation, he was put into the ICU unit for rest, quiet and quite a lengthy recovery period. Michael Ironi was under constant observation with no visitors allowed. Not that anyone came to see him anyway, which made life a lot easier for the hospital staff, that were overseeing his well-being.

His slow reconciliation back to consciousness alongside some sort of reality was slow, laboured and so very painful. The nightmares stayed with him all the while, the intravenous drip with the medication helped quell the ongoing, agonizing pain. Yet, delirium took him over as he cried, shouting out:

"BELINDA WHERE ARE YOU? I HAVE LET YOU DOWN AGAIN. ANJELLA HAS FORSAKEN ME, WHERE AM I?"

Then, drifting back into a drug-induced sleep, he was silenced for a while. That helped enormously with the discomfort and the strange memories that were washing over him, slowly fading as the medication induced assisted in a peaceful tranquil setting, to assist and aid his speedy recovery. The local news station and newspapers were awash with the story of the failed bank robbery. They told both viewers and readers, that two insurgents had blown the main door of the bank successfully. But then the second device had failed them, not having enough explosive to unlock and force open the strong room chamber. Michael was not aware of his big story, due to him being on the operating table. Also, he was not in a position to watch television, or read a newspaper.

Ramon had sat down with a relaxing cup of *choffee*, to watch the news. Guessing straight away that the attempted robbery was where Michael had been to get his severe injury, Tristina turned to her daughter:

"I see another bank robbery has taken place, this time in Mombassa. This one failed, the two robbers blew themselves up. That makes me think of Michael, funnily enough, Anjella."

"I wonder if that was him? Perhaps it was and his crimes finally caught up with him. He blew himself up in the process, getting to cocksure of himself, knowing Michael. That would be a shame. I guess someone will miss him. Adhiambo is asleep, I am off to bed, see you both in the morning."

"Yes, you will, darling."

"Goodnight, precious."

"Come on Ramon, I think we ought to hit the sack, it is getting late."

"So it is, come on my queen, let us retire to the royal four-poster."

For a change Anjella was the first one up. She now had the kitchen to herself. Getting the large skillet out, she throws some beans, corn kernels, white and red onions along with bell peppers into it. She tops it with her own *mchuzi* mix, making a quick and easy *githeri* for breakfast. As it cooks away Anjella gets Adhiambo up, helps her wash and clean her teeth, the same way Mummy brushes hers. When they both get dressed, Anjella goes back into the kitchen, while Adhiambo rushes into her grandparents' bedroom announcing, after jumping on the bed and kissing both Nana and Grandpappy.

"Mummy told me to tell you both, that breakfast is being served, it is *githeri*."

"That sounds wonderful little girl, we will follow you to the kitchen."

"OK, Grandma, hold my hand."

They both get up, go to the table and sit, as Anjella dishes up,

"Are you both coming with me, when I take little miss pearl here, to school?"

"We would love to come with you, Anjella."

"Come on then Tristina, let us finish here and go and get ready."

"OK, Mum, Dad, we will make it a family outing."

Anjella drives while the lively little Lulu sings to both of her grandparents. Singing softly and slowly, the words of *Lulu Kilya*. This made her grandmother cry, due to flood of memories it brought back of when she used to sing it to Anjella, as a baby, to get her to sleep. It worked every time.

"That was exceptional my darling. Who taught you that song and how to sing it so well?"

"I do not know, Nana. The words were all a jumble at first. Then this tune came into my mind. Then the words just seemed to fall into place."

"You are such a clever little girl. You take after your mum, in so many beautiful ways."

The little treasure that was Adhiambo smiled contentedly, knowing her song was fully appreciated. At the same time wiped away Nana's tears, with her delicate little fingers.

"Do not be so sad my lovely grandma, I will make you happy."

She stands up on her grandmother's lap, putting her arms around her neck, pulling her very close. She kisses Tristina gently, with all the affection she can muster. In return Tristina pulls and hugs, squeezes her granddaughter. Kissing her little warm lips for a very long time. When they had both finished, Adhiambo looked her grandmother in the eye.

"I love you, Nana, never go away and leave me, will you?"

"I will not ever my sweetheart. I will be here for you, whenever you want or need me."

"I want you for always please, Nana."

"OK, my glorious cherub, always it is."

"OK, everyone, here we are at school."

Anjella cries out, they all line up for a final kiss from adorable Adhiambo, all getting the usual cuddle as well. As she walks proudly to her school, they all wave to her and Anjella telling her:

"We will be waiting for you, when you finish."

"OK, Mummy, love you lots."

"Love my precious, always will."

They watch her go in, then get back into the car. Tristina sits in the front with Anjella, driving off to the hospital where she works. Tristina asks her daughter;

"Are you sure you have not been teaching that song to Adhiambo?"

"No, Mum, she just started singing it to me, in the bathroom, as I washed her this morning. But thinking about it, I did sing it to my stomach, when she was kicking me, when I could get no rest. It helped me cope with the incessant pain. After a while the kicking subsided when I sang it to her, so perhaps she liked it and remembered it."

"What a memory she must have, to be able to piece it together. Then put it to that singular tune, then to recite it and sing it, to us all, without one mistake."

"But you used to sing it to her Tristina, when she was a babe in your arms, when Anjella was at school."

"I know Ramon, along with the other two songs I used. It always got her to sleep, when she was restless."

Now Michael was on the road to recovery, slowly regaining his senses. His sense of self, along with the preservation of said self. He knew he was not going to let that bank beat him a second time. He would need a prosthetic hand, then he would recharge the job and do it all by himself. Slowly, cautiously he let himself heal properly, no rushing no shortcuts. He needed to feel his verve for life to return, his strength, his mindset, his vigour to continue with the job in hand. One of the nurses came to his bedside.

"So, you are back from the dead. I thought it only polite of me, to come and check on you, Michael."

"Very thoughtful thank you. How long have I been here nurse?"

"A lifetime, over three months now here in ICU."

"Can you remember how I got here?"

"Apparently you just appeared at our main entrance, on the verge of passing away. But with a long intricate operation, we managed to keep you on this side of the pearly gates."

"I take it you were not able to save my detached hand?"

"We are terribly sorry about that. But it had been kept in an old shirt, was decomposing, was lifeless. It had been detached for so long, by the time we worked on you, all the nerve endings and arteries were dead. So it got discarded."

"Do you think I could see a doctor, please, nurse?"

She goes off in a hurry, soon returning with a doctor in tow. He sits on the bedside chair

"So sir, you are looking a lot fitter than when we first admitted you here."

"Thank you, I feel a lot better, I probably look a lot better too."

"Did you have a question?"

"Yes, I did. How much longer will I need to stay in here?"

"Actually in ICU? Another five days."

"Then what happens to me?"

"Probably a week in one of the general wards, then it would be up to you and what your own plans would involve."

"Is there anyone I can talk to, about replacing my hand?"

"Yes of course there is, but she is off today. I could get her to come and pay you a visit tomorrow morning, first thing."

"That would be lovely, thank you so much."

"Do you feel like some solid food today?"

"That would be great, Doctor, as long as you think I am well enough to take it."

"I will inform the kitchen, we will see you later."

Michael slips back into his bed, making himself comfortable as he drifts back into a slight slumber, much to his own annoyance. The hospital prosthetic surgeon turns up for Michael. She sat very comfortably on the chair at his bedside, just making sure the patient was awake and fully aware of her presence. Then assisting him to sit up, she smiled and reseated herself,

"So young man, what would you like to know?"

"If you can help me, by replacing my lost hand?"

Michael lifts up his left arm, showing the surgeon his stump. She looks at it admiringly.

"Of course, we can, it has been left in a great condition. But it will be rather expensive."

"What will it cost me?"

"The hand itself will be 275,000 shillings, the fitting will be 75,000 shillings. Then the weeks of physiotherapy would amount to 115,000 shillings."

Michael Ironi looked at her, while he thought about his future with the Light of Africa.

"That is a princely sum I must say. Still, I need to get it done. How would you like the payment?"

"We would like it all up front, please."

"That is OK."

"It is not a reflection on you Michael. We used to offer it half before, then the other half after the operation. But we found, to our dismay, that many of the patients were doing a runner, before they had paid for the second instalment."

"That is not a problem. I have my card in the drawer. What if I pay now, then you come and collect me, once I am ready to be moved to your department?"

"OK, Michael, I will just go and get he mobile terminal, so you can make the payment."

The surgeon soon returns with the payment terminal, she gives him the receipt then tells him:

"We will come and collect you in about ten days. Then take you to my department, will that suit you?"

"Yes, see you soon and thank you."

Life back home only got easier. Michael, all but forgotten now and Anjella grew into her job, research was her life and she enjoyed it immensely. Finding her own circle of friends and associates, she brought them home to dinner, only too proud to introduce them all to her vivacious daughter, mother and father. The little jewel that always glistened, that was her beloved Adhiambo, who had become the centre of her life in all that she did. She had in the meantime got a small fridge to house Dad's supply of Tusker. They had redecorated the house with new furnishings and a fresh coat of paint. So now it was a home for them all. Adhiambo was growing, not only in confidence, popularity, knowledge and other skills. She was also looked up to by her own circle of girl friends, who came around all the time, to play, study, eat and just generally get in the way, as children do. In the new cabinet were bottles of Kenya King gin, Old Monk rum, also all the components to make a *dawa*, everyone's favourite cocktail. Of course there was also tonic as well as bitter lemon, to go with Tristina's gin. The rum was for Anjella, who needed no mixers, as she preferred her drink neat. She only ever drank if she was not working and if she was drinking socially. She never drank alone, or in front of Adhiambo.

Ramon went over daily to check on their own home, only making sure it had not been disturbed, or broken into. His granddaughter's seventh birthday was just around the corner, so Gramps brought some extra chairs back with him, in readiness for her party. A party piece she had learnt as well, was the school motto in Latin, which was *In Opere Et Veritate*. Which translated into *In Deed and In Truth*. Also, with Nana Tristina's help she had learnt the words to *Kavuli Tutu*, to sing aloud before she attempted to blow out the candles on her cake. This weekend Ramon was doing a barbeque for Anjella's friends, who were paying them a visit on the Saturday afternoon.

Michael has been transferred out into the general ward, where he had suffered in silence. Then at last the prosthetic surgeon gives him a personal visit on the Friday afternoon. Smiling as usual looking very tantalising and provocative, without knowing it, she tells Michael:

"You look a lot fitter, more sober than when we last met, Michael."

"I feel more aware of everything around me now, Doctor, now I am finally out of ICU. But I do have this irritating, infernal itch, that constantly aggravates me. But when I go to scratch it, there is nothing there to scratch!"

"That is only your mind playing tricks and games with you, because that part of your limb is no longer there. Once you get your new hand attached, it will fade and ease with time. So that you will not feel the focus of attention, on Sunday afternoon you will be moved to my department, OK?"

"Thank you, Doctor."

"We will let you settle in for the rest of Sunday. Then Monday we will commence with the intricate fitting. Then once you are happy and comfortable with the attachment, then we will get you using it. Aquainting yourself with getting the most out of it."

"That sounds great, looking forward to Monday already, Doctor."

The surgeon rises, shakes Michael's right hand.

"We will be waiting for you, until Monday morning young man."

"It will be a pleasure to be under your directions, Doctor."

Just as she leaves, dinner starts being served. Michael is given a tray, with a plate of goat *karanga*, along with a slice of almond cake for his dessert, along with a cup of black tea.

Sunday afternoon comes along quite quickly, when two orderlies approach his bed.

"Good afternoon, sir, we assume you know about your move to the prosthetic department?"

"I do indeed, how are we going to get there?"

"Everything is in hand, we will get you into this wheelchair, then take you there now, if you feel you are ready."

They take him to the staff lift and ascend a couple of floors. There, they wheel him into the ward, where at the moment he is and will be the only participating patient on this ward.

"I am sorry to say sir, but you are the only one here. The good thing is, you will get all the attention, aid, assistance you will require tomorrow morning. Until then you just lay back and enjoy."

"Thank you both for your help."

They both help him out of the wheelchair, onto and into his designated bed. Making sure he is comfortable, they both leave him to his own company. The surgeon appears very early on the Monday morning, with her staff of three nurses, who wheel in a small trolley. Then all four of them stand around his bed, while the nurses make him very comfortable. She looks at him.

"I see you are already, were you anticipating our arrival young man?"

"I was and I am. Excited is a vast understatement."

"Good, that shows acceptance of the situation. Your willingness to learn, to adapt will make the operation so much easier."

"So, what happens now?"

"We put the new limb on your arm, to make sure you are comfortable with it. Also, that it fits and touches the parts of your arm and wrist that it needs to reach."

"When are you satisfied with that?"

"We will take you to our own private theatre, perform some microsurgery, with your new limb."

"Then, after that?"

"Then you will start learning how to make it function, so that it will become part of you. So that you start to use it, without thinking of it as a separate part of you. So that it matches the workings of your good hand. As you are the only patient here, my three nurses will give you all their time and experience in getting that right, before you leave."

They all smile at him, all looking very proficient, amicable and knowledgeable.

"So are you ready to start Michael?"

"I am indeed, I am all yours."

So donning her surgical gloves, she slowly and gently removes his dressing, until she gets right down to the stump. Addressing it very tenderly, giving it a very good and thorough appraisal, she continues to smile.

"This is just about perfect. We have enough of all the major nerve ends to work with. So, let us proceed."

The three nurses surround her, attaching the new limb. Once it is as snug as it can be, all three attendants stand back thus allowing the surgeon to see the fit.

"So Michael, how does it feel?"

"It feels very strange. Just to sit here watching it do nothing at all. But a hand on the end of my arm, nonetheless."

"I guess it would feel slightly unreal, perhaps a little unnatural, a kind of novelty effect. Now does it feel too tight, too lose or uncomfortable? Does it feel like an encumbrance, or does it feel part of you?"

"It feels part of me all right. I sit here and look at it, I can see it is my hand, on the end of my arm. If I can accept that now, then everything else will be so much simpler for later. It feels very comfortable, not the slightest bit out of place."

"That is excellent, Michael. You are certainly on the road to a one hundred per cent recovery, with thoughts, notions and interpretations like that."

"Did you plan on doing the surgery today?"

"Oh, yes, Michael. We are going to take you the theatre now, get scrubbed, then we will start in about half an hour."

"Amazing, I am all yours then until the end."

They dress him in a surgical gown and help him into the wheelchair before transporting him into the empty operation room. Then the surgeon and nurses all go and get changed and ready. The anesthetist puts him under, counting down with him:

"Ten, nine, eight, seven, six…"

Then Michael goes very quiet, the nurse turns to the surgeon:

"He is all yours now."

The prosthetic surgeon tests him first, just for her own satisfaction.

"Michael, Michael, are you asleep?"

There was no response, no murmur, as the surgeon checked his eyes.

"OK ladies let us get on with the operation."

The microsurgery was long, tiring and labour intensive. Patience was imperative, a big necessity. Silence was the order of the day. All four of them worked, understanding the importance of not disrupting the surgeon's concentration. Then all four of them feel gloriously happy with the completed procedure. Then, putting his arm and now new hand into a sling, they move him to their recovery room, with a constant twenty-four-hour observation by one of the nurses, who all took it in turn to keep an eye on Michael's well-being and steady recovery. Slowly he came around a little groggy, but smiling as he dared himself to take a look at his arm, with its new appendage attached. His eyes traversed down his arm along his hand, suspended in front of him. Flexing it automatically, he felt it work and respond immediately.

"Nurse, nurse!"

She comes rushing in to his shouts, she smiles quite openly at him, not apologetic as she rubs his arm.

"Are you pleased? Do you feel good?"

"Very pleased, I feel terrific nurse."

He leans across kissing her quickly, as a token of his thanks. She gets up off his bed, flashing her long, lithe legs. Michael grins approvingly as he sees her scanty underwear, as her uniform rides high.

"I will just go and get the surgeon." she tells him brazenly. The specialist comes back with the nurse following on behind. Going straight up to his bed, removing his sling. Michael makes it work almost instantaneously for his private audience. All stand transfixed, as they all watch it work, doing as he instructs it, perplexed by the instant effect his thoughts and deeds have upon it. Admiring the work, the all-consuming passion of the surgeon and her nurses had dedicated to his well-being and outward appearance.

"So, trying it out Michael, does it come up to your expectations?"

"It does indeed. It seems to react just like my other hand. I just think of doing something, lo and behold my new hand does it for me."

"That is the idea of linking it into your nervous system. So it is part of you always, from the very beginning. After today, tomorrow morning in fact, we will show you the full scope of its uses. I will be on call, but the nurses will be your daily instructors." So the week flew by, constantly exercising his mind with his hand, until it became at one with him. He mastered it almost immediately. All three nurses were very impressed with his motivation, which hastened his advancement. The surgeon came down to visit him on the Thursday afternoon. She spent three hours with him, testing the hand, with Michael in full control. Both he and the doctor were thoroughly intoxicated with the patient's accomplishments. Gaining the full control and use of the limb, in such a short space of time.

"So how does it feel now Michael?"

"Like a man possessed, at one with the universe. Once again master of my own destiny."

"That is very good. In that case are you happy to sign your release form, in the morning?"

"That would be fantastic, Doctor, do you mean it?"

"Of course, that means you can get back to living your life once again young man."

"That would be exceptional, crazy."

"Everything is fine then. Lola you stay here with Michael please, finish off the instruction. Deanna, Daya come with me please. We have a new patient to organize."

Lola goes up to the office, looking for the release forms. While she disappears, Michael fondles himself beneath the sheets, having wanted to relieve himself for such a very long time now. Gratified that he could apply the right amount of pressure to be in full control, he could feel himself stiffening as he closed his eyes to exert more tension. Just at that moment, the sumptuous Lola decides to sit at the other end of his bed. She smiles very openly at him, he cannot help himself as she pulls up her dress, revealing her long, supple gorgeous legs. Also revealing and showing him, that she has no underwear on. At this he pulls slow and hard as she tells him:

"You are a very naughty boy, Michael, I know very well what you are doing to yourself. Try and stop it now."

"I am very sorry, Lola, if this embarrasses you, but I cannot. It has been so long since I have been able to achieve an erection, I just need to finish myself off."

Lola throws back the sheet, astonished at what she reveals.

"Come with me to the recovery room, where it is more private and where I can lock the door. Pull your trousers back up."

She just loved the sight of his sexual organ, all primed, aroused and hard. She gently runs her fingers along his rod — he was on fire, which made her wet in an instant. She then rubbed Michael, feeling him flex a little more. Following Lola into the silent room, she locks the door and draws the blinds. Lola removes her uniform as Michael now drops his trousers once again. She sits him into a chair, then takes him orally as she sucks on him gently,

"My, this is a whopper, so damn delicious."

First she gobbles his paramount manhood, then having satisfied herself she goes over to the nearby trolley, applying some transparent gel to her inner thigh, leaving some on her fingertip. Whereupon she returns, then rubs into Michael's surging weapon. Then in the reverse cowgirl position, she clambers over him, sitting onto him, as he lays back to accommodate her. She slides all the way down, sighing as he enters her nimble, willing mound, taking the slight curvature of his muscle in her stride. Michael fully penetrates Lola's sweet haven, then pulls, jerks and twists on her mighty nipples. Then he is soothing, caressing and massaging her soft, silky bosom. His fingers walk across and over around her large elaborate aureoles. She pushes as hard as she can down on his throbbing unrelenting pole as he tries to shunt himself deeper into her. The two of them just luxuriating in their closeness, heat and Lola's womanly perfume. She still jostles atop of his formidable crown.

"I love your breasts Lola, what cup are they?"

"EEEs, also my nipples are very sensitive, as you might have noticed. They just love being sucked hard and long, Michael."

Michael rocks to and fro, twirling her robust teats, pounding her wet, sticky snatch. Lola knows she is well lubricated as he dips his fingers into her cream, then licks each digit in turn. The nurse groans, snorts as she grinds a little wildly, smearing her cream over both of their recumbent bodies in the process.

"Ooohh, my oohhh you are a beserker, so tempestuous Michael."

"This is all your doing, nursie, your lithe body has enchanted me. You flaunted yourself in front of me, giving me the instant hots."

Withdrawing from Lola, sitting her down, then getting inbetween her hot, enflamed thighs, he pushed his tongue into her sopping wet, fragrant pussy. Lapping lasciviously at her abundance of free-flowing juices, he thoroughly enjoys his session of cunnilingus, with his favourite nurse. She now gets onto the floor on all fours, allowing him to plunge himself straight into her pink sweetie, as deep as he can. Pile driving, he makes Lola's thighs quiver and shake. Knowing that the nurse can feel all of him, deep within her receptive loins, his strokes take longer as his swollen dome bangs, striking all points south in the nurse's nether regions. Her sensory receptors love the averse physical contact. His dire purple crown making her writhe as his full length strobes her aching nest. Her whole body is awake and moving to the incessant thud of this man. Lola had no other recourse than to move, dance and jiggle to his personal tune, as his muscle raged inside her provocative, irresistible body. She shudders, unable to help herself, as she climaxes once again. The two naked bodies smell of nothing except Lola's sex.

His energy level upped, pounding, pillaging her vibrant, resilient mound once again. Knowing he was full, he made sure every thrust agitated her whole torso. Holding Lola down in place, he grunted as he shunted down hard to keep himself in place. Then he was ejaculating with a violent force into her trembling, overwrought inner thigh. Thick, sticky, white entwined, leaving both more than satisfied. They just knelt there, bonded by the carnal expression they had just glorified with each other.

"You are exceptional Lola, the most beautiful nurse I have ever tasted. Thank you so much for helping me, relieve my tension and frustration."

"It was my pleasure, Michael, I really enjoyed you. Just adored the ride you gave me. Now I know you are definitely good for your release tomorrow. I will come and check in on you, later."

"I will look forward to that, Lola."

She smiles, stroking his arm, now wiping his disarming penis with a moist wipe, with slow attentive motions, making him all eager again.

"Ssshh, I can do that, nurse, you are getting me excited and frustrated once again."

"Sorry, Michael, I just cannot help being a nurse."

She gets dressed, then helps Michael open the door and blinds before wheeling Michael back to his bed, then waves to him. He grins.

"See you later, luscious Lola."

"You will, I know for sure."

She leaves the ward as Michael now relaxes, then reflects, figuring out how to take the bank on his own, before returning to Nairobi. What was going through his mind was that he had no explosives or transport, no cash to actually buy anything that could enable him to do the job. So the main bank he decided was totally out of the question. So it would have to be mini hold-ups. He would have to gate-crash smaller branches between here and Nairobi, just rob then in situ. All he had to do was get a hire car, he had a balaclava in his knapsack, he knew that for sure. He walked over to his bedside locker, pulling out his sack, to see what else had survived his ordeal. In there was a woolly hat with the cut-outs for his eyes and mouth. The dummy pistol, the mini Indian club with the fragmented glass embedded in it, along with a map. That would have to do for now, he did spot a box of powdered latex gloves on the trolley, so he tucked those into his holdall as well. Those then were the tools at his disposal, so he would have to make the most of them. He would at least arrive in Nairobi, with something to show for his leave of absence.

The Light of Africa would have suspected he was one of the bodies found, as he had not been able to contact anyone, after such a long period of time. The only person that knew of his existence and survived, was Ramon. He would not have told a single being of his relief, nor his personal singular involvement with Michael. So it could stay that way, for the safety of his precious Belinda and Anjella. Also, if he was extremely lucky, he could get back in time for his daughter's birthday. He would even put himself out and purchase her a present or gift. Slowly he fell asleep with all these thoughts going around in his mind. Then he was disturbed, sat bolt upright in the chair, rubbing both of his eyes.

"So sorry to disturb you sir, it is only the evening meal. Would you like tea or coffee?"

"A strong black Kenyan would be fabulous."

So she poured him a mug of coffee, to go with the *mutura githeri*, alongside the *maandazi*.

"You are a life saver, Mama, thank you so very much."

The older woman smiles at his gratitude.

"You are very welcome young man. I hope you get well soon."

"I am on my way tomorrow. So I thank you for your service mama."

He gets up, hugs her very close, kisses her on both cheeks and lips, telling her:

"You keep real safe, now."

"I will, my boy, you too."

She leaves fully bolstered by his attention and good wishes, loving his kisses and hugs. The first she had received in many a long year. Michael enjoys his food and large mug of coffee as he sits back down, reviewing his map so as to decide where to stop, on his way back to Nairobi. It would be completely random, a bonus, an overwhelming surprise for his control officer on his unannounced return to the fold, some time over the weekend. He climbed into his bed feeling a little whacked. Sleep came easily, his hand relaxed as he did not awaken during the night. He was only woken up by Mama, again, as she did the breakfast rounds.

"Good morning, my dear, so what would you like this morning?"

"Good morning, Mama, and what a fantastic one it is, too. A black Kenyan along with something sweet please."

She pours the hot coffee, putting it alongside a generous slice of almond cake.

"Thank you, Mama, please keep safe for me."

"I will my dear, see you again, perhaps."

She leaves while Michael has his coffee and cake. Then he gets dressed, ready to leave the hospital. Deena comes in with the release forms for him to sign. Putting his signature to them he kisses Deena,

"Thank you so much, for a very pleasant stay."

"It was a real pleasure, to help you get back to normal Michael."

Finally, free and finding his feet, he made his move, taking his knapsack with him. Now to locate a car hire firm. Lola told him to look out for one on the B8, the Bambiri road. She could not remember the name, but nearly everyone used it to cover the 274-mile journey back to Nairobi, rather than use the public transport system. If they had the money available, of course.

He was following her directions and there it was. Marines Car Hire Limited. Going in and perusing the selection of automobiles, he looked over a nondescript car that would not draw any attention to the driver, regardless of what he does, or intends to do, during the course of his long trek back to Nairobi. That is just what he wants, he smiles to himself as the attendant approaches him.

"Yes sir, can I help you at all?"

"You can indeed young man. I would like to hire this car, if at all possible?"

"Certainly sir, where would you be going?"

"Back to Nairobi."

"That is very convenient, we do have a pick-up service there. If you can tell us where you are going precisely, where you will leave it, then we can retrieve it for you."

"I will leave it in the car park of the Sarova Panafric Hotel. I will leave the keys at the front desk, ready for you to collect."

"That is superb sir, shall we do the necessary?"

After showing the salesman his driving licence, signing the paperwork and paying the required amount, he is out, gone and on his way. Driving out of Mombassa, he keeps to the back roads, driving a little cautiously at first, getting used to the controls and transmission with his newly acquired hand. once he felt happy that he was the master of his automobile, that all was within his grasp. He put his foot down, joining in with the Friday morning traffic in Mombassa. Threading his way through onto the major roads, finally on the B8 he laughs out loud, screams an obscenity, relishing the overt danger, he is going to put himself under, just to regain the trust, popularity and recognition, for his self-serving attitude and demeanour, for the Light of Africa.

Having escaped the mayhem of Mombassa, he has his list of stops already pegged out on his map. That, and a sheet of paper with instant directions for him to follow as he drives. He pulls over to a small coffee shop, taking a well-earned black breakfast tea, drinking it hot, feeling the bite at the back of his throat. Going back to the car, he looks looking at his map for his first engagement. It was not far away. Moving his knapsack onto the front seat in readiness, he drove on calmly, self-assured and nerveless, in complete control of his emotions. Drawing up to the first bank in Mariakani, he noticed at once that it had an electronic barrier at the car park. So he left that one well alone, not wanting to get trapped within its confines. Continuing to drive along the main thoroughfare, through the town, he spyed a bank with an open door and no evidence of security. Parking putting his hood up, the latex gloves on both of his hands and his dummy weapon in his right hand, the mini club in his left hand, he goes straight up to the teller drawing his weapon, throwing his empty knapsack over the counter, then he makes an express command:

"All of the money in there, otherwise you are dead my friend. Which would mean I would have to help myself anyway. So please hurry up."

The teller was too afraid to answer back. She tipped all the cash into the empty sack along with the other two tills that were behind the counter. Michael, a little excited at getting his own way, gets back into his car, making his getaway before the alarm is raised. That was very straightforward, uneventful, the perfect trick. He only hoped that all the others would be just as quick. This time he went through the town, escaping onto the freeway, enabling him to put his foot down, coasting at sixty miles an hour instead of ambling along at thirty, through the back streets.

Driving for forty-five minutes, he slipped off one of the exit stations, disappearing into one of the restaurants, for some light refreshments. Taking some *mishkaki* and *irio*, followed by a slice of semolina cake, with the date filling. This seems a much smaller community at Maji Ya Chumvi. Gathering his thoughts, his willpower, gumption, gearing up with his own sense of survival and self-preservation, he drove directly into the centre of town. Locating another bank just on the edge of the main road, he parked in the nearby empty car park, right on top of its exit. Then donning his robbery outfit, he walks so confidently into the bank. Which only has one young female customer in attendance. Walking right up close to her, he draws his weapon and put it hard against her back, so she could feel it was there. Keeping her in between himself and the teller,

"Lady, please tell the man what I am pushing against your back."

"It feels like the nozzle of a gun, it is hurting me."

"Now nothing will happen to her, as long as you put all your cash in here."

Giving him the knapsack and, then without daring to look at his aggressor, the teller starts to fill it with all the available cash he has at his disposal.

"Hurry up or she will be on your conscience for a very long time. Death does strange things, to those that are involved and become part of it."

The teller empties all three drawers as quickly as he possibly can into the holdall. Then he returns it to Michael, who in turn twirls the young lady around, kisses her on those two divine lips, smiles and winks before he retires to the entrance. He leaves the female customer in a quandary, not sure whether to cry or wave him goodbye. Knowing now that she would not be able to get the money, she needed to do her shopping. He drove out of Maji Ya Chumvi, not in a mad rush or hurry, but quite swiftly finding his way up to the major road once again. Pulling over to the side, he removes his mask and gloves, laying his weapons on the floor of the car. Moving off once again, he keeps to the main road for a swifter exit. Mixing himself in the flow of traffic already on the freeway. Looking continually for any sign of a chase, or sounds of sirens, but nothing seems to be following him. So he moved over into the inside lane, taking a breather, while he looked for the exit to Samburu.

Just before the required exit, a fuel station showed itself. Pulling into the welcoming shade, he refuels and gets his oil and water checked along with the tyre pressures. Giving the attendant a tip, he drove onto, into Samburu, which seemed to be a rather quiet suburb. The first bank he came to was closed. So continuing to drive down through the centre, he found a facility that was open and doing business. With only his dummy pistol, knapsack and peephole balaclava on, he strolled straight in the premises, scaring the living daylights out of the lone female teller who was in attendance. Pointing his weapon directly at her, he held her eyes with all his intensity.

"No noise, if you please, just empty your tills and drawers into here. I do not want to hurt you in any way, my most gracious lady."

She nodded as if in a trance, giving him all that was available. Taking the holdall from her quivering hands, he kissed the back of her hand twice as he took it.

"Thank you, so much, young lady."

She just looks at him, far too scared to do or say anything in return. Once plundered he leaves the bank, he scoots off in his car, putting the air conditioning on, making himself ready, for the two-and-a-half-hour trek across the Taru Desert. He drove away not looking forward to this part of his journey home. This time he puts his foot down before racing away. Venturing into fourth gear, then up onto the Nairobi road, he heads towards Voi, then the Tsavo National Park. It was a long, hard slog, taking it nice and easy on the deserted uninteresting desert road, pacing himself and his vehicle, in the early afternoon heat. His heart pumped, exhausted but he felt glad to have made it across the Taru in one piece, through Voi as well as the Tsavo Park. Finally, he made it into the relative safety of Mtito Andei town. He found a small hotel where he parked in the spacious car park. He took the time to check his vehicle over, the oil would need topping up, along with a refuelling stop as well, as soon as possible. He then went and got himself a room, where he showered and freshened up as best he could, then reappeared for dinner. Ordering the *Nyama Choma*, his personal preference being the goat, *Kachumberi*. Followed by a slice of the very tempting *Mkate Wamaya*. He even allowed himself a cold Tusker, as he would not be driving again until the morning. He enjoyed it all immensely, cooked to perfection. Then retiring to his bed, and slept soundly right through the night, until 07:00 hours. He took a cup of vanilla tea with his *makte* and *githeri*.

Settling his account, he then moved out to a nearby petrol station, refuelling, as well as getting his water and oil topped up. Once again, he made his way up to the freeway that was the B8, finally heading home. Driving a little more carefully, he looked out for the exit for the B7. He wanted to pick up Kitui town it was easy enough to spot. He took the required exit station onto the B7, following it into Kitui town. It was alive and full of markets, the to-ing and fro-ing of people, getting ready for the morning's activities. He spotted one of the banks just opening its doors. Heading over that way, he parked directly opposite, facing the correct way for a simple escape and evasion dash afterwards.

He slipped his mask and gloves on as he sat in the comfort of his car, his hand weapon at the ready. Then strolling straight into the bank, he found no one but the teller in the building. Michael put his finger up to his lips, keeping the weapon at chest height, as he looked very intently at the older man.

"All the money in here now. Do not talk, just do it."

So he did, scooping all the everything that was available, into the already heavy knapsack. It was now full to bursting.

"Thank you so very much. Would you come round this side for me?"

So the older teller came and did his bidding. Michael struck the Indian club hard against his cranium, putting him to the floor, out like a light. Then he walked out of the bank as though nothing had happened. Closing the door behind him, he got into his car and then he was away, without a backward glance.

"Nearly home, Michael," he says aloud to himself, as he mustered the energy to drive out of Kitui, back onto the B7. Now driving and not needing to stop for anything this time, he drove enjoying the first part of his journey. Over the Chyulu Hills, past the sweet overpowering smell of Kibwezi town; an area known for its essential honey production. Then finally to the car park, of the Sarova Panafric. Leaving the car locked he went to the front desk.

"Excuse me, could I have the keys for room 326?"

"Certainly sir, it is good to see you back."

"Thank you so much. Could you see that the representative for Marines Car Hire gets this set of keys, when they come calling?"

"I will indeed sir."

Michael goes to his room, placing his knapsack and his other paraphernalia into his wardrobe, then locking it. Undressing, he takes a long overdue shower. Then getting dressed into something very clean, He takes a large wad of notes and hides them in a hidden pocket in his heavy coat. Then walking over to the premises of his control office, he knocks on the door with the required code. He was let in. a new and nervous acolyte asked Michael to stay where he was. Mr Ironi did so, remembering his days as a junior and how hard it could be to make a suitable impression. The acolyte went into Jomo.

"There is someone here to see you, Jomo."

"Who is it?"

"Michael of all people."

"Are you sure, I thought he was dead?"

"No, he is here in the flesh, alive and kicking."

The door opened to reveal a large smiling face. Michael strolls in, Jomo not quite believing his own eyes.

"Damn Michael, it has been an age. Come sit down and tell me the story."

"Have you got a cold one for me?"

"Of course I have."

Jomo pulls out a brace of Tuskers from his cooler. Decapping them he passes one over to his mucker.

"Well Jomo, with the bank in Mombassa, the IED I made to blow the vault had a short circuit. I gave it the statuary fifteen minutes, then moved into investigate. It just went off of its own accord. It killed my two oppos outright. It took off my left hand, I managed to get out and hide. I also managed to get a lift to the nearest hospital, where they managed to get to me just in time."

"So your two mates are dead, and left at the scene?"

"Yes, I am assuming the police put that down to a failed attempt. By the two bodies, they would have found at the scene. Probably putting them with the remnants of the car that we stole as well."

"So where have you been all this time?"

"Most of the time, in the Mombasa General Hospital, recovering along with their more than capable surgeons, who were attempting to keep me alive. Which I might say, they did very well. Then a visit from their plastic and prosthetic surgeon who came to see me, at my request. So here I am now, with two good hands. I am able to use my new one, just as good as my old one."

"Let me have a look Michael."

Michael shows Jomo the work and craftsmanship that went into restoring his hand.

"That is amazing Michael."

"I also have a bonus for you and the Light of Africa."

"What would that be? Hold on hold on, when did you leave Mombasa?"

"A couple of days ago now."

"OK so what is the bonus you have for us?"

"Take a look in my knapsack, but go very careful."

Jomo undoes the chords holding the top of the holdall in place, keeping the sack tied, carefully loosening the top of the bag. Taking a look inside, he cannot believe his eyes once again.

"Is this full of cash?"

"It is indeed."

"So where did you get all this from?"

"Some very swift personal raids I made on my journey home, to make up for the failed robbery in Mombassa."

"This will help us no end. Where did you make your raids?"

"They were in between Mombassa and Niarobi. The first was in Mariakani, then Maji Ya Chumvi, then Samburu. Then finally I called into Kitui town. Then I made my way home. Then my first port of call was here, to let you know I was still in one piece and fighting fit."

"You have been busy on our behalf. It was very rewarding as well."

"Oh yes, I am very glad you think so, Jomo."

"We will not require your services again, for a while. But this prize haul has made a difference. I will put the usual percentage into your bank account. Take a couple of days off, enjoy yourself, go out. Then come back and see me on Monday, Michael."

"OK, thanks for the beer."

"No problem, you earnt it."

Michael left thinking of what to get his beloved Belinda for her birthday. Going back to his hotel, he recovers the cash he hid away. Then venturing to the taxi rank, he gets a ride to his house. Knocking on the door, he can hear the sweet tones of Anjella as she approaches the front portal. Opening the door, she is completely surprised, shocked to see him standing there in front of her.

"Good grief, Michael, how the hell are you?"

"I am good, a lot better than I was, or have been lately. But there is no need for you to know about that, or anyone else for that matter."

"Come in, I thought you had forgotten all about us. It is ages since you promised, to come round and visit more often, so that you could get to know your daughter a little better. Adhiambo? Come and see who has decided to come and pay you a visit, at long last."

"Dad! Hi, Dad, what is up with your left hand, have you had an accident?"

"Yes, but only a small one, a mere trifle."

Anjella comes over to look as well, having missed it the first time around. She takes in her hand, feeling it and unable to leave it alone, not believing it is prosthetic.

"Well spotted Adhiambo, it is prosthetic and a very good one as well, if I may say so. What happened here then Michael, for you to actually lose it?"

"I just burnt it very badly and had to have it replaced. Now it is OK. I have come round to invite you all out to dinner. Because it is Belinda's birthday tomorrow. I would also like to buy her a present as well, if that is conducive with everyone here?"

"That is very nice of you, Michael, we would love to. I am sure Adhiambo would love to go and choose a present with her daddy."

"Yes, I would. I do not know if I would like anew dress, or something for school."

"If we all go out now, how about we take you shopping for a new dress. Then you will have your mummy and nana to help you choose. Then you can tell me what you need for school. Perhaps we can sort that out together? Then all go out and have some dinner together as a family."

"OK, Daddy, that sounds like a proper birthday wish, spending the whole day with you."

As they all get ready, Anjella turns to Michael.

"As you are being so generous and, in such a good mood, would you like to join us tomorrow, for Adhiambo's birthday party?"

"I would love to. Providing no one objects to me being there and included."

"I would love you to be there, Daddy, at least for this once, if you can?"

"The more the merrier, I say." Ramon added. Tristina smiles and kisses her husband on the cheek. She tells Michael:

"You can control the hordes of children that will be coming round to our little home, tomorrow."

"In that case, I would be honoured to come to your party, my dearest daughter."

Then altogether they ventured into the shopping precinct that was Westgate. Letting his beloved Belinda look and choose where she wanted to go. Michael and Ramon both took a backseat as the three ladies went hunting for a beautiful party frock, for the young birthday girl.

"Ramon, do you still keep our little secret?"

"Of course, I do, Michael. I am glad to see the hospital were able to do such an excellent job, in restoring you to one piece."

"So am I. Everything is good up to now, I can only thank you, for your help."

"I am only glad I got there in time for you."

They both see the three women disappear into a female clothing shop. So they wander in that direction, staying outside, giving them the space to see what the young madam would like, not wanting to interfere in her choice at all. But Belinda comes dashing out of the shop, looking for her father.

"Daddy, I know this is a birthday present, but can I wear it to my party tomorrow?"

"Of course, my sweetness. Once I have bought it for you, you can wear it whenever it suits you."

"Oh, thank you, Daddy. Are you and Grandpa going to come in and see what I have chosen?"

She holds out her arms, even at this age. Michael picks her up, she kisses him on the lips. He kisses his little *mondo* back hugging her close, whispering to her:

"Grandpa and I will follow you into the shop, to see what you have chosen Belinda. A very happy birthday Belinda."

"Oh, thank you, thank you."

He puts her back down, she rushes over to her mum and nana,

"Yes, I would love that one. Daddy says I can wear it for my party tomorrow. What do you think Dad?"

"I think the pale lemon suits you, it highlights your natural beauty."

Michael goes forward to pay for the item that has caught Belinda's eye.

"So, what would you like for school, my precious?"

"Could I have a tablet?"

"Of course, you can. Do you know how to use one?"

"Of course, Daddy, they show us at school."

"Come on then, let us go and look and find one for you."

Michael takes her into a shop that sells computers, she points out the one that they use at school

"This one I know, Daddy, because we use it at school."

"Will you be happy with that particular one, Belinda?"

"Yes, I will, Daddy."

"Can I help you at all, sir?"

"Yes, we would like this tablet, for the young lady."

"OK, sir, I will go and get you one."

"Does it have parental control available on it?"

"Yes, it does. I can set it for you, if you would like me to, sir."

"That would be very kind of you."

The assistant comes back, opens the box, removes the tablet and switches it on. He runs through the whole menu of controls. Belinda's eyes lighting up as she watches. Then the assistant implants the parental control, making it safe for the young lady to use.

"Thank you for your help. So what is the damage?"

"Forty-five thousand shillings."

Paying the assistant, then turning to the birthday girl,

"Would you like me to wrap it, for tomorrow?"

"Yes, please, Daddy."

"OK, I will keep it for now, and you can have it tomorrow, my gorgeous birthday girl."

"OK, Daddy, give it to me, when everyone is there to see."

They both come out of the shop, holding hands. Michael has the present under his arm.

"Did you get the one she wanted, Michael?"

"Yes, I did Anjella. I also got parental control put on it as well."

"Well, that was good thinking on your behalf."

"I know Anjella. So are we ready to eat, people?"

"Yes, Daddy I am hungry."

"If the birthday girl is hungry, then I guess it is time to eat. What are we waiting for?"

They jump a taxi. for the short drive to their favourite restaurant, Fogo Gaucho. Going in and waiting to be seated,

"A table for five, please."

The waitress smiles as she leads them to a quiet little corner. Once they are all seated around the table, the waitress who had been waiting very patiently asks:

"Would you like to order any drinks?"

"Yes, please. Two Tuskers, one Kenya King and tonic, one Old Monk and a splash for the birthday girl."

Adhiambo turns to the waitress smiling, "Could you make it the guava juice splash, please?"

"Of course, young lady."

The waitress leaves, but returns shortly afterwards with the order. After placing the drinks on the table, she asks, "Are you ready to order, sirs, madams?"

The whole table nod at each other, all agreeing that they know what they would like to eat. Belinda takes pride of place.

"I want the *mishkaki* and the *irio* please, Daddy."

"I would like the *mishkak*i with the *githeri*."

"OK, Anjella. I would love some of your *sukuma wiki* with your superb *karanga*."

"OK, Ramon for me, the *mutura matoke* and a *mahararagwe chapati*, with a bottle of the Leleshwa merlot shiraz."

"OK, Tristina, I am going to thoroughly enjoy *nyamachoma*, goat, *kachumbari* rice."

The waitress leaves to fulfil their order.

"Michael how did you really hurt your hand?"

"We do not need to discuss it here and now, while we are in company."

"So when will you tell me?"

"When we are somewhere a little more private."

"Anjella, wait until you get home. You and Michael can have the kitchen to yourselves. You can both discuss it at length there."

"Remember, you have other ears listening as well."

"OK, Mum, Dad, I will find out later."

Adhiambo looks very cross, looking directly at her mother.

"Stop causing trouble, Mummy. We should be happy, all my family are here together for once, that doesn't happen very often. We're all around the same table, please do not spoil it now."

"OK, my *mondo*, happy birthday, my little pearl."

They all smile as Belinda kisses her mummy and daddy, in equal measure. The food came along with the wine, allowing the birthday girl a little taster, as a treat. It was enjoyed by the whole family. The waitress returned to clear the table.

"Would you like to order dessert?"

Michael turns to the beaming, bright, very happy birthday girl.

"So, Belinda would you like a sweet?"

"Yes, please, Daddy, I would love the sticky date pudding with some ice cream."

"OK, precious. I will have the walnut and halva cake please."

Tristina then speaks up.

"For me, the *mkate wa maya,* please.

Then Anjella smiles at the waitress.

"Could I have the sweet potato and coconut pudding, please."

Ramon, the last to order, asks politely, "A slice of the apple and walnut cake, would do me admirably, thank you."

Having dined together and really enjoyed each other's company. They all go home together. Indoors, Anjella turns to her mother and father,

"Would you keep Adhiambo amused, please, while I talk to Michael?"

"Of course, we will, Anjella."

"Thank you, Mum."

Anjella and Michael go together into the kitchen, closing the door behind them. Adhiambo turns to her nana.

"What are Mummy and Daddy going to do?"

"Just talk, my little *nyar kingi*. Sort out a few things. would you like to learn a new song, while we have the chance?"

"Yes, please, Nana."

"This is called *Kanyoni Kanja*. It goes like this:

*Kayoni Kanja*
*kanyoni kanja*
*gekugwa nja na mitheko*

*ndakoria atiri*
*ndakoria atiri,*
*wamichore wat'inda ku?*
*Ndatinda kori*
*ndatinda kori*
*ngiaragania mbirigiti*
*na mbirigiti*
*na mbirigiti.*
*Na ndinainukia magoto.*
*Magwa iriaini*
*magwa iriaini.*
*Gwa cucu wa kamerujia meru!*[7]

"OK, Nana, that is a pretty song. I love it, I love it, I do, I do. Will you teach me it all?"

"Of course, my precious. We will go through it slowly."

In the kitchen Michael sits with his partner Anjella, telling her exactly what happened to his hand, how it happened, what he was doing at the time. But crucially leaving out the bit where Ramon came and gave him assistance, to get to the hospital. He shrouds that in a relatively believable lie. Anjella felt his new hand, as it gripped hers in return.

"You say you paid to have this done at the Mombasa General Hospital?"

"Yes, it cost me a small fortune. But I got a very precise and neat job in the process."

"It is, Michael. Now I guess you are back and whole again. You will be flitting in and out of our lives, much the same as before?"

---

[7] For translation, see glossary

"I am afraid so. But I will come and see you all, when the time allows. I will carry on living at the hotel."

"OK, Michael."

"That is so, you and Belinda, do not get involved in anything I do."

"You promise to come and see Adhiambo, now you are back with us?"

"I will as often as I can. What time can I come to the party tomorrow?"

"Come when you are ready. You can help us prepare for when the children start arriving, at about three o'clock."

"OK I will look forward to that. Also, I want you to look after something for me."

"What would that be, not a gun or anything like that?"

"No, no nothing like that. Just some money. Stash it away somewhere, so that only you know where it is hidden. An emergency fund, in case you, I, we ever need it in a hurry. Keep it safe for all of us."

"OK Michael, give it here to me."

He hands over the pack of notes to her trembling hands. She takes it from him and puts it into her rather large bag for now.

"Come and have a drink, Michael, please."

They both come out of the kitchen, into Nana teaching Adhiambo the *Kanyoni Kanja* song.

"Dad would you get us all a drink? It has been such a wonderful day."

While Anjella goes into Adhiambo's room, to secrete the bundle of cash; Ramon makes a round of the *dawa*, with some magic moment vodka. The cash hidden away, Anjella comes back to join the party.

"Mummy, can I have a drink?"

"Of course, my *mondo*, how about some passion fruit?"

"OK, Mum, that would be lovely."

So they all sit together, helping the birthday girl sing the song she had just learnt. Tristina, Anjella, Ramon, Michael and Adhiambo, all sing as best they can. The little pearl enjoyed all the attention, as she always does.

"Come on, Adhiambo, time for bed. Another big day tomorrow, with all your friends. You will need a good night's sleep my *mondo*."

"OK, Mummy I am coming."

Starting with her nana Tristina, she goes round them all in turn, finishing with Michael. Giving them each a big affectionate kiss, with a hug and a whisper of "good night", in each very attentive ear. Then she runs to catch up with her mum, who gets her to bed. She reads her a bedtime story, until she falls fast asleep.

Michael leaves for a good night's sleep as well, not bothering to ask if he could stay, knowing full well the reply, before he even thought he might be invited to spend the night in his house. Ever since the time of him pleasuring himself in Anjella's bedroom, that was never talked about, neither of them were ever close, no chance of ever being so. Most of the time they only communicated to keep Belinda on the straight and narrow. But for the moment things were good between them. Putting the bottles in the bag, a small gift for all the children, in the shape of Kojo the Magician, for their entertainment. The tablet was wrapped in a pink ribbon, hiding away the cash gift hidden inside to spoil his Belinda even further. Catching a cab, knocking on the door, Tristina answering, smiling:

"Come on in, Michael. Everyone is up and working towards the party."

"OK, first Belindas' birthday present, then the bag, just to top up the drinks cabinet."

"Thank you very much, Michael. Just join in, would you like a vanilla coffee?"

"That would be wonderful, Tristina."

He goes out into the kitchen all ready to pitch in and give his assistance.

"Can I help anyone people, or will someone tell me what needs doing?"

"You could make some chicken tikka sandwiches, or the ham and peach. Or cut those long sausage rolls, into mini ones. You could make three or four jugs of the mango/guava and passion fruit squash."

"OK, Anjella, no problem."

Michael gets the four jugs, making two of the mango/guava squash, then two of the passion fruit variety as well. Then getting a large tin of fruit salad, he sprinkles the fruit across all four jugs, then puts them all into the fridge. Cutting the sausage rolls as required, then he helps Ramon with the various sandwiches while Anjella and Tristina were placing all the jellies in the fridge. Then he slices the almond cake, *mkate wa mayai*, apple and walnut cake, the walnut honey and date cake, along with the coconut and sweet potato pudding, *maandazi*, the walnut and date cookies, all onto plates and covering them.

"That is just about everything. Let us all take a well-earned breather."

"OK, Anjella, just so that you know, at about five o'clock, Kojo the Magician will be making an appearance. I hired him for the party. I hope you do not mind?"

"That was very thoughtful of you Michael. They will all enjoy that."

"I do hope so Tristina."

"They will enjoy that. It will be a big surprise, I know."

Belinda now appears into the room, making that comment as she enters, in her brand-new party frock. She twirls wanting to be admired by everyone. The whole captivated audience clap for her, all smiling and laughing as they enjoy her open display of youthful joy and happiness.

"So are you ready for your all friends, my little treasure?"

"I am indeed, Mummy."

They all slowly start to show up, all knocking on the door. Anjella tells all the parents they are more than welcome to stay and, enjoy the party as well. But all of them take this rare opportunity to let someone else look after them. While the mums and dads take the time off to vanish and enjoy a little them time, while they had the chance to be alone, all the children go rushing off into the big garden, all going wild, chasing each other, playing tag, skipping and kicking the various balls about. They even chase the feral cats into everyone else's garden. Just children being children and enjoying every moment of it, causing havoc while the adults lay the table, with all the goodies that were cooked and prepared earlier for their enjoyment.

"Are you all hungry? Come on then, the table is all ready for you!"

They all come in, finding a convenient seat. Then all tuck in to the glorious food laid out on the table before them.

Tristina and Ramon go around the table filling the glasses with the cool fruit cocktail Michael had prepared. Then the fruit and ice cream appeared much to everyone's delight. Then the cakes and other sweets were put on the table for them to help themselves when they fancied more. There was a knock at the door, Michael attended the call to the front portal.

"Hi, Kojo, do come in." His table had been set up. He put his case of tricks on it, then looked at them all.

"Good afternoon, children."

"Good afternoon." they all responded.

"I am Kojo, the Magician. Here to entertain you. Are you all ready to be magicked?"

They all scream back at him, with a wilful over enthusiastic sense of anticipation:

"Yes, we are."

So Kojo with his tricks, his balloon shaping and little comedy act, kept them amused. He made Adhiambo a pink pony, getting her up in front, so she could help him with some of his tricks. Which delighted her and all her friends at the party, especially the audience participation, where they could all join in the fun. It gave Anjella, Tristina, Ramon and Michael a chance to tidy up and refresh the table, so there was now some room, so that Belinda could open her presents in front of everyone.

"Well Kojo that was superb, thank you so very much for coming."

"Thank you, Michael, for giving me such attentive children. It was a real pleasure."

"Here is a little bonus, you take care now."

"That is very kind of you. Thank you and you enjoy."

All the children came back to the table, watching the young birthday girl unwrap all her presents. Reading the labels out loud, then thanking each friend in turn, as he did so. Then came her big moment. Anjella and Michael bring in the birthday cake, putting it on the table. First of all, Adhiambo stands and sings the *Kanyoni Kanja* song. Then slowly all the other children join in with her, loving all the showing off they do between them. All her girl friends join in together, to sing to her.

> Afya njema na furaha,
> afya njema na furaha,
> afya njema na furaha mpendwa wetu Adhiambo,
> afya njema na furaha mpendwa wetu Adhiambo.
>
> Maisha bora marefu,
> maisha bora marefu,
> maisha bora marefu mpendwa wetu Adhiambo,
> maisha bora marefu mpendwa wetu Adhiambo.[8]

Then they all applaud, shouting at the birthday girl to blow out her nine candles. Then they stand out of the way, letting Adhiambo have all the room she needs. Then with one big huff and puff, she blows out all nine candles in one attempt, making her birthday wish at the same time. Then Anjella comes forward.

"Would you like a slice now, then I will cut you all a slice to take home as well?"

"Oohh yes please."

---

[8] For translation, see glossary

"That would be lovely."

"Two pieces of cake, are we allowed?"

"Of course, this is a birthday party."

"We are very lucky."

"Thank you Mrs Ogwayo."

All the girls now catered for, Tristina now takes the cake into the kitchen, cutting further pieces, to put into all the goodie bags that they made up for Adhiambo's friends, for when they go home. There were nine of them, one for each of the girls at the party.

"Now girls…"

Anjella stopped, she could see that the birthday girl, as well as all her friends, were more interested in her presents, than listening to her. So she left them to it, putting on some music in the form of Muthoni Ndonga, better known as Muthoni Drummer Queen. Her opening song is Kenyan Message[9]. Also, Anjella includes Adhiambo's other favourite, a rather new face to the popular music in Kenya, the vibrant Cece Sagini. The music was enjoyed and danced to by all the girls.. Anjella went to sit down with her mum, dad and Michael, enjoying a glass of the fruit cocktail, from the last jug that had any left in it.

"That was a qualified success, I think."

"It was that, Anjella."

"Thanks, Mum."

"Any party where everyone enjoys themselves, is a good party."

---

[9] Muthoni Ndonga is also known for her *Blankets and Wine Festivals*, which attract a lot of African musicians.

"It is Michael and they are very quiet now, being entertained with all the birthday presents."

"It is rather relaxing now. What is the time?"

Tristina looks at her watch.

"It is nearly seven o'clock, the mums and dads will be arriving soon."

Shortly after that last comment, the first of the parents start to arrive. With first knock at the door, Anjella gets up to answer.

"Come in please, have a seat. Adhiambo would you get Daeja's bag from the kitchen please, her mummy is here to take her home."

"OK, Mummy, no problem."

After the first parent arrived, the other eight followed slowly afterwards. Adhiambo said, thank you to all the mothers and fathers, for allowing her friends to come to her party. She gave each friend and her mother a kiss, as well as her friends getting their individual goodie bags, before they all left. The birthday girl was all smiles, joy and happiness, going around each of the adults kissing each in turn, with the pop music and the voice of Cece Sagini, still playing in the background.

"I had such a wonderful time today. Thank you all so much for everything."

"We are just happy you enjoyed yourself so much."

Ramon gets up, pours a King gin and tonic for Tristina, an Old Monk rum for Anjella, along with two *konyagi* vodkas, for Michael and himself. A small glass of the fruit cocktail was provided for the smiling Adhiambo. Giving everyone their glass, Roman raised his:

"A toast to our beautiful, birthday girl."

A chorus of:

"Our beautiful, birthday girl."

All five chinked their glasses, in respect of Belinda's ninth birthday, then all taking a small sip, they relax and enjoying imbibing. Then Anjella turns to her daughter:

"Come on, young lady, school tomorrow. Time for you to go to bed. Say good night to everyone."

Adhiambo goes round to everyone, saying her goodnights. Going with her mum to bed, Ramon and Tristina get up and go the kitchen, to attend to the tidying and washing up. Anjella returns.

"Well Anjella I am going to say goodnight to you all. Thank you for what was a superb day."

"Do not leave it so long until we see you again, Michael."

"OK, Anjella, goodnight Tristina, Ramon."

They both come from the kitchen.

"Goodnight, Michael, come back soon."

He kisses Tristina on the cheek, then shakes Ramon's hand.

"You take care, Michael."

"I will, Ramon."

He walks out into the warm night air, wending his way back to his hotel. To start with Michael is as good as his word. He comes at every possible moment, to see Belinda. He interacts with her, takes her out at the weekends, actually starts to know his own daughter, after all this time away from her. Belinda gets the chance to know him, then his visits get less frequent, so by the time of her next birthday, he is not there to celebrate it with her. Nor is he there when Anjella gets promoted to the head of her department. At the same time, she gets an invitation to attend the World Health Organisation, as part of the hospital's deputation, because of her work with malaria. Anjella also while she has the time calls her friend Miss Suzie Wokabi, the chief creative officer of Suzie Beauty, asking her if she could find her daughter Adhiambo a small Saturday job. Just so that she can earn herself some money and, hopefully, become a little streetwise in the process. Suzie tells Anjella if she comes to the office, she will most certainly find her something to do, that will give her a sense of fulfilment.

In the meantime, Michael has been moved out to Luug, a township in Somalia. Where he has been directed to find a convenient hideaway, where the Light of Africa can build a small training camp, for the instruction of bomb making, for their converts. He had been given a name to contact on his arrival. But that contact had already been discovered by the Somalia army, by whom he had been put down along with three other followers before his arriving in Luug. So for the moment Michael is keeping a low profile, still fully intending to cover his function in founding and funding a local bomb school, for the addicts and so-called freedom fighters.

He notices the local garage has a couple of well-worn vehicles on their forecourt, so went up to the proprietor:

"Excuse me, are either of these vehicles for sale?"

"Sorry, no. I use them for spares. I do have one round the back, if you are interested."

"Would you show me?"

"Of course, it will not be a problem."

He takes Michael to the rear of his workshop, letting Michael have a good look, lifting the bonnet. Then going to get the key, he started it up for him.

"That sounds good, nice and even."

"It should, I repaired it, I have even used it."

"How much to take it away now?"

"Seven hundred and fifty Somali shillings."

"I do not want you short changing yourself. I will give you fifteen hundred."

"OK, it is a deal. You give me the money now, then the car is yours to take away."

Michael takes out a fistful of notes, giving them to the mechanic.

"Can I bring it here anytime, if it needs any work doing on it?"

"Of course, I know the car inside out."

They shake hands, the mechanic puts the bonnet down for Michael, putting the money in his pocket. having acknowledged each other, Michael drives off, while the mechanic goes back to working on the pickup that he has in his workshop. Knowing that this day has been a very good one already, Michael was very happy, due to the fact he now had a locally licensed vehicle. So now if he drove, he would not stand out in the crowd. Now he could increase his options for his terrorist outpost in the wilds of Somalia. He needed to be very careful, being an insurgent in a rabid country like Somalia. Trust was not an easy thing to come by, so he needed to work alone. That way he only had himself to blame, if anything was to go wrong.

He eventually finds a defunct building, most of the structure was sound and solid. It had a cellar, which proved to be a bonus. It was well off the beaten track, away from prying eyes and very loose tongues. One of the outbuildings was big enough to conceal his car, so all was well. He decided to spend the night there, just to see how busy it actually got; to see if there were any busybodies about. In case armoured patrols came this way, he slept in the outbuilding, lying in the back of his vehicle. Nothing disturbed him, he stayed there well into the latter part of the afternoon. All he saw all day long was, a couple of goatherds go past. They did not see him, tucked away in the outhouse, watching their movements. This would be his school then so, moving out, he went back to his original hideout. Making a pitstop at a local garage he found an ATM, where he withdrew cash from his Kenyan account. Then he bought the basics that he needed, from various numbers of outlets, all with cash payments. He hid as much as he could in the boot of his car.

Then he left nice and early, to reach his new ground zero without attracting too much attention to himself. Once there Michael Ironi spent a good couple of hours checking to see if anyone else had been there in his absence. The piece of twine he had left on the cellar door was still in place with the same knot. So with some self-satisfaction, he felt it was safe, or as safe as it would ever be, here out in the wilds. So transferring all his basics to the cellar and re-sealing the door with the twine, he sat down with his bottled water, opening his bag of goat samosa. Taking his time, he decided what he really needed was an account here in Somalia, under a false name. Then obviously some money to put into the account would be very helpful as well. Then a thought struck him, as daring as it was, it probably would work, just once. A little deceitful perhaps, but all the money acquired would at least stay in Somalia. But it would just be in a different bank. All he had to do was find a town big enough to have two banks. So that would be the next job for tomorrow. Drive out and find a large town, other than Mogadishu. In the late evening he made a move, refuelling on the way back to his original haunt. He lay down and slept. Then with a cup of tea and some *mkate* to bolster himself for the morning's trek. He drove until he found what he wanted. Finally, on a road, or what passed for a road, here in Somalia, he ventured deeper into the country, now far away from the Kenyan border.

Not feeling quite so relaxed, but ever watchful, as he ventured towards into town centres, he looked for one with at least two banks. Probably few and far between, he thought to himself, but find one he would, wherever that may show itself. That would be his first stop, approaching the town of Merca. He spotted two banks, both on the edge of the main thoroughfare. Both look active and open, surprisingly not very busy. So if he were to do it, now was the time. So he put up his hood, along with his balaclava, and took his dummy weapon in his right hand. Going into the first bank, which only had the teller in attendance, pointed his weapon outright at him.

"All your paper money in there now."

Forcing his new holdall into the teller's hands, as the young man took it Michael hit him hard with his clenched fist, while still holding the fake gun. The teller went down like a lead balloon. Then climbing over the counter, Michael helped himself to all the notes that were readily available. He then made a very swift exit back to his car. Removing his hood and woolly balaclava, he put both items underneath the passenger seat. He then took his time counting the money, making sure he knew how much he had. Then he calmly joined the queue of the second bank. As it came to his turn, both he and the teller wished each other a good morning.

"So sir, how can we be service to you, this grand morning?"

"I would like to open an account with your bank, if I may?"

"Certainly, sir, just give me a moment."

The young female leaves her till, then returns with another older-looking gentleman.

"Please come this way, sir."

Mr Ironi gets shown into an office, where they both sit. The older gentleman looks at his new client and smiles.

"Will you be making a deposit today sir, with your new account?"

"I will, I have the cash on me now."

"What sort of account would you be interested in?"

"I would like a current account, as well as a savings account, if that would be possible?"

"Of course sir, that would be a wise move on your behalf."

They go through all his details, for both of his accounts.

"How would you like it split, Mr Dalmar?"

"I would like it 60/40, in favour of the current account."

The manager counts it all out, in front of his new client. Going back to his computer, he fills in the required amounts.

"Right that is all done for you. Your two accounts are now up and running, you can use them whenever you are ready."

"That is great, thank you, for your time."

"No, thank you, for your custom, Mr Dalmar."

Shaking hands, they both walk to the door of the office. Michael departs to his car, driving back to his hideaway. First, he cooks some of his goat over hot coals. Then he gets a superb night's sleep. Checking his car, which all looks in good working order, He heads out onto the road once again. Driving into Kismayo, he walks through the main road. There were two banks here as well. One where he had opened an account, the other quite a small independent concern. Then he drove over to where he planned to have his training school. Feeling comfortable as he sat in the sun, he drank a couple of cold beers, from the chiller, which was in the boot of his car. Enjoying the seclusion and he smiled to himself. He was miles away from any influences or outside interferences. Then he remembered his daughter, Belinda, and missed her all over again. But his job had been his life, since he had been fourteen, scouring the streets for a living. Fortunately, the Light of Africa took him under their wing, he had slowly worked his way up and into the organisation. So now he really enjoyed his work, he would have time for them both at a later date. They probably had forgotten him already, so not to worry. Onwards and upwards with the acquisition of explosives. Anyway, he had one more little job to complete tomorrow. Then he had everything in place, so he could leave, ready to return to Kismayo.

Sleep was the key to an early start. So he would head down to the Amal Bank, relieve it of its funds, then pay it all into the First Somali Bank, into the account of Abshir Dalmar. Then he was in place for a peaceful existence. He had moved out from his original living quarters, what little he had was now in the car with him. As he drove to his pyrotechnic college, out in the sticks, his vehicle ended up hidden away in the outbuilding. In his living base down in the cellar he slowly collected together all the components he needed to make various IEDS and EODS; to kill, maim, injure, one or one hundred and one. His craft, skill and knowledge were all powerful when it came to the art of dismembering, slaughtering. But he still found it difficult to engage in small talk, along with the smooth tonguing and entertaining young ladies. But the rather enterprising Abshir Dalmar was more concerned with furthering the cause of the Light of Africa.

He had emailed his contact officer, informing him that the college was all ready to take students, and where it was. That if the students were going to use vehicles, they had better make sure they were registered in Somalia. There was less chance of them getting checked, or standing out in the crowd, within the eyes of the local police force who worked alongside the military. Abshir was checking out all the local military installations, barracks garrisons, police stations and any and all government concerns. So now on completion of their training, the students had something to actually practise on. The board outside his college read as Kulanka Soomaalida Soomaaliya Iyo Sharciyada[10].

The chairs and tables were all brought in, a little at a time, all kept safe and hidden away in another outbuilding. They were sourced from a variety of outlets, so now everything was ready for the forthcoming instruction, lectures, demonstrations and procedures. All anyone would need to know about how to kill an adversary, without even trying. So drawing a Tusker from his fridge to relax in the cool air of the cellar, he studied his books as he sucked the beer from the bottle. After a short while, he finally got a reply from Jomo, telling him to expect half a dozen students, who would be attending his college very soon. They would be a mix of Somalis and Sudanese, there would be four male and two female operatives attending his first course. They had all paid the requisite fees, so they were

---

[10] Somali College of Politics and Law

expecting a hard core, intense training regime. So that they could conduct lone wolf attacks, if need be, all across their countries. It would be down to him and his instruction, if he was successful, that would extend operations across two borders, with three operatives in each country. Providing they managed to stay in one piece, of course.

So his intentions were to train them to his standard. Starting from owning an alarm clock, turning it into an IED, as well as disguising an oil drum as an EOD, with or without timing devices, a delayed fuse, remote control, mercury tilt enablers or even pressure pads on any EOD. He was relishing the idea of having his own audience, his own students to play to.

Meanwhile Anjella was patiently waiting for her passport to arrive. She had Adhiambo put on it, which was a wise move, then she only needed to go to the Swiss embassy, to get her visa. Enabling her to travel to the World Health Organisation, to talk about her work against malaria and the mosquito. She had never been outside the borders of Kenya before, so she was looking forward to her trip to Europe. The World Health Organisation was funding the trip and all the expenses, so it was going to be something rather special for the whole fortnight. She was going to be staying in a plush hotel, so what was not to enjoy? Tristina and Ramon were both excited for her, even though Adhiambo was not going. She was going to be looked after by her two devoted grandparents, of which she did not mind, she always had great fun with them. She always felt special in their company, like a little *nyar kingi*. So if her mother had to go away, she would miss her, but her grandma and grandpa would make up for it.

So strong was her bond with her mother, it would never be splintered, snapped or sheared. The love just stretched as far as it needed to. They never felt any strain or superficial flaws, but they would between them make up for the separation, on Anjella's return. Another birthday passed when Adhiambo's father did not show his face. But mum and daughter were fending for themselves quite adequately, with the help always of Tristina and Ramon. So Mr Michael Ironi was not being missed at all. Slowly he was drifting from their memory, Belinda had trouble remembering what he looked like, but she had everything she needed, without him being involved in her substantial life. She was content with all the attention that was given to her at home, she was doing very well at school, where she had all the friends she needed. She was a well-adjusted, young female at the age of thirteen. Adhiambo had a very strong will, lots of determination and a photographic memory, which aided her studies. She had not been affected by the turmoil in East Africa, all the upset and terrorism within its borders. Anjella had continued her work, her contact with the World Health Organisation had not stopped since the first set of lectures she had given about four years ago. She had been asked back every other year since, to continue with her updates on the advancements she had made. She had made contacts within the international community, which had helped her no end to improve her studies, along with the legitimacy of the papers she had written. Anjella was now more involved in her research, social life, her daughter's schooling and the future of the Kenyan woman.

Anjella had just come through the front door, seeing her daughter studying alone, smiled went and sat beside her.

"My dearest Adhiambo, would you like to come with me, to Geneva? I will try to make it during your holiday time, so that you do not miss any of your school work."

"I would love to, Mum, are you sure I will not be in the way?"

"I am positive. If you would like, you can come with me to the World Health Organisation and watch me."

"That would be really special to watch you mum."

"It would, I cannot make any promises, but we will see."

"OK, Mum, you just tell me, if I can or not."

"I will my darling, you can be sure of that."

Abshir had adjusted to his rather lonely life, out in the outskirts of Dolo. He had received his first influx of students, they had all passed his directions with flying colours. Their final project was to blow up a police station, with an IED, plus a timing device. They set it up, placing it at the rear of the station. They all got back to Dolo with five minutes to spare. Then they watched the reporting of it, an hour later on their television. Abshir was very impressed, especially with the two females' apprentices, who seemed to be more committed to the ideology than their male counterparts. Which turned out to be the right perception on his behalf, as the four male insurgents ended up wasted on their third bombing programme. Whereas the two females were still achieving great success, in all their endeavours, twelve months on.

His classes had grown from six to a round dozen now, which he enjoyed even more. They were still mixed students, he did try not to fraternize with them too much. But with his latest class, he had taken a real shine to one of the female acolytes. It would seem at the same time that she paid a lot of attention to him as well. He had already learnt that she was a practising Muslim. But she did seem to enjoy her freedom a little too much, which disturbed the male students. But she would not be tied down by all its teachings, even its philosophy of female degradation and enslavement. She never wore any head covering, always wore pastel shades in her clothing and never black. Her eyes were always simmering, passionate, wanting excitement. Then one day after a long course of instruction, she came up to Bashir quite openly, confronting him eye to eye.

"Can I come to your quarters?"

"Of course, is it for extra tuition?"

"No, it is to have sex with you. I am not a virgin, but I want to be penetrated by a soldier of Al-Wasse'e."

"I am not a soldier of Al-Wasse'e. I am an expert bomb maker, here to show you all my expertise, my craft. So that you can disrupt, destroy and destabilise governments and their official backing."

"In that case it does not really matter, I just want sex with you before I die, one way or another. You will qualify as a soldier and, now is a good time for me."

"In that case come in and make yourself comfortable."

Bashir first locks the door.

"I want you to undress for me now, Bashir."

"If that makes you feel more comfortable, more relaxed then I will."

He slowly undresses, until he is completely naked. The female, Yaya, takes her time, seeming to enjoy the tease and anticipation she brings to his loins. Now a real man is involved explicably in her private little game of intimacy, she feels all hot and wanton herself. First of all, she tantalizingly unbuttons her tight-fitting primrose kameez. Followed by her half-cup bra as her enormous, pendulous breasts roll out, magnificently. Both are topped by seventy-five-carat gold-plated nipples, all set to pop at a moment's notice. Her aureoles covered almost half of each splendid orb.

"My oh my, those aureoles are stunning Yaya. So rich, dark, dimpled, massive."

"Do you know what, Bashir, no one has ever fully appreciated them before now."

"But they are exceptional, your boobs and nipples are truly breathtaking."

"Ah yes, everyone comments on those babies, all the time."

Yaya rolls down her shalwar, removing her kameez, slipping out of her four-inch open-toe stilettoes.

"I see I have aroused you, with my little striptease Abshir. That is some beast of an organ you have there, my teacher!"

"You are a divine woman, such splendour I have never seen before. You have so much to spare, a fine young, dazzling, exotic woman. It is very hard not to show my appreciation my pleasure, when I stand here naked before you."

"I know Bashir, but this is the first time I have had hard evidence, that really shows a mature liking and acceptance of me. To see it so close in all its splendour and glory excites me beyond belief. You are steaming hot, I can see that for myself."

"Yes," he replies as he rubs his hands all over his raging, shiny, bulbous sticky crown.

"What is that for teacher?"

"It is all for you. It is what you wanted after all. Hot, thick, surging meat to penetrate your sweet, lusting loins."

"I cannot wait to feel your thick indulgence rip through my eager body now, Bashir."

Coming up behind her, he then slipped his muscled, rampaging weapon as it throbbed, pulsed, in between her two tight, curvaceous buttocks. Sinking his full length, then he holds her hips as he lavishes his petulant shaft along her very tight butt a few times, both of them thoroughly enjoying the contact.

"That is gorgeous Yaya, tight, so damn delicious. That is some muscle you have there, I could feel you hanging onto me, on my every stroke."

"Bashir you are the first to go there. I enjoyed it as well master, your thickness astounds me."

Then the throbbing, tensile teacher, having enjoyed Yaya's delights, kept her in that position. Posturing above her, teasing her again with his rod, he then slips smoothly into her warm, welcoming wisp of a bushy pussy. Straight in all the way in until he came to a stop, with his hard hilt the only thing stopping him from going in any further. The slight curvature of his ramrod locks him deep within her tasty, relenting thighs. At the same time, he pulls and jerks on her mighty nipples, his soothing caresses fondle her soft silky sensuous bosom. Running his eager fingertips across, over and around her large, elaborate aureoles, He shunts himself into her supple body a little more, just staying there, inserted, luxuriating in her severe closeness, heat and womanly perfume. Her hands come round squeezing, jiggling his hardened balls. She shoves herself backwards onto his round, rigid, upright shaft and formidable crown.

"I think you are enjoying this as much as I am, Yaya."

"I am really enjoying you Bashir. No one has been so sensitive or caring as this before. This is probably the first time I have been able to enjoy sex with anyone at all, as a sharing process."

"Your breasts are gorgeous, silky, substantial and soft, what cup are they Yaya?"

"My breasts are EEE, my nipples are very reactive too, especially if they are sucked."

Abshir rocks to and fro, twirling her plump, juicy nipples between his thumb and forefinger. Then he pounds her cute quim. She is now well lubricated, his fingers dallying, dipping into her bush and cream. Licking them he tastes her sweetness as she groans and sighs, as he now bangs her wildly, smearing and splattering her juices over both of their bodies.

"Oooohhh, my ooohhhh my you are a wild one. Can you not contain yourself, master?"

"This is all your influence Yaya. That tempestuous and erotic body of yours is giving me the hots for you. I want my release, but it will not come."

Abshir withdraws so as to get the young, stunning student to lay back, as he gets in between her legs. He pushes his tongue into her delicious, fragrant snatch. Lapping and licking he lunges at her abundance of sticky cream.

"You relish oral sex, Bashir, I can see and tell."

"It is something special, when it is done properly."

He has licked her dry, but leaves her quim still pink, swollen, moist and ready. Her thighs quiver and shiver until, kneeling over her, his eager mouth latches onto her enormous nipples. Sucking and nibbling he can feel them grow instantly. tenderly he suckles, licks and chews her teats, as Yaya sits silently smiling, loving all the attention being given to her by

Abshir. She has never been spoilt so much as this by a man, by an older man who knows a few tricks. She is truly pleasured by all that he does to her. He runs his oral muscle across and over her massive, all-encompassing aureoles. He loves the uneven texture and density of her soft skin. He just adores her magic, her charisma and illusive charm.

"Now you lay back Abshir."

As he does so, she holds him in between her small, soft, diligent hands. Opening wide she takes his swollen dome, along with parts of his pulsing shaft, into her warm mouth. She gobbles, slurping on his very sensitive, shiny head. Pushing the tip of her tongue into the swollen eye, teasing, tormenting, torturing him. Poking and prodding, she probes as she squashes, juggles and rubs his tentative gonads. He jerks up, Yaya all ready, as she delights in drinking from his fountain of man milk. As he erupts into her closed mouth, she devours him until the flow of juice subsides as she licks her lips hungrily.

"Mmmm, that was sticky, thick, so much. But I got you, Bashir."

"You are a veritable expert at felatio Yaya, that was superb."

"But I see you are still hard."

"Would you like more, Yaya?"

"I would indeed, teacher."

She climbs over him, pressuring down on his upright, beaming shaft, taking all of him in one straight hit, right down to his hilt. Yaya grinds against his inferno of an erection, exciting herself as she climaxes quickly. Well lubricated, she rides him hard. His excessive lunging taking him as deep as she is able, feeling every inch of his of his hard, stubborn muscle. She rubs herself against his thudding flesh, but Bashir, unable to contain himself this time, trembles as he shoots his milk into Yaya's young, delicious, volatile body.

"It was a glorious endeavour on your behalf my *kapala jeung guru*. Just what I wanted, needed and desired, your sticky milk so hot and now inside me. I can sleep and dream of that experience now all night long, while I lay in your arms, Bashir."

"You will be a very welcome guest in my bed tonight, Yaya."

They kiss as he picks her up, folds back the sheet and lays her down before lying next to her. Yaya sidles up to him as he wraps his arm about her stunning tender body. She slowly slips into a deep, sound slumber.

Anjella has renewed both passports, hers as well as Adhiambo's. She had also managed to revise her lecture periods, they now coincide with her daughter's summer break. So now at the age of fourteen, she was looking forward to her first trip abroad. Tristian and Ramon were going to go back home for that period of time. So they would be able to put their house back in order, as it had been some time since they spent any amount of time there. But first Ramon was going to take them all to Nairoibi airport, so they could see Anjella and Adhiambo off. The time had arrived for the journey of a lifetime for their granddaughter, so with them both gone, to enjoy the celebrity of being at the World Health Organisation. Adhiambo to enjoy her mother's lectures, to learn new ideas in a new country, a new environment in the heart of Switzerland. It is a completely different country to Kenya.

The cold was the first thing that Adhiambo noticed and felt right down to her bones. She was shivering as she rushed into the foyer of the rather grand hotel they were booked into, to gain its instant heat and warmth. She urned to her mother.

"Mum, that is bitterly cold out there."

"I thought you might notice that, not the same as home is it?"

"No it is not, but I am sure I will survive, Mum."

"Anyway, now we have the key to our room, let us go and get ready for dinner."

They both take a shower, change and go down to dinner.

"So mum, what are your lectures about this year?"

"There are two main themes really Adhiambo. The first is about attempting to clean our water supplies in Kenya. The second, is trying to create an inoculation, that could give everyone an antivirus, that protects us from the plasmodium. Then, in return for the female mosquito biting us, once it has absorbed our blood, the antivirus kills the mosquito as well as the malarial parasites."

"That sounds a very clever device, Mum."

"It would be, if we could trace what disrupts the mosquito and plasmodium, but leaves the human being alone."

"So, what other blights could that potentially do away with?"

"Well, young lady, seeing as you ask, clean water could possibly rid us of schistosomiasis, cholera, Rift Valley fever, along with chikungya."

"Then how about the death of the female mosquito?"

"Well that would terminate the African mosquito. The male mosquito would not be able to procreate, so slowly we would generically see the end of yellow fever, dengue fever, Zika, encephalitis, and obviously malaria."

"So how close are you, Mum, to discovering this magic formula for your anti-virus?"

"We have between us devised three serums. We are working on the percentage mixes of the various compounds, to see which would be the more fatal dose, to browbeat the mosquito into submission, but at the same time, not lethal to the human being. So will you be coming with me, to the World Health Organisation tomorrow?"

"I would love to very much, Mum, will I be able to, at my age?"

"Of course you are, Adhiambo. So I think we both need an early night, as it will be a very long day tomorrow."

"When will we get a chance to go out and explore, Mum?"

"My lectures and questions are normally for the first three days, because I like to listen and see what other people are achieving in my field of work. So after that we can go out and explore together. Is that OK, my *mondo*?"

"Of course, Mum, I think I am going to enjoy this."

Having sampled the cuisine and hospitality of the hotel, they both retire to their room. Going to they fell into a deep sleep almost instantly. Neither of them woke until the alarm went off, which only disturbed Anjella. Adhiambo was so comfortable, she just slept on. Anjella roused herself, bathed, clothed and checked she had her lectures and all her notes for the day. Then spent the next five minutes trying to wake her precious daughter from her very deep slumber. They went down to breakfast together, handed in the room key and caught a taxi to the World Health Centre.

Bashir was in contact with Yaya, who was out in the Sudan. She was doing great work, not only in the Sudan, but crossing the border into South Sudan as well. By disrupting peace talks and aid for feminine relief, in actual fact she had killed some of the charity volunteers as well as destroying and disrupting their newly set-up distribution and collection points. She had also blown a police station apart, killing most of the local security force in a single attempt.

Now his college was gaining a distinguished reputation amongst those in the know. This bought a lot more third-party advocates and students wanting to take part on his course, to learn his techniques. They provided he had advanced notice of who was attending and the numbers involved and where they were coming from. He was more than satisfied. The fees did not concern him, that was Jomo's area of expertise. He received all nations gladly into his school of anarchy. The government of Somalia was still recovering from his last attack on the Ministry of Defence, which involved a single EOD alongside a brace of IEDs, laid into the network of a small air force base, along the coast. Easily achieved when a single female insurgent took the guard away from his post to fornicate, while the three male terrorists entered the base, with such ease of purpose.

So his new influx of students were just arriving, a band of happy male delinquents, thinking they were going to be the next big name in terrorism. So with a class of a dozen male insurgents, all eager to start, Bashir eyed them one by one, if he thought they were going to be up to the tasks ahead, then the final test would have to be something really special. Bashir did have a plan B, just in case they were not that special. That was an easier target, where they could not fail. He would see after the six weeks of intense training. All the instruction took place in the cellar whereas the practical work and demonstrations were all conducted out in the plains of

Somalia, away from any civilization whatsoever. The construction technique took place after the first two weeks of instruction and close demonstration. So that left them with four weeks, to get a grip on the mastery of explosives and the delicacy of their chosen trade and craft. Everything he had taught them had to be absorbed. So in the final seventh week he set them tasks, all in groups of four. All working together as units, the idea being that if something went wrong, from the four, there would be enough individuals who survived, to complete the task in hand.

Now the seventh week was here, where Abshir gave them the task and objective and what they had to achieve. He addressed them all of the twelve in the classroom:

"You have the whole arsenal and quartermaster stores at your disposal. I want you to stay in your three cells. Your objective is the government building in Mogadishu. I want at least one IED to go off inside. Not forgetting a single EOD to disrupt the main entrance, just before the IED blows internally."

"Will you be here to answer any questions Bashir?"

"Yes, I will be in my office. Do not forget, talk, discuss, approve, then operate. All three cells can interact, so you all know what you are doing. What are the most important things to remember?"

"Timing."

"Yes."

"Knowing where we should be."

"Correct."

"Communication and talking to each other."

"Most certainly, now off you go."

So all twelve have the map on the wall, a pictograph of the government building, spread across two tables. First, they discuss as a consortium of a dozen. It gets a little heated, the discussion nearly comes to blows, then they all remember they are all on the same side. So it simmers and dies down to a more reasonable volume. They decide that all twelve of them will carry a short fuse IED. The EOD will be a remote control, laid out the night before. The doorway was blocked by a security barrier, so one of them would have to put a small drum by the security box. Even two would be wiser, just in case one was discovered.

The three cells of four insurgents should have the IEDs easily to hand, so they could distribute them about the building, without drawing attention to themselves. Now they had a plan between them, it was time to piece together the IEDs and, the EODs. They made sure they were all safe, until they were required. Cells two and three were constructing the EODs. Cell one made the IEDs, making thirteen; the extra one they wanted to try, before exposing the other twelve to anyone's pockets or case. Just on the off-chance of an accident. By the Wednesday afternoon, they have decided to fit the IEDs with a time lapse fuse.

Taking the thirteenth improvised explosive device out into the dunes away from the school, they lay it down so they could all see it. Then all of them retreat far, far back, well out of its reach. The timer was set for two minutes, with a ten-second delay. They all looked at their own timepieces, watching the seconds tick by, then the delay; nine, eight, seven six, one. Then boom!

"Nice one, timed to perfection."

"That means the other twelve will be just as subtle."

"Very direct."

"Now we can go out tomorrow night, to set up the two EODs."

"So I think we should all adjourn for dinner and a beer."

The dozen students all return to the cellar where they lock everything away for safekeeping. Then they all join Bashir in the canteen where he has made a goat *karanga* along with some *mahararagwe na chapatti*. All help themselves to a tusker, then all ladle out their own stew. They sit discussing the task and operation that lay ahead of them, for Friday, which was their pass or fail day. They all slept very contentedly, no dreams, no palpitations, no sweats or nerves. Getting up they remain relaxed, not letting any tension build up. When Thursday evening arrived, they all jumped into the van with the two EODs. Then they parked as close as they dare, but not seeing a way in. So driving further around the building, they found an alley, where they could park unseen, in the far recesses of the alleyway, then it was just waiting. About midnight there seemed to be some movement. If there was a change of shift, probably the barrier and box would be left unattended in the wake of the guards talking and taking a smoke together. The dozen usurpers, as quietly as possible, humped the drums over to the box. One they put inside by the fan outlet. The other went inside the forty-five-gallon drum that was cemented into place, supporting the upright and the horizontal barrier that was restricting entry into the complex.

Returning to the van they continued down the alley. With no light to guide their way, they eventually came to the metalled road, the other end. Joining the non-existent traffic, then switching the vehicle lights on, they wended their way back to the safety of the school. Where Abshir was waiting for them.

"Is it done, everything in the right place?"

"Yes Abshir."

"One is in the security box."

"Tucked underneath out of the way."

"The other placed inside the barrier drum."

"Both at the foot of the stairs, of the Somali Security Office."

Abshir smiles.

"That sounds like a good job. So that just leaves the mini IEDs tomorrow morning. Make sure you all come back tomorrow."

"We will Abshir."

"Go and get some sleep boys. Make sure you are all well rested, for later in the day."

"We will all return."

The rest of the early morning passes by, the dozen insurgents all rise bright eyed. Jumping in the van once again, they wend their way to Mogadishu, all with their personal IEDs on their person. Parking the van well away from their target, they all saunter as individuals towards the building, that was their target. Nonetheless, all were stopped and searched for weapons of any kind. They gained entry, all headed in different directions, into corridors, offices, window ledges, water closets, the back of stairs, pillars and chairs. All explosives are set for twenty minutes, with a fifteen-second delay. They had realized between them that the EOD that was placed by the fan had been discovered and was now in the backyard, along with some empty gas cylinders, waiting to be removed. Now all twelve IEDs had been placed, the terrorists departed the facility making their way back to the van. The first one back sat in the driving seat, the second took the remote control. Then the rest just filed into the van. When all the students were there, the door was closed. They drove off in the direction of the college, then the remote was triggered, to the delight of the dozen. The two EODs wrecked two sides of the complex, killing the four guards that were on shift at that time. Shortly afterwards the twelve IEDs reacted like a tornado, ripping through the interior of the security building. Completely tearing apart the old government building, They left death and carnage everywhere as the twelve made it back in one piece. Disappearing instantly into the cellar, Abshir was there waiting for them, patting all of them on the back as they filed in.

"That was a grand job, you have all passed with flying colours. I think this is going to make the Somalis rather disgruntled, I think they will be looking for the infiltrators almost immediately."

"Thank you, Abshir for your most lucid instruction. Without your knowledge and guidance, we could not have performed so well for you."

"So now I think you should make your way back home, for the weekend. Before anyone starts to search for the culprits."

All shaking hands and hugging each other, they jump back into the van.

"Make sure you get fuel at the first chance, then you will be OK with your full tank."

"We will Abshir, see you again perhaps."

Driving from the cover of the outbuilding, they start their long journey back home. While Abshir watches the news content on his laptop, amazed at the amount of destruction, death and personal violation that had just happened and introduced into the life of the normal Somali. With no regret he listened intently, learning that all resources that were available were going to be used to find the evil perpetrators of this abominable act. Already the Somali air force was involved, with their helicopters scouting and scouring their plains for any unusual movement along their borders. Now, Abshir tells himself, he should have kept those twelve boys here, until late after the local sunset. But it was too late now. His own vehicle was ready, but he was not going to move until the last shred of light had left the sky. He was now in the process of securing all his buildings, locking everything down and shielding the cellar away from prying eyes, so it was now as secure as it could be. The college sign had been removed. All his personal stuff was in the car as the sun said goodnight, disappearing slowly below the mountains, Abshir went to the car. The moon was in its first quarter, so not a lot of light was available. He drove slowly so as not to be noticed as he headed towards the Kenyan border. He crossed back into Kenya unopposed by anyone, not seen not followed driving at the required speed. He was hoping to make it to Nairobi, some time in the early evening.

Just pulling over, he listened to the latest report on his car radio. He learned that one of the choppers had intercepted a van, with twelve male occupants inside, driving towards Tanzania. They were now in custody and being questioned. This could be awkward, might even mean having to take Anjella and Belinda with him, to try and mask his activities and blend in with the crowd. Where would he attempt to run and hide himself? Considering this for a minute or two, as he drove on he concluded that Europe would be his favoured choice, but how would his daughter and partner take to moving so far away? There would only be one way to find out, that would be to confront them, when he had the chance and ask, no not ask, but tell them, they all had to move out of Kenya. But he would have to discuss it first with his control officer, Jomo. The sun was coming up now, so he pulled over to a roadside coffee shop, taking a sip of the hot liquid, along with a bite of the freshly baked bread, he felt in better spirits. Finishing his coffee then driving on, he stopped only one more time to refuel. Then he surged on ahead to Nairobi, his first port of call, the office of the Light of Africa.

"Michael so nice to see you. But you should still be in Somalia."

"I know, but I think there could be problem there."

"Why, what has happened?"

"Did you hear the report, about the explosion of the Somali government building, this morning in Mogadishu?"

"Yes of course it is all over the radio and television. The latest is they have stopped a van with twelve young men in it. Ahhh, I see, has it got something to do with you?"

"Yes of course, the twelve students are mine, from our bomb school. That was their final project, to see how much they had learnt."

"A good job they made of it, as well. You do teach to a very high degree Michael."

"Thank you very much Jomo. That van was the insurgents trying to get back to Tanzania, now the Somali air force has them, I am sure they had parted with all the information the Somalis require."

"I see you do have a problem. That puts a different light on everything now."

"That was my thought exactly."

"What do you plan to do?"

"I think I am going to disappear, for a short while somewhere."

"Where were you thinking of running to?"

"Europe was my first thought."

"Good choice, you will not be noticed so much there. Who could help you?"

"Ishmael could probably get the paperwork I need."

"I am sure he could. Yet it will take a couple of days. Have you thought about taking anyone with you, to assist with your cover and identity?"

"Yes of course, my daughter and her mother. Even though I have not seen them for years. I know what their reaction will be, obstinate, belligerent and not very helpful at all. That is of course, if they actually remember who I am."

"I do not want to lose you Michael, you are our top operative after all. You will be very hard to replace."

"Well Jomo, thank you for the sentiment. But I'd rather be gone for eighteen months and return all refreshed. It's far better than getting caught and being locked away for twenty years or more and, not being able to return at all."

"I guess you are right there."

"Also, if you need funds, the Somali First National Bank, in the name of Abshir Dulmar, the account number is 0011438."

"OK, Michael, I got all that. Where will you go first?"

"To see my daughter and her mother, try and talk them both round to moving away for a while. If not, I will leave and go on my own."

"I hope it does not come to that. It will be far easier with a family in tow."

Adhiambo loved spending time with her mother. She attended the three days of lectures that her mother gave to the audience of the World Health Organisation. Laying out all their investigations and the current research and results that went with their findings, just as she had told her daughter right at the very beginning, over dinner at the hotel. She got a well-deserved lengthy applause, at the end of her question period. When Anjella had finished and approached her seat with Adhiambo, a research scientist Miss Emelia Koso, from the United Kingdom, touched her arm wanting to talk to her directly.

"That was very impressive Doctor Ogwayo."

"Thank you Doctor Koso. Call me Anjella please."

"In that case I am Emelia. Now Anjella, how would you like to come and visit us, in England?"

"Where do you do your research then Emelia?"

"At the Hospital for Tropical Diseases, in Central London."

"That would be sensational, but I would need to contact my director first."

"If he agrees and it appeals to you, let me know. You could phone from here, if you wanted to contact him right away."

"Are you sure?"

"Yes, at no expense to you whatsoever."

They all go out into the main foyer, going to the concierge to get a call put direct to her hospital. After the call Anjella is all smiles, turning to Emelia.

"I would need a visa and permit, Emelia, also would it be possible for my daughter to come as well?"

"Yes, we can do that at the British embassy, here in Switzerland."

"Are you sure Emelia?"

"Yes, I checked when I arrived. Just in case I required their assistance, before I listened to your presentation. Where are you based at the moment, Anjella?"

"I work at the Nairobi Hospital for Women and Medical School."

"Perhaps we could do an exchange or interchange between us."

"That would be a fantastic idea, Emelia."

The three women leave the centre, talking and laughing, discussing the possibility of a new life, that seemed so improbable, to the two East Africans. Emelia takes Anjella and Adhiambo out for dinner. As they order and continue their very open discussion, Emelia turns to Adhiambo:

"So young lady, would you like to visit England?"

"Of course, I would, such an adventure I have never dreamed of before. Would this involve me as well?"

"I think it could, if your mum decided to come and work with us, for a while."

"Would I find a school easily out there?"

"You would, I know one close by to me. Your English sounds very proficient, better than some of the locals who have lived out there, all their lives."

"I enjoy English, I understand and can be understood, if I need to attend school out there."

"You both think about it, your director has said yes. I will come to your hotel in the morning, for breakfast. You can think about it now, then tell me what you think tomorrow. If you say yes, we can go to the embassy tomorrow morning first thing."

"OK, Emelia, we will talk to you tomorrow morning."

The cab drops off all three ladies at their various hotels. Anjella and her daughter go up to their room, closing the door. They hug each other tight, not daring to let go. Then Anjella looks Adhiambo straight in her wonderful brown eyes.

"A chance of a lifetime my dear daughter. To work in the United Kingdom, who would have guessed that."

"It will be, Mum, for both of us."

"How about you, Adhiambo, a new school, college, university, a new life entirely. Would you like it, look forward to it?"

"Yes, I would enjoy it, a different country, a world away."

"So, what do you think we should tell Emelia tomorrow?"

"I think we should go for it, while we have the chance mum. But do you want to go?"

"I would love to go, experience all that I can."

"So it is decided then. When we see Emelia in the morning, we can tell her, yes, Mum."

The morning soon comes around, they both go down to breakfast, enjoying the croissants, toast and muesli, along with the selection of jams. Anjella sees Emelia enter the breakfast room, she stands up shouting over to her friend:

"Emelia, over here, good to see you."

Emelia sits down, while Adhiambo pours her a coffee,

"So what did you decide, ladies?"

"We decided between us, it would be an adventure we could not afford to miss, so we would love to come and join you in England."

"I am so pleased, when do you think you could come and visit us?"

"We would need to go back to Kenya first, to straighten out a few things."

"OK Anjella."

Anjella turns to her daughter.

"So how about if we left early, sort everything out, including your schooling, young lady. Then we go out to the UK!"

"Super idea, that would be cool, Mum."

"If we make it about two weeks then Emelia."

"That would be great, Anjella. So how about we take a trip to the British embassy, now."

"Ready when you are, Emelia."

The three women leave the breakfast room, all very happy in each other's company. Hailing a taxi, they were presently dropped off outside the embassy. They go in together, Emelia going up to the concierge, showing her some paperwork, then turning to her two friends.

"Come on, Anjella, Adhiambo, this way, have you both got your passports?"

They both hold them up, come forward, then all three go straight into the visa department. There the two visas are given quite freely, with no fuss, along with Anjella's work permit and her daughter's study and work permits, for a period of forty-two months.

"Thank you very much."

Emelia takes them both outside, once again looking for another taxi.

"Let us all got to the airport and, get your flights taken care of, shall we?"

"OK, Emelia, we can do that now."

The cab takes them directly to Geneva airport. They go in straight up to the Kenyan Airways stand. Anjella approaches one of the attendants.

"Good morning, I wonder if you can help me?"

"I will certainly try to madam. How would you like me to assist you today?"

"We would like to fly back to Kenya, as soon as possible please. I have two tickets for my daughter and myself, but they are for six days' time."

"That should not be a problem, let us see what we have available."

The very attentive attendant goes through her flight plans and schedules.

"Here we are, we have two seats available on a late flight on Friday, at 20:30 hours."

"That would be splendid."

The young female assistant smiles taking the two tickets from her, then replaces them with the two replacements.

"With the compliments of Kenyan Airways."

"Thank you so much, that is very kind."

Emelia walks over to her, with Adhiambo at her side. "So when do you fly back?"

"We fly back out on Friday night at 20:30 hours."

"OK I will come and pick you up, on Friday evening. So let us go exploring." Emelia takes them out to see St Pierre, a twelfth-century cathedral, the Palace of Nations, the United

Nations building. The Musée D'Art et D'Histoire, then finally the Place Du Bourg-De-Four, the shopping and dining plaza. Having eaten and enjoying each other's company so much, they had forgotten about the passage of time.

"Let me take you back to your hotel."

"If you do that, then at least stay for a nightcap."

"OK Anjella, I will."

They head straight to the bar, Emelia ordering for both of them, with a soft drink included for Adhiambo. After a couple, they part company. As promised Emelia comes to see them both off at the airport:

"Anjella, please do not forget to email me with your flight details when you come over to England. I will come and pick you up, you can stay with me, until you find your own home."

They all say their goodbyes, hugging, as they walk into the departure lounge. Ramon is waiting at the other end, to pick them both up from Nairobi Airport. He takes them both home to a glorious family dinner of freshly cooked *matoke sukuma wiki mishkaki*, with the coconut and sweet potato pudding. Anjella hugs her father, his granddaughter kisses him.

"Missed you, grandpa, lots."

"I missed you, my precious pearl."

"Mummy has got some exciting news for you and Nana, when we get home."

"So how did it all go this time, with both of you?"

"It was very memorable, lots of interest in what we are doing."

"A wonderful country Gramps, so completely different to here at home."

He parks up outside, collects the suitcases, whilst his granddaughter and daughter go rushing in to see Tristina, who is busy over the stove, checking on dinner.

"What a wonderful sight, Mum, seeing you again."

They both kiss each other, hugging as Adhiambo wraps her arms around both of them, now tied, entwined in a group hug as her grandma kisses her on her head.

"Come on people, let us sit down, eat before it all gets cold and ruined."

They all sit down holding hands, as Ramon says grace. Then they all partake of the meal as one very happy family. Anjella is the first one to speak, unable to keep her news to herself any longer.

"Mum, Dad, I have some very exciting news to tell you both. I want, no need to tell you now, so we can all discuss the implications, for us all."

"OK, Anjella then tell us please."

"I will, Mum. I have been offered a job at a hospital in England.

"That would be very nice for you, would it include Adhiambo going with you?

"Whereabouts in the United Kingdom would you be going, Anjella?"

"Yes, Mum, it would include your dearest granddaughter, coming with me. It would be in Central London, Dad."

"Would you need a visa and work permit, Anjella?"

"Yes, Dad, I have already got those. I managed to get them in Geneva, at the British embassy, with the help of Emelia my friend, who offered me the job in the first place."

"What about Adhiambo, what will she do?"

"Mum, she will continue her schooling, without a doubt. She also got her entry visa and study permit, like me for forty-two months."

"That will be wonderful for you both."

"I know, Mum."

"What would you like to do with your house?"

"I would like to keep it, Dad."

"In that case would you like us to look after it for you, Anjella?"

"Would you do that for me? Would you have the time? What about if Michael came back?"

"Of course we would find the time to look after your home. If Michael came back to claim it, then we would move out for him."

"Have you seen or heard anything of Michael, since we were away?"

"Not a word Anjella, we have no idea where he is."

"Ah well, I would have liked to tell him, but if we do not know where he is hiding, it is going to be rather difficult to communicate with him. Well tomorrow I will see my director at work, so I can tell him, what we plan to do, Mum, Dad"

"You will also have find time, to take me and talk to the governor of my school, Mum."

"Yes, I know my sweetheart. I will come and collect you tomorrow afternoon, we will pay him a visit then."

"OK, Mum."

"Do we have a bottle of Leleshwa Sauvignon blanc Tristina?"

"Yes I believe we do Ramon, out in the kitchen."

Ramon disappears into the kitchen, bringing with him a bottle of wine, along with four glasses. One for each of the ladies, of course one for himself. He opens the bottle as they all smile so happy to be together. He pours out the wine into all four glasses, holding his up high, as he gives the toast.

"Here is to you and Adhiambo, a bright, bold brilliant future, for you both in England."

"Cheers, Dad and, thank you."

"Thank you so much, Gramps."

"That was a beautiful sentiment, Ramon."

They all had a second glass, then Adhiambo kissed everyone goodnight, heading to her bedroom for an early night, excited at her future prospects. Anjella yawned, closing her eyes, feeling half asleep.

"You look done in Anjella."

"I am, Mum, never felt so tired as this, for a long time."

"You go to bed then, Anjella, if you are tired. Your dad and I will tidy up, then we will come to bed."

"OK, Mum, Dad, thank you very much. Have a good night's sleep."

Anjella had called her two soulmates, Suzie Wokabi and Jeanette Oromo, asking them both out to dinner, telling them she had something very exciting to tell them. As they ordered dinner, Anjella told Suzie and Jeanette, that she was going to move to England, to work. They both screamed with delight, jumping up to kiss and congratulate her. They both got Anjella to promise, once she had a place of her own and was settled in, she would tell them, so that they could both come over for a holiday.

Michael woke up nice and early, showered, dressed, then decided to go round to see Anjella and Belinda, to inform them together of his urgent need to get out of Africa for a while.

Wanting to know if they would both come with him. There was only one way to find out, so he caught a cab, hoping to have breakfast with them all. Paying the driver, he knocked on the front door. It was opened by his daughter, who seemed shocked, taken aback, surprised and lost for words. Then, after the initial confrontation, she gasped:

"Goodness, Dad, are you trying to give me a heart attack? Come on in."

He follows her into the kitchen, where they are all partaking of a family breakfast. Belinda points to an empty seat.

"Sit down, Dad, join us please."

Michael sits down, Ramon gets up to fetch a cup and plate for him, so he can join in with the meal. He smiles a little awkwardly.

"Good morning, how have you all been?"

"We are all fine thank you. Where have you been for the past five years?"

"Right down to it, hey Anjella? Well, I have been working in Somalia, at a college teaching."

"So what bought you back here then?"

"I needed to leave due to complications, of the teachings I was giving. That is why I have come here, this morning to talk to you both."

"About what in particular?"

"I need to leave the country, as soon as I possibly can."

At this Ramon gets up, taking the arm of his wife very wisely.

"Come on Tristina, it is time for us to leave. This is, I am afraid to say, not for our ears."

"What do you mean?"

"I mean this could get loud and, possibly, very destructive. If we stay it might even get more so, because of our presence. You know what Michael can be like!"

"Anjella if you need us, text or phone, we will be indoors."

"Where are you going, Grandma?"

"Adhiambo we are off home, just until the three of you sort this out. We do not want to make things worse, by being here."

Tristina takes Ramon's hand, then leads him out to the car. They make their way home, not wanting to be involved in a slanging match, if things boil over. Especially as Adhiambo's father had not been involved in her life for such a long time. Knowing it could get violent, if they stayed there, which would antagonise and rile him without a doubt. Michael was thick-set, imposing man, with an overgrown, conceited, violent temper. He was used to getting his own way all the time, every time. He was the most successful operative for the Light of Africa which had now bought him infamous recognition and infamy.

After the capture of the twelve students in the van, now the whole of East Africa would be on the lookout for him. Especially the security forces and the police of at least four nations, who had him marked down as a public enemy. He had been able to evade them up until now. But for how much longer? They were getting close, he could feel it. Time to do a runner, he needed a passport, someone else's preferably, to get off the African continent. He went to his buddy Ishmael.

"Ishmael can you do me three passports, that will get me away from here?"

"I can indeed. Where would you like to try and contrive an entry to?"

"How about the United Kingdom?"

"Let me just check."

He checks through his online database, of the latest stolen passports for the UK.

"Here is one for you, a Simony Boko who has a wife and daughter. Been a resident now for eight years, would that do you?"

"That would be just about perfect. See if I can disrupt a thing out there; cause a little disharmony along the way. How much for the three of them?"

"Seventy-five thousand shillings."

"OK, seventy-five it is. I will bring the cash when I pick them up. When will they be ready, the Light knows I will be disappearing for a while?"

"Give me four days, just to be on the safe side. You keep safe Simony Boko, with your wife and daughter."

"I will, see you in four days."

"Count on it, Simony."

Michael left making sure he was not followed. Returning four days later to retrieve his fraudulent documents, as well as to pay Ishmael for his work. So now he was sat with the three passports in his pocket, just about to explain what he wanted to Anjella and, his grown-up daughter, Belinda.

"Would the two of you like to come with me, to the United Kingdom?"

"Not really, Michael."

"Why not, Anjella?"

"Because Adhiambo and I are already going to England, to a new posting with my research work."

"No, I do not believe you."

"We are, it is already organised, we have our visas, work and study permits. All legal as well."

"I am sorry to inform you that if you go, you will both travel on these passports."

Defying her to say different, he throws down the three fake documents on the coffee table.

"They have our new names, which gives us passage into England any time we want. I know this is my fault, so we travel as one happy family."

Anjella lifts one of the books, looking inside.

"Boko, what is this, stolen and fake?"

"Of course, they were not cheap either."

"In that case, Dad, I will not be travelling with you, under someone else's name. I will stay here with Nana and Grandpa, you and Mum can go together."

"You see, you scare your own daughter so much, that she does not want to travel with you. Nor do I. YOU GOT THE DOCUMENTS YOU CAN TRAVEL WITH THEM."

"My work got me into this mess…"

"Dad, you do not work."

"What do you mean by that?"

"You get paid to blow things up, kill innocent people. Disrupt and unsettle governments, all on a very large scale. That is why you have to leave Kenya."

"How do you know?"

"I am not stupid, Dad. Your false hand, all those disgusting photos you keep on your phone. The dead bodies, demolished buildings, the explosive devices. They are not photos of chance, but souvenirs of reckless endeavour of someone that kills for money and likes looking at his trophies.

It is not for idealism, just some sort of perverse pleasure. So I will travel on my passport or, I do not travel at all."

"That goes for me as well. You travel on your illegal documentation alone and, make good your escape. We will travel in the knowledge, that we have done it all legally."

"OK, I use my passport, you both use yours."

"But we still do not need your company, Dad. You are the desperate one, needing our company. Does that give some sort of cover, flying with two women?"

"Yes, in fact it does, Belinda."

"You pay for the flights, seeing as how you are on the run. You will always be on the run, so you need to make the most of it, until you are killed. Perhaps we will be better off then."

"They are not quite the right thoughts, my darling."

"Sorry, Mum, but Dad is trying to dictate how we travel. This burden is of his own making. Why should I care? I do not want to be associated with him and his carnage. He does not care. Let us go to England, kill a few people, maim innocent children, blow up a few buildings. See if anyone really cares about the Light of Africa. There are so many terrorist organisations, the normal people all they care about is wiping them out. I am on their side in that discussion. So you do not really achieve anything, attain any goal, even with your private schools. Which indoctrinate young, untainted minds with your evil. Then with the separation of male and female students, all your hate preachers that never preach joy and harmony. Everyone just wants them dead. You have no goal or great plan, only death and carnage to your own people. Which in turn brings drought, famine, plague and disease. Then in the final conclusion, when you are cornered, you turn and run away. If anyone tries to stop you, you exterminate them like a piece of garbage. Finally, one day when you are not looking, it will be your turn to get shot. A fatal bullet penetrates your heart, with the hate and venom of someone that wants to see you dead at their feet. Or an unseen drone will obliterate you and your comrades. Then you do not get up, then all this false crap about being a martyr will mean nothing. If you swallow all this righteous shit, Dad, you must be some sort of deadbeat. In some backward-looking religion, that you do not even believe in, or pay adherence to. You get forgotten, with no grave marker, eaten by crows, ravens, maggots and worms. So here is to a long time being dead and forgotten, Dad."

Michael, in a flaming temper, goes over to his beautiful young daughter, sneering, then he cracks her face with the back of his hand. Splitting her lip and making her nose bleed, catching her cheek bone and bruising it heavily.

"Careful what you say, girlie, in my presence."

"You are not my father! I could not care less. Hit me again, perhaps it makes you feel like a real man, punching a fourteen-year-old girl. Just like the killing of all those unknowns you slaughter daily, with their backs to you. A real hero, you cannot even face them when you do it."

"Anjella, you had better take her out of my sight, before I hit her again."

"Hit me again, Dad, perhaps it gives you a hard-on, hitting defenceless women — killing innocent children."

"GET HER OUT OF HERE NOW!"

Adhiambo goads her father even further, she taunts him one last time smiling at him.

"Will it make you feel like a god, if you take my virginity, while you hit me. Does that make you the bigger man, a bigger terrorist, in your Light of Africa, if you debase your own daughter? Incest is allowed, is it?"

Anjella pulls her shocked, now sullen and anguish-filled daughter out of harm's way. She now received the second back-hander intended for Adhiambo. She reels from the force of the blow, the vicious slap knocking her backwards. But quickly she regains her composure Anjella then replies with a firmly planted, stress laden kick in between Michaels parted legs, with the ferocity that Ramon had shown her the first time he demonstrated this maneouver. As he went down clutching his genitals, Anjella, and her smiling daughter, Adhiambo ran to the bedroom, locking the door behind them.

"THAT WILL NOT HELP YOU!" Michael shouts at the top of his voice, as he starts to rise very carefully up to his feet. But then a crashing rabbit punch[11] meets him putting him down once again. That sent him sprawling across the coffee table, destroying it totally. The Luo Lake Goddess laughs out so loud, it makes the house tremor. Then she goes into the bedroom, where her two *nyamin*, sit huddled together on the bed. Then she reveals herself to them both.

"My glorious *nyamin* you are both safe. But you need to be very careful with this ignorant man. Go to your mother and father, be safe there."

The Luo Lake Goddess hugs and kisses them both, then is gone. They drive to Tristina and Ramon's house. Anjella tells her daughter:

---

[11] A short sharp chop with the edge of the hand to the nape of the neck

"Adhiambo my sweetness, my one true joy, you will have to be very careful with your father. He is very unstable, arrant and virulent."

"I know, Mum, he is a iniquituous pig. My father, who knows nothing about religion. Even though he tries to spout it off, he does not have a clue. A moron who lives without love or compassion, a complete waste of time, energy and space."

Michael finally manages to get up off the floor, along with the cuts and grazes he acquired with the punch and smashing into the table. Then again with a blast of his growing loss of temper, he shouts as loud as he could, at the empty bedroom, Thinking Anjella and his insipid daughter were still cowering in there:

"I swear that wretched Belinda is going to be the death of me. She is far too clever for her own good. I will have to keep her in check. Any way, who hit me in the neck?"

He then storms out of the house, going back to his hotel room, to clean himself up.

On reaching her mother and father's home, they both rush in crying, as Tristina and Ramon take both of them into their open arms. Both Anjella and Adhiambo sob, weep quite openly, then Tristina stands back looking at them both.

"It looks as if you have both been in the wars, your faces look very sore, come on come into the kitchen and tell us all about it."

All four of them go into the kitchen, Ramon getting out the first aid box, while Tristina runs some warm water to wash the pair of them. Anjella tells her mother and father the story.

"Oh, Mum, Dad, it was that fetid man, Michael, hitting us both."

"He is the Devil. You both going away with him? I am not sure that is such a good idea."

"Yes, Nana, but we were both saved by our goddess, she came to our rescue."

"Of course she did my *mondo*, she is always with the both of you, keeping a watchful eye."

"Yes, Mum, she came to see us, while we were hiding in the bedroom. Would you and Dad come back with us, just in case he decides to return, to carry on?"

Ramon has their daughter embraced in his arms, Tristina holds on tight to their precious granddaughter, kissing her, trying to ease her pain. Ramon tells them,

"Give me the keys, you both sit in the back with Mum. We will drive back with you, to keep you safe."

Warily they all walk back indoors, Ramon getting the vacuum cleaner to clear up the mess that Michael left behind him. Anjella and Adhiambo sit on the sofa cuddling, as Tristina makes some fresh vanilla tea. As Tristina comes in with the tray, Anjella looks upto her, trying to smile.

"None of this matters, for now, until we get to England. Where we can look forward to a more settled life there."

"You do not believe that for a minute do you, Mum?"

"No, I do not, my child, not while we have your father in tow. It will not help us all the time we are associated with him. It will help us escape the mayhem of Africa, along with your dad, for as long as we decide to stay out there."

"I only hope I can make some more friends out there, as well as move away from his circle of activity. I do not want to be involved with his culture of hate, greed, carnage and rebellion. With some pseudo-religious beliefs, that do not actually exist. Well, only in his primitive mind. My father is corrupt, corrupted amd corruptible, tainted. Just an out-and-out waster, mongrel, charlatan. If I ever get the chance, I will shop my father, then start a whole new life of my own."

"I hope you get the chance my *nyar kingi*. But do not ever let your father know that you want to trade him off for a better life.."

"OK, Mum, but if I want to live without him, without his influences, as well as inhospitable guardianship, we will have to manage by ourselves. We have up to now, so why not continue that way?"

"We just need to get to England, then it will be so much better, for the two of us."

"OK, Mum but you will have to be careful too, we both need to survive this ride, OK?"

"Yes Adhiambo, we need to tread very carefully around your father."

"Mum when you go to work, I am coming with you."

"OK my precious, but we can go later, when our swelling has gone down. Along with that nasty bruising, which will have to fade, or everyone will be asking where we got it from."

They all sit down to enjoy the cup of tea Tristina had made. Then the unsavoury Michael storms into the house, just about to shout Anjella down, when he sees that Ramon is sitting there just waiting for him to start. So being the coward he is, he just says nothing. Anjella turns on him right away.

"So, Michael, is this the way you are going to treat your daughter, from now on?"

"It will be, if she continues to talk to me in that fashion."

"She has had second thoughts about going to the United Kingdom, if she has to go with you. So you need to be very careful, how you treat her or, she has told me, she will stay her with her grandmother and grandfather."

"OK, so she stays here, where is the harm in that?"

"There is no harm, hard man. It just means that I stay here as well. Then when our bruises and swellings have gone down, Adhiambo and I will travel later, without you. We will do our journey with our legal passports, which means you can go by yourself."

"Hold on, hold on, if I am going to be paying, we go together when I say we do Anjella."

"We do not need you to pay, so we can go when we like Michael."

"OK, so you are both independent of me, you do not need me, I understand, Anjella"

"Michael, you do not understand. We have not needed you for the best part of our daughter's life. Then all of a sudden you decide to come onto the scene, where we are meant to be beholden to you, for some unaccountable reason. It will not work. You have not been part of our life ever. So that will not change."

"OK, Anjella, I understand, it is a role-reversal thing. But at this moment in time, I need the both of you."

"But will it work with the way you treat your daughter? I think not, especially as she does not trust the bully and self-serving waster you are now Michael."

"Then she needs to keep her thoughts to herself, until we go our separate ways. Then we will get along just fine Anjella."

"OK, she does not want to talk to you anyway."

"She does not have to, as long as we stay a family unit, until we get past immigration,

"We can do that I am sure, Michael."

"When were you thinking of telling work?"

"I was going to go today. But now it will have to wait."

"Why Anjella?"

"Due to the beating you gave to the both of us. Now with Adhiambo's split lip, bleeding nose, along with the heavy bruising around her cheek and eye. My black eye does not look too good, either."

"Neither of you had those problems earlier."

"Not until her coward of a father hit her, then hit me as well."

"She needs to hold her tongue, she is only a little girl of no great importance."

"When we get to England, you can find your own housing, far away from us, thank you."

"OK, I will. At least then I will not have the burden of looking after the two of you."

"We will be better off on our own. We will survive longer by ourselves, without a hapless, inimical jerk getting in our hair anyway."

"Anjella I will come back at the end of the week, to see if you have made a decision or not."

"OK, Michael, but do not come any sooner."

Michael turns around and opens the door, walks out then slams it as hard as he can, as he leaves the premises very bemused. Tristina looks at her bewildered daughter.

"He has gone for now my darling. You just need to get through the immigration process at Heathrow, then you can go your separate ways."

"Good. I could never live with a thug, that is all he is now, Michael will be all alone, thank goodness."

Tristina and Ramon were not very happy nor gratified that Anjella and their granddaughter had after all, agreed to travel with the despicable Michael Ironi. Especially after the condition he left both his partner and daughter in, when he was alone with them. But they all sat down to a gorgeous dinner of *karanga*, followed by a sumptuous sticky date pudding.

Adhiambo went with her mother, waiting in the car while Anjella went in to see the director of the hospital. He was very happy to hear that she had been offered a position in London. He did state that he would like her to return eventually, to replace him at some point as the director. Anjella said she would love to be involved further with the direction of the Women's Hospital. But at this point in her career, she needed to explore the world, to see what it had to offer her, within the scope of all her studies. He agreed with her, also stating that it would look great on her CV. They parted the very best of friends, hoping to see each other again in the not too distant future.

Then on the same afternoon, mother and daughter went to Adhiambo's school, to inform them of her intended move to England. The headmaster told them both that they would be very sorry to lose Adhiambo, and her influences she had given them all. The fact she was an excellent student, a role-model for all the other juniors that had gone there to study, since she had been at the school. But they realised this was a fabulous opportunity for the young lady. They wished her all the best in her environment and her future life. He told them both, if they were to return the following day, there would be a school report awaiting their collection, to give to the new headmaster, wherever that might be.

Michael comes waltzing in on them all, on the sunny Friday afternoon, while they are all enjoying a refreshing cup of tea.

"Good afternoon, one and all."

They all look at him, without replying. Then Anjella looks through him, telling him very aggressively:

"We have managed to sort out Adhiambo's school, along with my position at the hospital. So you can book the flight, whenever you are ready."

"OK, Anjella, if I got one for Monday, would that suit you?"

"Yes, Michael, that would suit us both."

"Then let us have a look now."

He has brought his tablet with him, checking in on the Kenyan Airways site. There is a flight out on the Monday evening, at 17:30hours. So he books three seats, paying for them there and then. Then turning to the two still seated females he informs them,

"Anjella, Belinda, I will come and pick you up at 13:45hours."

"OK, Michael, see you then."

So he leaves, as they go back to their tea and *maandazi*[12]. Anjella turns to them all:

"We had better enjoy this weekend together, it could be our last one for some time."

"It could be, Mum, but I am sure we will be back for a visit at some future date."

---

[12] See glossary

The whole weekend is spent in each other's company, as all four of them enjoy and indulge in the delights of Nairobi. Anjella helps herself to some of Michael's stash. Then she hid the rest away, out of reach of prying eyes and itchy fingers, until Monday when she would take the rest with her. Then the time finally came for all of them to say goodbye, to each other. Affectionate kisses, long tight hugs followed tears and sobbing. Then finally came a touching of hands not wanting to let go of each other. A long sad adieu and bon voyage, as Michael finally pulled away, heading towards Nairobi Airport in the hire car. Offloading the suitcases, he left the keys at the office, then went into the complex to book onto their flight to Heathrow. Anjella has already emailed Emelia, with all their details. Adhiambo took the inside seat and slept through the whole flight. Anjella took the inside seat and enjoyed the evening meal with a little shiraz. Then she put her seat in the relaxed position and slept a little uncomfortably. After dinner Michael partook of a brace of Tuskers, which kept him company, while he watched the films through the whole eight-and-a-half-hour flight. It was very restful, only flying at about two thirds capacity, flying at 38,500 feet. It took them from thirty-two degrees of Nairobi, Kenya, into the early hours of a seven-degree misty Saturday morning, of Staines, Middlesex.

Having collected their baggage, they slowly walked through immigration,

"Excuse me, sir, would you come with me?"

The officer takes Mr Simony Soboko, into a nearby interview room, while mother and daughter carry on through. There in the arrival lounge is Emelia waving at them both, shouting at them. Anjella turns to her daughter.

"What do we do about your father?"

"We leave him here. He said we go our separate ways, so we go. If you wait for him, I want to go home now. I do not want him spoiling the rest of my life, no matter where I live."

"OK. Then, here we go precious. Hi, Emelia good to see you again."

Emelia, Anjella and Adhiambo all kissing and hugging each other, smiling, all too happy to be in each other's company.

"I hope you do not mind, but I have made beds up for you in my spare rooms. Until you manage to find somewhere to live."

"That is fine Emelia, we are just so happy to be here."

"Come on then, let me get you both home and to bed. Then we can do some exploring later."

They talk about Adhiambo's new school, Anjella's work, where Emelia lives in Plaistow and why it is referred to as the East End. Being only forty minutes away from Central London, it is no bother getting to work. When they get in, Emelia shows her two new guests to their rooms.

"You sleep as long as you like, we can talk properly when you get up."

With that Emelia leaves them to it.

"Well, Mum I am all for sleeping now."

"So am I, my sweetheart, come on."

So they both crash out together, on the double bed and sleep. Anjella along with her daughter's noses begin to twitch, as strange smells and aromas emanate from somewhere far below. They both get dressed, then follow their noses, leading them both to Emelia in her kitchen.

"Oh my, that smells absolutely wonderful, Emelia."

"What is it?"

"Well, Anjella, Adhiambo, it is referred to as a Full English here. It is in fact just a fried breakfast."

"What is that?" asks the young lady, pointing to the dark black sausage.

"That Adhiambo, is called black pudding. Very tasty, but sit down and you can try it all. I have just switched the kettle off, so you can make a cup of tea, or coffee, whichever you prefer. Just help yourselves."

As they do, Emelia dishes up sausage, bacon, black pudding, mushrooms, fried bread and baked beans, all topped with a fried egg. Then sitting down with her two guests, she ate with them. Watching them tuck in and really enjoy the meal, as they finished with two empty plates. Anjella turns to her friend:

"That was fantastic, normally back home we would just have fresh bread and a cup of tea."

Adhiambo smiles, seeming a little coy.

"Ask me then, Adhiambo, I know you have a question that is eating you up."

"I have two in fact, Emelia. The first is, what is the black pudding made of?"

"I am very glad you ate it first. It is made from pig's blood and a selection of herbs."

"You would not think that could be so tasty. It was delicious Emelia."

"It was completely different from anything I have ever tasted, Emelia."

"I know Adhiambo, Anjella. I am just so glad you both enjoyed it so much. So young lady, onto your second question."

"Is there a girl's school near here, Emelia?"

"In fact, there is. I will take you and your mum on Monday. How does that suit you both?"

"That is amazing Emelia, could I walk there?"

"It would be a long walk. On Monday we will go by car, then you tell me if you could walk there."

"I will Emelia."

"So for the rest of today, would you like to go out and explore?"

"I would love to. Where could we go Emelia?"

"I know we could go to Tower Hill."

"What is there, Emelia?"

"Anjella, there is the Tower of London, you might have heard of it. It is where they keep the Crown Jewels on display."

"That sounds very enthralling. Mum, let us go there."

"OK Adhiambo, we can go."

"Before we set out, Anjella, do you have a bank account?"

"No, Emelia, I have money on me, but no account."

"So the first thing to do, is take you to my bank, so you can open an account. It is only a short walk."

"OK, Emelia, we can do that first, how far is it?"

"Only in East Ham, a Lloyds."

So they all walk out together, up to Browning Road, going into and up to the information desk. The young woman looks up smiling:

"Good morning, ladies, how may we help you this morning?"

Anjella steps forward, asking:

"Could I open an account please?"

"Of course, madam."

She gets up, taking the party over to an empty desk, then turning getting Anjella to sit.

"So do you have money to open the account with?"

"Yes, I have Kenyan shillings, is that OK?"

"Of course, madam, that is fine."

The Lloyds cashier takes all the relevant information, takes the bundle of shillings, counts it all out. Then showing Anjella the exchange rate and what her money is worth in sterling. She pays it directly into her account, then looking up to Anjella asking her:

"Would you like cheque book along with a debit card?"

"Yes please if that is possible."

"Of course it is madam. What address would you like it delivered to, Mrs Ogwayo?"

"Twenty-four Cumberland Road, London E13, please."

"Certainly, they should be with you within five working days, Mrs Ogwayo."

"Miss Ogwayo is much more preferable please."

"My apologies, Miss Ogwayo."

Now Anjella's financial circumstances were sorted out, they made their way up to Upton Park, then onto the District Line to Tower Hill. Where they all enjoyed the rest of their fantastic day.

Simony had endured a long and infuriating investigation at the immigration office. The officers were very thorough. He had showed them his passport, bank details, his address, both his visas, his national insurance number and his general practitioners address, even though he had been here for eight years. But he finally made it to his new residence in Bow. There he had a good long rest, then texted all his friends and associates in Kenya and England, letting them know he had finally made an entry into the United Kingdom in one piece.

But he had no idea where Anjella had got to. As far as he was concerned, he wanted to keep that way. He had no immediate plans, except to sleep. Then to see what was what once he had awakened from a good rest, then having a clear train of thought. All in the name of greed, power and retribution. Being a callous, soulless asshole, he did not care that he was in another country. He thought he could just carry on his way of life, with scant regard for anyone else. He was a brainless jerk, who only cared about himself and his self-serving platitudes.

Having slept and had something to eat, he walked the local shops, looking for outlets that sold the items he would require to construct his home-made deathly devices. Then he looked further afield for possible targets, ones that would raise awareness of the sudden infiltration of the Light of Africa. His eyes lit up, at the prospects in The Arcade Market Square. Then just across the way, in Cordelia Street, a school and a police station that stood so close together, so very tempting. Then he caught a bus to Canning Town bus station, crossing the A13 beneath Newham Way, onto the A124 Barking Road, up towards Plaistow. There he followed his nose, until he came across another police station, between Cumberland Road and Esk Road, on the A124. There not too distant in Jutland Road, lay another bonus — a school. So there in the space of 120 minutes or so, he had found his first two targets. Now he just needed to source the equipment for his improvised explosive devices. That realistically needed to be very compact, using small local shops as much as possible, using cash in all transactions, then keeping all his items out of sight in his cool, damp basement. He did not want to draw any undue, unwanted, unwelcomed attention upon himself, so soon after his arrival here. Buying bits and pieces slowly with his normal day to day shopping, he finds and accumulates all the items he needs for his specialist task. In this way he commits himself to working during the night, making sure all his doors and windows are locked and shuttered, so that he does get any unforeseen, nasty surprises of his own.

The days pass by in his rather solitary existence, but it was for the greater good, or so he thought, with his own rather disputed, weak beliefs. He still at times dwelled on what Belinda had told him, weeks ago. But still he could not think for himself, after all the years of indoctrination by and from the Light of Africa, this was the only code he lived by. The only way of life he knew, having survived and thrived on the excitement of it all. So consumed were they that nothing would gravitate him away from their demands and his catechism of survival. Eventually, the two devices were all ready to use, one sealed in to a cigarette packet, another in a matchbox; a third as a standby in a Tic Tac container. They were all left neatly on his worktop, as he decided to go upstairs, to get something to eat as well as a drink, to clear the dust and fumes from his dry throat. It was coming up to a long weekend, involving a Friday and Monday. So he guessed the Thursday night would be a good moment to hit the locals with a bomb, a bit of carnage and destruction. So he just lay on his bed contemplating his reckless side, which had always helped him survive. So now on foreign turf, he was hoping that it would see him through here as well.

Thursday night came, the streets were full of people out enjoying the beginning of the Easter weekend. In stealth mode, Simony strolled along Bow Common Lane Upper, into Brabazon Street, along into Chrisp Street, then over and into Southill Street. Finally finding himself in the Arcade Market

Square. He planted one of his devices at the rear entrance of the police station. Priming it for forty minutes, he walked unnoticed into Kerbey Street up to Cordelia Street, putting the cigarette packet and Tic Tac container down at the base of the rear fire escape, setting those both for twenty-five minutes. Then he departed down Grundy Street, Canton Street, along Kildare Walk, Pigott Street, Stansby Road and along Cotall Street. Finally, back into Common Lane Upper and away from his misadventure. As he walked slowly back to his house, he heard the first device explode, followed shortly by the detonation of the other two. Calmly walking past Tower Hamlets cemetery, then he dialled 111. A voice spoke:

"How can we be of assistance?"

"The bombing of the police station at the Arcade Market Square, along with the school in Cordelia Street. It was the work of the Light of Africa, your friendly terrorist operatives."

Then he cut himself off, disposing of the phone at the same time. Then he headed back to his dwelling for a good night's sleep and a restful weekend, wanting to see how the officials dealt with the mess he had created all by himself.

"Well gentlemen, this is a right shambles. A telephone call is the only lead we have. Come on, let us go and see what we can do. The Light of Africa is a new one." Commander Helen Ball, feeling wretched inside and out, stays resolute after her short resumé of the situation. She leads her team out.

The Counter Terrorism Unit move out, into the Arcade Market Square and get to work.

So Adhiambo had been introduced to her new school and the headmistress, Rachael McGowan had welcomed her, to

Plashnet School for Girls, in Plashnet Grove, Canning Town E6. She had been impressed with the headmaster's report, from her school in Kenya. Telling the young lady, that she hoped her work would not drop off, that the tutors were all there to help her at any time. Emelia and Anjella along with Adhiambo, had all been out together to look for somewhere to reside, knowing that the hospital would help them, in settling down, once they had found somewhere to live. The only address they had found that they liked was, St Andrew's Road, E13.

The three ladies were watching the TV, shocked at the local bombings. Adhiambo's ears prick up, when she hears that the Light of Africa, are laying claim to all the disruption, destruction and devastation. She suddenly thought to herself, surely her father would not have started his terrorist activities already. Especially under a false name! Then again perhaps it was not him, what was she to do? She would talk to her mother later, then see what she had to say about it. When they were upstairs alone in the bedroom, she sat next to her mother, before going to her own bedroom.

"Do you think Dad has got anything to do with this, Mum?"

"What makes you ask that question my *mondo*?"

"The mere fact that Dad is over here, somewhere. Also, they are saying that the terrorist organisation, The Light of Africa, are taking responsibility for it."

"I suppose he could be. I think if he was, he would be working by himself."

"Why, Mum?"

"He would not have had the time, to make any contacts, to set up what they call a cell. But then again, they might have had operators already here, who could have assisted him."

"OK, Mum, forget I mentioned it. Let us just enjoy the rest of the weekend with Emelia."

Sunday was spent indoors, watching TV, discussing St Andrew's Road and having a roast lamb dinner. On Monday, they went to see the Monument and walk around St Paul's Cathedral. Then Tuesday, Adhiambo was back at school, while Emelia and Anjella were back to work.

Simony was in his basement working on three more IEDs, making ready for his second target. He relished his work, it was the only thing he was good at. He had decided to put a couple of embellishments on all of his newly prepared devices. This he was hoping to have ready, in two weeks' time, for the May Day weekend. He had no one to rely on, except himself. So everything needed to work first time, because there was no going back now he had committed himself to this course of action. All three had delay fuses of a single minute, one packed into a large Smarties tube, one into a small water bottle, the last one into a plastic snuffbox. He had the same plan as before on the Friday evening, the beginning of the long weekend. He had his disposable phone ready for the call.

Anjella and her daughter had enjoyed the sightseeing around the city. They had learnt what the Monument was there for, having viewed the splendour of St Paul's. Then Adhiambo had knuckled down to her studies whilst her mother was enjoying her work with the other likeminded people at the hospital; all trying to eradicate the female mosquito, the spread of malaria and other waterborne diseases across Africa. The following Bank Holiday was soon upon them. But it was Anjella and Emelia's turn to work on the holiday. So Adhiambo on the Saturday and Monday used the school library to further investigate her homework, along with other subjects that she felt needed her immediate attention, so she was able to keep up with all her classmates. So as not to let anyone down, especially her teachers and the name of the school.

Simony appeared on his front doorstep, late into the evening. Simony had reached Godalming Road when the first of his IEDs had detonated. They all had flash incendiary, where the explosive sticks to whatever it lands upon, then just burns.

Simony made his way home, then phoned 111 and left the same message as before. Then, stamping on the phone, he slots the remnants in between the grates of a nearby drain, dropping it down into the murky depths. Then going indoors, he locks everything before sleeping the sleep of the righteous. Not perturbed, disturbed or infuriated by his vicious deeds, no nightmares, no visions at all. He felt completely at peace with the world and with his vile devices. He thought that seeking to equalise the world, with his deleterious, detrimental escapades, would make him happy. This, in his small mind, was his way of achieving that goal. But he did not realise his little bit of viciousness was inconsequential to the world at large. He was just a nuisance who needed to be stopped, that was a certainty.

The news on Saturday was all about the second bombing in the East End. The reporters telling everyone that the Light of Africa, had laid claim to this one as well. Adhiambo was really worried, Anjella was at work, so being fifteen and very concerned, she decided off her own back to visit her local police station. She stood outside uncertain for a while, then forcing herself through the doors, she advanced up to the desk, where a big burly sergeant looked at her, smiling.

"Can I help you at all, young lady?"

"I think so, if someone is willing to listen to me, regardless of my age."

"In that case I think I know just the lady. Luckily enough she is here in person. I will just call her."

He picks up the phone, waits patiently then:

"Ma'am, I think I may have someone who may be of interest to you in your investigation."

"OK, Sergeant, I am on my way."

Commander Helen Ball comes out of one of the back offices, into the light of the main entrance. All smiles, she comes straight up to the young lady sat down on the bench, by the main entrance.

"So, young lady, do you think the information you have is very important?"

"I think the information I have could relate to the last two bombings you have had."

"What, here in the East End?"

"Yes, I do."

"In that case, come with me, please."

Helen takes hold of the young girl's hand, taking her over to the desk first.

"Sarge, get me Inspector Lewson, Tuley, and Sergeant Lona Vandy, please send them to my room."

"I will straight away Ma'am."

The desk sergeant is on the phone straight away,

"Ah there you are Inspector, the commander wants you, Tuley and Sergeant Vandy right away."

"OK we are on our way."

Commander Helen Ball enters her office. Sitting the girl down, she makes sure she is comfortable.

"First of all, I am Helen, so young lady, what is your name?"

"It is Adhiambo Ogwayo."

"Have you been here long, Adhiambo?"

"About six weeks, Helen."

A knock at the door, heralds three more people coming in. Inspector Lewson, is followed by his collator Constable Tuley and a female Sergeant, to keep Adhiambo comfortable in this company. Lona Vandy sits next to the girl, holding her hand.

"I am Sergeant Lona Vandy, call me Lona please. I am here just for you."

"Please do not worry Adhiambo, these are just here to listen to your story, Lona is here to keep you company, OK? So now what would you like to tell us?"

"When my mother came here, to England, it was with the offer of working at a hospital, after her appearance at the World Health Organisation."

"Which hospital?"

"The Hospital for Tropical Diseases, here in London."

"Can you remember who got her the job?"

"Yes, we are staying with her at the moment. It was one of the other doctors giving her lectures at The World Health Organisation, at the same time. My mother is Doctor Anjella Ogwayo, the other doctor is Emelia Koso."

"So, what does your mother specialise in?"

"Malaria, the mosquito, schistosomosis, Rift Valley fever and chikuwgnya."

"Where have you and your mother come from, Adhiambo?"

"Nairobi, Kenya."

"Where did your mother work in Nairobi?"

"The Nairobi Hospital for Women and Training School."

"Please Adhiambo, would you like to carry on? Take your time and tell us anything you think is important."

"When we came here, we travelled with my father, who was on the run."

"What was your father's name?"

"His name on his fake passport was Simony Soboko. It would not surprise me if it had not been stolen especially for his entry, into this country."

"What makes you say that?"

"Well his proper name is Michael Ironsi, he is a terrorist for the organisation that calls itself, the Light of Africa."

"Ah, now I see why you came to us. They are the firm claiming responsibility for these two outrages."

"Yes, he also has another name."

"What would that be Adhiambo?"

"Abshir Dalmar, that was for when he worked in Somalia. He is also wanted in Tanzania, Sudan, South Sudan and Uganda."

"Dear oh dear, he has been a naughty boy. This is superb information, do you think your mother would come and speak to us?"

"I am sure she would, Helen, if I asked her nicely."

"When would she be home?"

"About six p.m. tonight."

"Are you by yourself until then?"

"Yes, I am."

"In that case, Lona, take this beautiful young lady down to our canteen. Make sure she eats, then take her home. Then stay with her, keep her safe."

Lona takes Adhiambo down to the canteen, making sure she eats well.

"You have whatever you like, Adhiambo, as much as you like."

"Thank you, Lona, do you think I have been of any help to you?"

"I think you have done us a great service by coming to us like this. Hopefully between us, we can stop this happening a third time."

"Then I am pleased I came to see you. I keep wishing I had come sooner, but I was not sure anyone would listen to me."

"But you have spoken to us now, that is very important to us Adhiambo. There is no rush, you enjoy your dinner. I am assuming Adhiambo is a tribal name?"

"Yes, it is, Lona, it means Born in the Evening."

"How absolutely beautiful."

"How long have you lived here, Lona?"

"I have lived here for twenty-three years now."

"Do you like it?"

"Yes, I do. The freedom I have is unbelievable."

"Where are you from originally?"

"My family came from Sierra Leone."

"What a crazy world, here we are talking to each other, when in another world we might never meet."

"I know, freedom makes all the difference, as you will learn, Adhiambo."

"I think I already am."

"Are you ready, Adhiambo?"

"Yes, I am, Lona, what does that mean, your name?"

"It means Exotic, which I am. Then, let me take you home."

Lona takes the short journey back to Cumberland Road, from the station at Adine Street, on the Barking Road. They sat talking about East and West Africa — what they both remembered. The lives they had left behind, their memories, their chat drawing them ever-closer to each other. Laughing at the good times, they tried to explain away the not so good and downright bad times. Just then the front door opens, as Anjella and Emelia walk in.

"Good evening, my *mondo*, who is this young lady?"

"Hi, Mum, this is Lona, a sergeant in the Metropolitan Police."

"Why is she here with you, what have you done?"

"Nothing, Mum, I promise. Lona is here because I went to them, about Michael and the bombings."

"We were wondering if you would corroborate your daughter's story?"

"Yes, I would love to."

"Would you like to do it here?"

Anjella turns to her friend Emelia, smiling:

"Would that be OK with you, Emelia?"

"Of course, Anjella, I will just go and put the kettle on."

"Mrs Ogwayo could I go and get another couple of officers?"

"It is Miss, of course you can. I can wait for you, Sergeant."

"Call me Lona, please, I will be back very soon."

Lona Vardy returned with the commander, inspector and Constable Tuley. As they turn up and sit down, Emelia brings in a large tray with a large pot of tea, six cups, sugar, sweeteners and various biscuits. The commander looks directly at Anjella,

"Would you like to tell us about Michael Ironi, Miss Ogwayo?"

"Well I knew him from school, he was a bully then. He never learnt anything. He did not even understand that Nairobi was the capital of Kenya."

"So when did you notice he started mixing with the layabouts of Nairobi?"

"When he was about thirteen, he started missing school, everyone noticed it. Eventually he left and never came back. He became an explosive expert at a young age. He was then shown how to make improvised explosive devices and I think, the other thing is called explosive ordnance disposal. He even had his own school out in Somalia."

"Can you remember what it was called, Anjella?"

"If I recall it was the Sudanese College of Politics and Law."

"Can you remember where it was actually situated?"

"I know it was in Somalia, but which town or village, I am not sure."

"This is all splendid stuff. Now is there anything else you can tell us, that might help in our investigation?"

"When we came here into Heathrow, he was pulled over to one side by one of your immigration officers. So they might be able to help, with the information they gathered."

"When did you arrive?"

"Tuesday the 15th March."

"Incredible ladies, if you can think of anything else, please let us know."

"We will, Helen."

"Adhiambo, I will be at the station so just give me a call, if you need me."

"OK, Lona, I will not forget."

On the return to the station, Constable Tuley phoned Heathrow's Immigration Control.

"I am after finding out about a Simony Soboko, that passed through your department on Tuesday 15th March. Apparently one of your officers pulled him over. Do you have fingerprints — anything in fact?"

"Ah yes, here he is. We took all ten prints, I will send them to you, along with all the other relevant information we have."

"Superb, thank you so much."

Tuley goes down to the evidence department, digging out the throw-away phone, they found after the first bombing. It had thumb print along with a partial forefinger as well. Comparing the one from the phone with the set he had received from Heathrow immigration, he found a match. Then when he thumbed through the paperwork, this alias Simony Soboko gave his address as Harley Grove E3. Tuley Sensed this could be the breakthrough they needed. Calling Inspector Lewson over to his desk, he explained what he had discovered, along with the implications of the fingerprint. A smile appeared on Lewson's face, he called Commander Ball, who dropped everything, to make her way down to the incident room. Excited and brimming with joy, the commander rushes in through the already open door.

"So we think we have our man?"

"We think we have our man, he could be, ma'am"

"So are we sure or not Lewson?"

"Yes ma'am, we are as sure as we can be, at this moment in time."

"OK, we will go tonight. I will get SO13 now, before he can do any other damage."

Commander Helen Ball picks up the nearest phone, calling the desired department.

"I want them now, at my disposal, but discretely of course."

"You got them ma'am. Where do you want them to debus?"

"The police station on the Barking Road, on the junction with Cumberland Road."

"Got it, they are on their way, will be with you very shortly."

The desk sergeant was in the yard, awaiting their arrival. Waving to them.

"Just follow me please, gents."

He took all of them into the large section room, where all the daily briefings took place. They all sit as the commander stands to take control of their use, in this situation.

"Gentlemen, we are in a position to capture the renegade bomber who torched the stations at West India Dock Road, along with the one in the Arcade Market Square. He also ignited the two schools in Cordelia Street and Wades Place.

We tend to think he resides in Harley Grove, Bow. We are under the impression he has a basement, which is where he makes his IEDs. No noise, no sirens, no lights. We will come from the back via Pudding Mill Lane, on the A118. Through Wick Lane into Tredegar Road, parking at Bow Road Station. We'll meet on foot, along Alfred Street and Benworth Street. I want both ends cut off and no movement whatsoever along Harley Grove. Then on your section leader's say so, force entry, front,back and in through the basement, if there is an entrance there as well. We want him alive and in one piece. Have a good day, boys, see you back at Bow Road Station."

They all sat there in the silence that followed, contemplating the more concise orders now being given to them by their chief inspector. While Commander Ball got her squad assembled, ready to get involved once the culprit had been nullified and removed from the premises. The time was 23:45. They all mounted the unmarked vans, drove quite happily, without drawing any attention from Adine Road on the A124, past West Ham and into Abbey Lane, then back onto the A118, coming off at Pudding Mill Lane. This took them across the Old Ford, into Wick Lane and down into the yard of Bow Road Station. At 00:55 everything was in place, everybody was ready to go. Then at 01:00 the house in Harley Grove was breached and entry gained by forceful means. The SO11 secured all rooms, Michael Ironi was found tinkering with another small IED. He was immobilised with the basic policeman's hold, allowing the Counter Terrorism Squad to go through his arsenal, his paperwork, his laptop and other personal equipment. All were gently being tagged, photographed and itemised as per evidence protocol. Then having everything they required, and making sure the house had not been booby trapped or hot-wired by any IED, EOD, or any other explosive device, SO19 were left there to safeguard the premises while the Counter Terrorism Squad loaded up all their cache along with the prisoner, making their way back to the Yard. By now they all felt quite confident there would not be any more brutal bombings of police stations and schools in the East End.

Now the Squad was systematically going through all the evidence acquired from Harley Grove. The expert inquisitors were questioning Michael Ironi about his dealings in here, along with the dire consequences he had caused back in his home of Kenya, Tanzania, Somalia and the Sudan. He admitted to the bombings here in England, but denied all knowledge of any involvement in Uganda, Kenya, Tanzania, Somalia and the Sudan. In turn he was asking them:

"What is the Light of Africa?"

"You know well enough, Mr Ironi. Take him away for now, we will try again later."

His fingerprints were all over everything that had been bagged, so he was implicated in a large way. He was now the prime suspect.

"He is a nasty piece of work, sir."

"Callous, a heart of stone, Tuley."

"If we do not get him for anything else, we have him for how many counts of murder?"

"Enough to bury him for good Tuley."

They both go down to Commander Ball's office, to inform her of the slow progress they are making. Helen turns to her phone, telling the section sergeant she wants Sergeant Vandy in her office now. After a short wait the female sergeant knocks on the door of the commander's office.

"Come in, Vandy."

"You sent for me, ma'am?"

"Yes Lona, tomorrow I want you to go to the Ogwayos, just to let them know we have Michael in custody. I am not sure we need to mention court appearances just yet."

"OK, ma'am, that will not be a problem."

After school finishes, Lona dressed in civvies this time before she knocks on the front door. Still in her school clothes the young Adhiambo answers the door.

"Lona, this is a nice surprise, please come in."

"Adhiambo so how was school?"

"It is a lot better now I have finally caught up. It is so interesting now I know the same as my friends."

"I am here to tell you that we have your father in our custody. He was caught red handed."

"Good, it is where he belongs. Mum will be so happy as well. When will he go to jail?"

"Once everything is ready. He will go to court first, all the evidence will be given. Then the jury will have to decide if he is guilty or not."

"He is and should be locked away for the rest of his life."

"You do not like him very much Adhiambo, do you?"

"No. Not the way he ended up treating Mum and myself. He is less than a pig."

"I am sure he will go to prison, for a very long time."

"Will we have to go to his trial, Lona?"

"No. I say no, we would rather keep you out of the spotlight, if we can."

"I hope you can."

"When will your mum be home, Adhiambo?"

"In a couple of hours, Lona."

"You go and get changed then, I will take you out to dinner, if would like to come with me?"

"That would be lovely, Lona."

The young girl goes through her full wardrobe, thanks to the gifts both Lona and Emelia had given her. Feeling all a quiver at the thought of dressing up, to go out with another woman. Looking hard for something to impress, but in fact was not necessary with the sergeant. Then it struck her right in the middle, she had only just got it. The blush pink thick-strap pephem bodycon midi dress, along with her new scarlet satin peep-toe stilettos. She felt so grown up as she walked down stairs into the company of Lona Vardy.

"Good grief a Black Beauty[13]! What a stunning young lady you make."

"Thank you so much, I was not sure if it was too much or not."

"Spectacular, Miss Ogwayo."

"Come on then Lona, let us go and eat and I am starving."

They walk into Plaistow together, finding a nice little eatery. Coming across Kate's Restaurant in Balaam Street, they sauntered in together taking a table in a quiet corner. Lona looked across at the resplendent, redolent and alluring young lady sat opposite her, smiling and asking:

"Are you ready to order, Adhiambo?"

It seemed as though her friend was ignoring her, until she looked making direct eye contact with Lona's soft yielding olive orbs.

---

[13] Black Beauty is the name of a hybrid tea rose. A deep lush red, so red it looks black.

"You must think me so rude, I am so sorry I was just caught up in the menu. Yes, I will have the *kenkey* with the grilled *tilapia*. How about you, Lona?"

"No not at all, you enjoy yourself and your food. I am going to have the fried yam with the roasted guinea fowl."

They sit conversing in a little girl talk, both enjoying the food at Kate's. Then they get up and start walking back to Adhiambo's home. Lona turns as the young girl starts to talk to her.

"Lona, when my father goes to prison."

"Yes, Adhiambo."

"Will you let me know which one he goes to?"

"Of course young lady, as soon as I know, you will know."

On returning to Cumberland Road, Anjella and Emelia had already been home for a while. Lona is surprised at how long they had been out.

"Dear me, Anjella, I apologise for keeping Adhiambo out for so long. We only went out to get something to eat."

"Trust me it is not a problem, Lona, stay and have a cup of tea with us."

"Thank you, so much."

Lona sits down on the empty settee, where Anjella's daughter sits down beside her, feeling very comfortable indeed.

"Anjella we have apprehended Mr Ironi, we did so in the early hours of this morning. We just thought that you and your daughter should know."

"That is wonderful news. When will he go to prison?"

"Well, like I was trying to explain to Adhiambo, he will have to go to trial first. Then the jury will convict him or not.

Then the judge will have the final say on the matter, when he gives the sentence to Michael."

"Well, all I can say is, I hope he is locked away somewhere, where he cannot escape from."

"He will not get bail. So at least he is locked away, until the court case."

"Lona do have a *mandaazi*, they have just been freshly cooked."

"Thank you, Emelia, what are they?"

"A Kenyan doughnut and so very nice too, with tea."

Lona takes a little bite, soon to be lost in the flavour and the bliss of its lightness.

"That, ladies, is a little piece of heaven."

"Do you really think so, Lona?"

"Yes, Anjella, delicious."

"We are going to have a barbeque on Saturday, would you like to come Lona?"

"If you are sure, I would love to, what time?"

"Anytime after one o'clock, would that be OK?"

"Fantastic, I have to go now, it has been a tremendous pleasure, spending time with you all."

They all hug Lona, then she leaves, heading back to the Yard. Adhiambo goes and changes into her pyjamas, then comes back down, kissing Emelia then Anjella both, goodnight. Emelia turns to Anjella, smiling just before Adhiambo disappears back upstairs.

"Anjella, have you thought any more about finding somewhere to live?"

"I have, I just need to take my precious daughter there, to see what she thinks of our possible new home Emelia."

"Is it still St Andrews you like, Anjella?"

"Yes, it is as a matter of fact, Emelia."

"Then let us all take another look tomorrow, with Adhiambo, when we get home from work."

They both look at Anjella's daughter, as she smiles and nods very happily, telling them both she will look forward to it, when she gets back from school. Adhiambo has breakfast with both her mother and Emelia, before they set off for work. They drop Adhiambo off at school, on their way to the hospital.

Michael's defence lawyer does not hold out much hope for him, on the strength of the unequivocal evidence against him. Also, with him causing so many deaths of so many children, along with the police officers he had killed, he had no hope. But Michael wanted to plead guilty, so that was the plea his lawyer put forward for him. It did not help him any. Anjella and her daughter were not needed in the case. He was committed purely on all the other physical evidence against him. Helped by the forged paperwork, his passport and visas, his subversive acts here and over in East Africa. There was the horrific count of dead, mutilated and half-burnt bodies. All those he had driven to early graves, well before their time. So the judge gave him life. His final words were:

"In this case, life will mean life. This man is never to set foot outside of a jail ever again. He will be incarcerated for the full time of his natural life, to be finally buried in an unmarked grave. Once he is pronounced dead, by the governor of his prison, he will spend all his time in solitary confinement for his own safety. Also, so that he can dwell on the many deaths he caused, with his wilful and violent acts of terrorism. Take him away please."

The facility of choice for Mr Michael Ironi was Pentonville, London. On that same day, Anjella and her daughter were moving into their new home, in St Andrew's Road, not too far away from Emelia. Who was also there, giving them both a hand, to move in to their new surroundings. Lona had made time to be there, giving what assistance she could. She got a text from Helen, late in the afternoon, telling her the result of the trail. She turned to the other three ladies, smiling, shouting quite loudly in her excitement:

"GOOD NEWS EVERYONE, MR IRONI GOT LIFE. WITH NO CHANCE OF EVER GETTING OUT OR PAROLE. HE IS TO BE LOCKED AWAY, FOR GOOD!"

"That is super news, Lona."

"I am so glad you think so, Adhiambo."

"Do we know which prison he is going to be sent to?"

"Yes Anjella, he is going to Pentonville, here in London. His last wish was to be able to see at least one of you, some time in the near future."

"That we will have to think about. How would we go about that, if we wanted to see him? Especially if he is in solitary confinement, Lona?"

"I would have to find that out for you both. If either of you showed any interest in visiting him, Adhiambo."

"I suppose once would not hurt, but I would not know what to say to him, Lona."

"I think it would be more of a question of you listening to him. Letting him clear his conscience in one form or another. Anyway, you just let me know at any time and we will sort it out for you. If you do decide to go, do not ever give him any of your personal details. Keep everything to yourself, for your own safety and protection, and that of your daughter and friends, Anjella."

"We will not disclose anything of any value to him whatsoever Lona."

"Is Pentonville far away from here?"

"No not really. But when and if you are ever ready, we will pick you up, take you there, as well as bring you home once you are finished Adhiambo."

"OK, Lona, I will go at half-term, just in case my daughter wants to come with me, to see her father one last time."

Halfway through the autumn term, Lona picks up Anjella along with Adhiambo, from St Andrew's Road. Sergeant Vardy wore civvies, driving all three of them to Pentonville prison. Sat in the car for a while, thinking about what she was about to do, finally unable to reconcile herself to seeing Michael again, turns to both her daughter and Lona, telling them:

"I cannot do it. I know I will fall under his spell. I cannot go in there and face up to the murderer. I am ashamed of him, of me being involved with him from the start. I feel dirty, tainted, used, despoiled and contaminated by his body. Even worse, if I reconcile and forgive him, I am no better than he is. No, you must go by yourself, Adhiambo. Can you do that for me, I am so sorry to leave you alone, like this?"

Anjella's daughter goes to her mum, cuddles her tight close, lets her weep then cry on her, comforting her all the while. Then she wipes away her mother's tears, consoling her, telling her:

"He never did deserve you, Mum, I know what sort of hog he is, he should have been castrated at birth. You sit in the car and just wait for me. I will tell you everything he says, when I come back out, OK?"

Anjella kisses her strong, wilful daughter on her lips, not wanting to let her go off, by herself.

"Adhiambo, you have always known how to look after your mum. We have always been bound to one another, since we both nearly died at your birth. Please keep safe and come back."

Then mother and daughter kiss each other once again, Lona takes the young woman to the main entrance.

"Take this, Adhiambo, it will get you through to see your dad."

Adhiambo goes through, with just a casual search, then through to the visitor's area, where he was waiting for her.

"Hi, Dad."

"Belinda so good to see you, it has been a while."

"A very long time, we have not had you in our lives and now you want to talk to us."

"So, where is your mother?"

"She feels let down, ruined in so many ways by you. So she said she could not face you in this situation. So I am sorry to tell you, that I am only one here to see you."

"In that case, it will be you that I talk to, my very dear daughter."

"It will indeed, Dad."

"In that case I only have you, to fall back on."

"You have only me. If you feel guilty, it is far too late to start using me as your personal confessional. You need to own up to what you have done, learn to live with it. Do not try and blame me, Mum or anyone else you know, with this outcome. You murdered, maimed and killed so many children and other people, your apology or any sign of regret will not wash with anyone. Probably all you have you to look forward to is a long time passing before you die, which will make no difference in the larger scheme of things."

"I know I have come to the end of my relationship with the physical world. I know I was going to get caught at some time or other. It was probably better I got caught now. But would you do me just a single favour?"

"It all depends on what that favour is, Dad?"

"Belinda, I want you to talk to my firm in Kenya."

"How do I do that, they do not know me?"

"If I give you a number, in Nairobi, would you call it for me?"

"I could do."

"If I give it to you, would you remember it?"

"I am sure I would."

"In that case it is 254711883369."

"Who would I be talking to?"

"Jomo, my control officer."

"How will he know it is me, I could be anyone?"

"Use the words Kapala Jeung Guru before you say anything else over the phone. Then he will know who you are, that it will be safe to talk to you."

"Will you need me to get some sort of reply, retort, response?"

"Yes, it will be a directive, that I will need to respond to, as quickly a possible."

"So you will need me to come back to you here?"

"Yes, I will Belinda."

"In that case, I will see what I can do."

"See you soon, Belinda."

As she walks away from him, Michael Ironi disappears and is escorted back to his rather lonely cell. Adhiambo comes back out into the car park, sitting back into the front seat, strapping herself in as Lona whisks them all back home. Anjella makes three coffees, with which she brings with her a fresh *mkate wamayai*. Lona takes a bite, turning to both of her friends,

"This is absolutely divine, Anjella, "

"Thank you, Lona."

Then Sergeant Vardy turned to Adhiambo, wanting to know desperately what had passed between the father and his daughter.

"So, young lady, what did your dad have to say to you?"

"Well, Mum, he was a little contrite, he did admit that it would be a waste of time being sorry and apologising now for his bombings, as it would not bring back the dead. He was very sad that Anjella never came to see him. But said he understood why she could not."

"Was there more, Adhiambo?" her mother and Sergeant Vardy both asked together.

"Yes, as a matter of fact there was. Rather important I think, especially to Lona and the investigation."

"What investigation Adhiambo?"

"The one involving my father."

"Yes, but we caught him, he is now in prison for what he done. That will now be considered a closed file, Adhiambo."

"But what about all the troubles in East Africa, Lona?"

"We do not have any intelligence regarding his operations out there, young lady."

"But my visiting him might have opened the door on some of the terrorism that his organisation, might have been involved in, Lona."

"OK, then tell me what he told you, young lady."

"First of all, I have a Kenyan phone number, which is the contact number for Jomo, his control officer, Lona"

"Oh, my goodness, how did you get that from him, Adhiambo?"

"He, himself asked me if I would be able to contact this, Jomo, for him. I said I probably would be able to, Lona."

"Can you remember the number Adhiambo?"

"Yes it starts with twenty-five, the international code for Kenya, Lona."

"Then what else did he tell you in confidence, Adhiambo?"

"That when I used the number, I had to say three Sudanese words, before I ever said anything else, Lona."

"Oh, my, he has given a lot to you, on trust. But I suppose he has no-one else to talk to, so he has to tell you, my precious"

"Yes, Mum."

"Did he give you any other orders, Adhiambo?"

"Yes, Lona. I had to wait for a directive from his control officer. Then I have to visit him again, to inform him what the directive is."

"Would you be up to visiting him again, Adhimabo?"

"If it helps you to catch the rest of the Light of Africa, I will help you all I can Lona."

"You are brilliant Adhiambo. Just make sure you can remember everything he tells you. I need to go to the Yard, to see the commander right away."

Sergeant Vardy finishes her coffee, kissing the young girl and Anjella as she says goodbye. Opening the front door, as she exits, she passes Emelia on the way in.

"Hi Emelia, good to see you."

"Lona, a pleasure as always."

The sergeant drives straight to the Yard, asking to see Commander Ball. Knocking on her door, Helen answers:

"Come in, Lona."

Already having Inspector Lewson and her collator in her office, she looks directly at Lona.

"You look extremely excited or very agitated Lona, which is it?"

"I am very excited Commander. You know I was taking Anjella and her daughter to see Michael Ironi today."

"Yes, how did it go, their one-time visit, Lona?"

"First of all, the mother did not go in. She could not face him. So the daughter went in alone, to converse with him, Commander."

"Call me Helen, please. So she said everything she wanted to say to him?"

"As it turns out, Helen, it is more of the other way around."

"What do you mean, Lona?"

"Well, Michael has given his daughter three explicit bits of information, which could help us and the Kenyan police track down the Light of Africa."

"How so Lona?"

"Helen, first of all she has a mobile number in Kenya, that enables her to speak directly to Ironi's contact officer. Secondly, she was given the password, that gives her secure entry into the network. Finally, she will be given a directive for her father, with which he will have to respond, once she has made the call. Obviously, this means she will have to go back to see her father."

"That is astounding, did you get all this information from Adhiambo?"

"I did yes. But she got it all directly from her father. She has all the information safely tucked away. Just so that no one can jump the gun, making it all worthless, by trying to be a maverick, a self-confessed hero, by misusing it. Only the daughter has the intelligence, she should be the only one using it. But with our help and guidance of course, Helen."

"That was very wise of you Lona, a good move. I think tomorrow evening after school, we should go and visit our lady friends in civvies, take them out for dinner. Let's talk to them personally, to see how they feel about helping us, as well as the Kenyan police force, in tracking down and possibly ridding ourselves of at least one terrorist organization. What do you say, Lona?"

"I think they would love that, ma'am."

"Also, how would you feel about working with us?"

"That would be amazing Helen, are you sure?"

"I am positive. I will have a word with your station officer. Get you transferred to my unit, for the duration Lona. Would that suit?"

"That would be fabulous Helen, thank you very much."

"Be here at 16:00 hours tomorrow, dressed in civvies."

"You can count on it, Helen."

In fact, Lona was early, extremely early, so caught up in her new role, she did not want to let anyone down. She sat outside the counter terrorism unit's office, waiting very patiently. Then Tuley passed by.

"Sergeant Vardy you are early, very eager, that is good to see."

"Tuley I am so sorry, I just cannot believe I am working with the big boys now, I am anticipating a fraught few days, just did not want to let anyone down."

"You deserve your chance, just like everyone else. If this works out, it could even be a permanent move for you. Would you like a tea or coffee, while we wait?" Tuley asks Lona, as he opens the door.

"A black coffee please."

Lona takes the container of Splenda out of her bag, clicks two into her hand, then drops them into her cup.

"Were you seconded into the unit, Mark?"

"I was for my computer skills. Then it became a permanent posting. There is nothing else like it, Sarge."

"Call me Lona please. I just hope this goes well for all of us then."

"It will Lona. Let me just make sure that the SUV is ready for our use."

Tuley phones the transport department, enquiring after the availability at the motor pool.

"Yes Mark, it is already with you, in the back yard with a driver in civvies, just as you asked."

Just as they both finish their coffee, Commander Ball and Inspector Tristan Lewson appear in the office. Lona gets up already to leave, Helen turns to her smiling:

"Sit down Lona, take it easy. We can all enjoy a coffee together first, before we fly off. Is the vehicle ready, Mark?"

"It is Helen, along with the driver in civvies."

"Great stuff, Mark."

They all sit enjoying a coffee together, Helen looks over at Lona.

"Do you think you are going to enjoy working with us, Lona?"

"I am certain of it Helen, once I find where I fit in and the way you all work."

"Lona, I think you work our way already. As for fitting in, you have done a fine job of that already. You are the perfect fit and a very sharp tool, if I might say so."

"Thank you so much ma'am, for your vote of confidence."

"Call the vehicle up, Mark, we will meet him out in the front."

They all pile into the waiting transport. The driver makes his way from Central London, across into the East End, into Plaistow. Parking outside Anjella's home, Lona knocks on their front door, as she hears the rushing of feet to open it. Adhiambo answers, laughing so full of joy, as her mother shouts to her:

"Who is it, precious?"

"It is Lona, Mum."

Turning to the sergeant, she kisses her on the cheek,

"Come in Lona, we were just deciding what to have for dinner."

"In that case, why not come out with us, Adhiambo?"

"Are you sure Emelia is here with us as well, Lona?"

"Of course, it is fine, the more the merrier, young lady."

"Where are we going, Lona?"

"I thought we would take your mum, to where we went the other day Adhiambo."

"You mean Kate's, Lona?"

"Yes of course, where else my bright young thing?"

"That would be lovely Lona. You will both enjoy it there, Mum, Emelia."

They all come out as they are, all dressed very nicely, as is the case of the African woman. Always dressed to perfection, always dressed to suit their body tones. They all squeeze into the waiting car, as Lona gives directions to Kate's Restaurant. Then stopping as they all get out, all streaming into the very hospitable bistro. All sat at one overly large table. They all order from the fine and tasty menu. Then Commander Helen Ball makes the opening gambit to Adhiambo.

"I hear you are more than willing, happy in fact, to assist us in any way you can, young lady?"

"Yes, that is right Helen. If it means stopping these bombings here and back home, then however I can help you, is the right way to go."

"In that case, with your father, we would like you to be involved, to help us get through this with as little pain as possible young lady."

"That would be nice, so how do you want me to do this Helen?"

"You make the phone call, get the directive your father needs. Then we get the information back to your dad, then see what happens after that, Adhiambo."

"Are you sure, Helen?"

"Yes, I am Adhiambo, this way we perhaps we can apprehend and capture more than just your father and, at the same time do some good over in Africa."

"That would be nice, Helen."

"Tomorrow is Saturday, Kenya is two hours in front of us. So if we come at about 08:00, would that suit you all?"

"That will be fine, Helen."

So after Helen foots the bill for dinner, the driver drops Anjella her daughter as well as Emelia back to their homes, taking everyone else back to the Yard. The commander turns, looking directly ay Lona:

"Sergeant Vardy, you will manage the phone call in the morning, unless you have any objections? While you do that, we will be talking to our friends in Kenya, seeing what they know about the Light of Africa."

"OK, Helen, that will not be a problem."

Lona was sat on the sofa at 07:55. Alongside her was the unsure young girl that was Adhiambo. It was now 08:00, Michael's daughter dialled the number and, hearing it ring, waited very patiently. Then someone finally decided to respond the ring. She could hear the breathing on the line, Belinda said very softly into the mouthpiece:

"Kapala Jeung Guru."

"It is a pleasure to hear you. Who am I speaking to please?"

"Miss Belinda Ironi."

"Oh, how lovely, Michael's young daughter."

"Yes, that is right. He has told me to relay to you, that here in the UK, the Light of Africa has gone out. He desperately needs someone to switch it back on again. Would you have an electrician available at all?"

"Generally, our engineers work from 1117 Côte d'Ivoire. I will try to one for you, but it will be a very costly affair. Do you understand?"

"I do indeed, thank you so much for your assistance."

The line closed, going dead in an instant.

"Did you get all that, Adhiambo?"

Yes, Lona, but I cannot say I understood it all. Hopefully my dad will, and he can enlighten us, so we can dig a little deeper."

While this was happening, Commander Helen Ball of the Counter Terrorism Unit, was in deep discussion with Mr Mathew Kirai Iteere, the Kenyan Chief Constable, as he was sitting very comfortably in his office at Vigilance House, Harambee Avenue, in Nairobi. Helen was negating how much Mathew already knew about the Light of Africa. Mathew was telling her that Michael Ironi had been on their wanted list for a long time now. They were also chasing an individual named Atieno Ochieng, in conjunction with the running of said terrorist network. So any assistance the Met could give him would be invaluable and very much appreciated. Mathew did tell the commander, that the Light of Africa did work from somewhere, along the Nairobi River. Lona also phoned Helen, telling her of their phone call and what had passed between Michael and his daughter. Helen was impressed with the day's work, also telling Lona that she would phone back, as soon as she had arranged the visitation rights for Adhiambo. Lona made a Freetown breakfast for them all, a succulent mix of crab and rice. They got through three cups of coffee before Helen was able to return Lona's phone call. Sergeant Vardy's phone rang.

"Lona, I have got the paperwork, I will send it to the local station. You pick it up from there."

"OK, ma'am, we are on our way."

Lona along with Adhimabo went to the local police station sitting in the front office, waiting for their dispatch to arrive. Once they have it in their hands, they hotfoot it to their vehicle outside. Then onto Pentonville as quickly as the traffic would allow them. There, once again, Adhiambo goes in alone, going through the search procedure as before. Then into the visitors' centre, where once again Michael sits there, all in eager anticipation of his daughter arriving with the news he requires to hear. His daughter approaches him, sits down kissing him and holding his hand.

"Hi, Dad, I made your phone call."

"What did Jomo tell you?"

"You want it word for word."

"Word for word, Just as Jomo told you."

"Generally, our engineers work from 1117 Côte d'Ivoire. I will try to get one for you, but it will be a costly affair, do you understand?"

"That is all he said?"

"That is everything he told me."

"So, 1117 Côte d'Ivoire, is a nightclub in Bedford Square, it is just off Russell Square, in London."

"OK, Dad."

"You look eighteen, you need to be eighteen to get in, so I do not know how you do it, but get in."

"OK, Dad, I will have to work something out."

"He wants one of my accounts. Now you must remember the number, the name and the password."

"All right, Dad, but tell me slowly please."

"333117629, Abshir Dalmar, Belinda."

"I have got that set in my mind, now the password, Dad."

"That is, my left hand, Belinda."

"I can remember that, Dad."

"Tell them when you can be there, it needs to be as soon as possible Belinda."

"OK, Dad, but what will I do at this nightclub?"

"I will tell you that, when you come back from the next call Belinda. One other thing you need to know."

"What might that be, Dad?"

"The First Somali Bank, that is where the account is, Belinda."

"So are you still OK in solitary, Dad?"

"It is not so bad. I do look forward to seeing you my dear daughter. You are the only contact I have with the outside world now."

"OK, Dad I will be back soon, all being well."

"Phone them as soon as you get back home, Belinda."

"I will, Dad, I promise."

Adhiambo goes back to the car, Lona drives her back home. When they both are both safely indoors, sitting down, Adhiambo turns to Lona, a little unsure of where to start.

"Lona, this is going to be rather awkward."

"Why is that, Adhiambo?"

"I will need to gain entry into a night club, at some time or other. But legally I am still under age, Lona."

"I think we will be able to sort that out if we need to, for you to carry on with getting this information for us. How old are you now, Adhiambo?"

"I am sixteen coming up to my seventeenth birthday, Lona."

"I am sure the commander will want to know why, Adhiambo?"

"Well, first of all, I will need to contact the same person again, with some of my father's bank details, Lona."

"I see, that is going to cost your father big money Adhiambo."

"Lona, I think it will. If I give you the bank details, perhaps you can catch someone, trying to remove the money."

"Adhiambo, I guess we could. Where is the bank situated?"

"In Somalia, unless there is a branch here in the UK Lona."

"Come on my little girl, we need to go and see Helen."

The three of them are sat in the quiet, of Commander Ball's office. Helen looking directly at Adhiambo, with warmth and a big smile.

"Adhiambo! So do you have some more information for us?"

"Yes, I do Helen. The bank is the First Somali Bank, the account name is Abshir Dalmar, the number is 333117629, the password is My Left Hand."

"You have the most incredible memory young lady. Just like a storage center."

"I have a photographic memory. It enables me to remember most things. Whether I find them pictorially, or if someone gives me information, Helen."

"Ma'am."

"Lona this sounds quite official."

"It is I suppose Helen. Our young lady friend here will also need some form of identity that states she is eighteen. So that she can continue with this elaborate fabrication."

"OK, tell me why, either of you."

"Well Helen, the next step for me, whatever that might entail, means me going to a nightclub called 1117 Côte d'Ivoire, in Russell Square."

"Adhiambo what do you think you are going to find there?"

"In all honesty, if it is like most nightclubs, it is most likely to be a den of iniquity. Where all the cowards, bullies, thugs and terrorists hang out in one form or another. Not necessarily with the owners' knowledge, Helen."

"Yes, Adhiambo, what a good description of a nightclub, so what there?"

"Helen, I guess that is where I am going to be, introduced to Michael's replacement or representative for the Light of Africa."

"Adhiambo, so you think someone is going to replace him?"

"In one form or another I do. They have seen what he has already started here in the UK, so at least we will have a head start, in knowing who his apprentice will be, then you be able to deal with the problem accordingly Helen." Commander Ball, picks up the phone instantly:

"Adhiambo, Lona just let me call my contact in Somalia first."

Lona and Adhiambo both sit there in the commander's office in great anticipation, as she phones direct to Somalia, getting through to the office of the Chief Constable of Somalia, General Addihakin Said Dahir Said.

"It is good to talk to you once again Addihakin, we have some information for you that may be helpful. It concerns the Light of Africa and, one of their bank accounts."

"Helen that is great news, really."

"It is if it helps you capture them, Addihakin."

"Do you have the details of the account Helen?"

"Yes, Addihakin."

"May I ask, who gave you the details of this account Helen?"

"You can indeed, Abshir Dalmar Addihakin."

"Are you certain of this, Helen?"

"Oh yes, he is in prison for life, here in England."

"What do you hope to gain, by sharing this intelligence with us?"

"Well Addihakin, either one less terrorist, if you manage to capture the perpetrator who tries to take the cash from this account. Which will lead to one less financial source to this organization, if you manage to close the account. Perhaps even shed some light or information on their movements over there in Somalia."

"That would give us so much satisfaction Helen. Will you keep us informed? If we make any headway, I will return the favour to you."

"Of course, Addihakin. So the information is, the First Somali Bank, the account name is Abshir Dalamar, the account number is 333117629. The password is My Left Hand. So it could be an investment account."

"Thank you so much, Helen, we will be in touch I can assure you."

"Speak to you again soon, Addihakin."

The Commander turned to her two younger lady assistants.

"You make your phone call, Adhiambo and I will sort out your identity for the night club."

Adhiambo dials the Kenyan number once again, waiting for someone to respond to her call. As soon as the connection is live, she goes into action:

"Kapala Jeung Guru."

"Miss Ironi you have such a warm, receptive voice, I could sit here and listen to you all day."

"Thank you, Jomo. Now, the First Somali Bank, Abshir Dalmar, 333117629, My Left Hand."

"Belinda that is lovely, the next time you see him, thank him very much for me. This Saturday at the 1117 Côte d'Ivoire. Any time after 23:30 hours you are to introduce yourself to one of the dancers. She is Yaya, apparently she knows your father very intimately."

"Will she know me, or of me?"

"No, she will not. But he will be able to give you a very good description of her. She will also need financial backing."

"So is that all the information, my father will need?"

"It is for now, Belinda, thank you very much."

Her line is cut dead, she turns round to Lona and Helen, they both look at her, pleadingly.

"Talk to us please, Adhiambo."

"OK Helen. I will need to see my father again. I have the name of one of the dancers, who performs at the nightclub. I have to make contact with her. Supposedly she knows my father, too well for his own good. She will need financial backing."

"We can sort that out for you, Adhiambo."

"But why should you have to do it Lona. It is my father got himself into this mess, he has all these undisclosed bank accounts. Surely it is better to get as much as you can from him. Make him pay, so that he makes up for all the devestation he has caused over the years."

"Adhiambo, how are you going to get him to pay, in any way or form, for this new terrorist who is going to take his place?"

"I am his daughter, if I tell him he has to finance this person, he will — plus he knows her very well anyway. He will have to transfer money into a new account just for her. Then at the same time, you get to find another hidden source of money, which has been used by the Light of Africa, Helen."

"OK, young lady, but you need to tread very carefully, please do not push your dad too hard."

"I will be cautious, Lona, he will make the suggestion I promise."

"That is good, Adhiambo, in that case you keep on top of your school work. Enjoy the rest of the weekend, I will arrange for you to see your father Monday evening."

"Helen, I am so sorry it is taking so long."

"My very dear young lady, you do not understand, nothing happens straight away. It all takes time, most of the time it is a waiting game, and patience really does help. I am just glad that you and your mother are on our side, believe me. You are doing a superb job, so please do not fret. I would love to have you on my squad, working for me now. But who knows, one of these fine days?"

"Well Helen, I will see you soon, and thank you for that great compliment."

"It is my pleasure, Lona. Keep this special lady safe for me."

"I will Helen, count on it."

They both leave the Yard, Sergeant Vardy taking the young Adhiambo back home to her mother. Anjella is just dishing up dinner for Emelia and herself as they open the door. She turns to her daughter, blowing her a kiss and smiling.

"Have you and Lona had a good day?"

"Yes, Mum a really great day, I even got a compliment from Helen in the process. How has your day been?"

"Making headway as always, focussing on our objectives. We seem to crack one problem, then in turn that presents us with two or three more, but we soldier on. Are you staying for dinner, Lona?"

"I would love to, if you have enough of course, Anjella?"

"We have enough, and you are always welcome, Lona."

They eat together enjoying the meal, as well as each other's company. They get very comfortable with each other, striking up a tight little friendship. It gets late as Emelia leaves to go home. Then Anjella offers Lona a bed for the night.

"Are you sure, Anjella? I do not want to put anyone out."

"Of course, Lona, you are like one of the family now. If you feel guilty Lona, you can always make breakfast for us in the morning."

"That sounds a fair offer, Anjella, I will wake you up when it is ready."

They all walk upstairs, Anjella showing Lona her bedroom. They hug each other, both wishing each other a goodnight. Then Adhiambo comes over to Lona, kissing her on the cheek.

"Lona, thanks for a very good day."

"Adhiambo, it was my pleasure, see you in the morning."

Monday soon comes round, school is fascinating as always. At the end of the day, as Adhiambo gets off the bus with her friends, they say goodbye as they split and go their separate ways. She goes indoors, changing into something more comfortable than her school uniform. Then she sits down, waiting patiently for the sergeant to turn up, with her visitors pass, so she can go and see her dad. Lona arrives, blasting her horn. With that Adhiambo rushes out to jump into the waiting car. They drive straight to Pentonville prison, where Adhiambo goes through to visit her dad. He looks perplexed and annoyed.

"You, young lady, have taken your time."

"Do you know how hard it is to get a visitor's pass to see you? Stuck there in solitary, for the crime you committed."

"No, I do not, nor do I care."

With that his daughter gets up, picking up her bag and goes to walk away.

"Please do not go, Belinda."

"WHY NOT…?"

Then remembering where she was, she apologises to everyone, sitting down once again. Catching herself and breathing deeply, she wipes away a tear.

"You only think of yourself all the time, you are ignorant and self-centred. You make such senseless remarks, I am not likely to come here any more, to see a murderer, Dad."

"OK, my beloved, Belinda, I am so sorry that you are stuck in the middle of all this. It is my fault, I should not be raging at you, I should consider myself very lucky, that you take the time to come and see me."

"I know, it is hard enough as it is. What with my school work, my exams starting shortly, then you getting agitated and jumping on my back, Dad."

"OK, what did Jomo have to say this time, my daughter?"

"He said to thank you very much indeed. This Saturday at the 1117 Côte d'Ivoire, any time after 23:30 hours. I am to introduce myself to one of the dancers, her name is Yaya, apparently you know her intimately, Father."

"Did he say anything else, Belinda?"

"I asked him if she would know me, Dad? Jomo said no, but you would be able to describe her to me. She will also need money, as well."

"Yes, I can tell you what she looks like. But how am I meant to give her financial support, stuck in here."

"I have no idea, Dad, that is one for you to figure out, all by yourself."

"See if you can get a visitor's pass for Friday, after school. Hopefully I would have thought of something by then."

"OK, Dad, all being well I will come and see you Friday."

Adhimabo leaves him, then travels back home with Sergeant Vardy. When they were sat comfortably indoors, Lona turned to the young girl.

"So what did he have to say for himself this time, Adhiambo?"

"Well Lona, first of all he got cross, because it had taken so long for me to get a visitor's pass."

"What did you tell him, Adhiambo."

"I told him I could stay away, not bother with him any more. Then I got up to walk out on him."

"Did that make him happy, or see any sense, Adhiambo?"

"No, it did not make him happy at all. But he did apologise, which is a very rare thing for my dad."

"Then the proper discussion ensued, I suppose?"

"It did, he is going to describe Yaya to me, as well as how he is going to provide for her, during her stay here. So I have no idea what to expect in that case. Providing I can get another pass for Friday, Lona."

"OK, we will get that sorted out for Friday. We are still waiting for your identity for Saturday, Adhiambo."

Adhiambo finds it very difficult to concentrate on her studies, but manages to do so and work through the confusion that her father is causing. She forces herself to focus at school, and the closeness of her friends helps so much. Her first set of exams are very near, so she must do well, she tells herself. On the way home on the Friday evening, her best girl friends invite her out. But she has to tell them that this weekend is spent with her father. He comes to pick her up from home, so she cannot delay. But she promises that she will go out with them, the next time they offer. They all call out as they go in different directions.

"See you soon, Adhiambo, enjoy your weekend with your dad."

"I will, see you all at school on Monday."

She changes straight away, just in time to see Lona pull up outside. The young girl rushes out hugging Lona, then they drive off to Pentonville, to see her father. She goes in, sitting down very quietly, making no noise at all, feeling a little self-conscious from her last visit.

"It is good to see you, Belinda. I thought perhaps you might not come, this time."

"I was thinking about it. I do not know how much longer I will be able to get the passes to see you. So I thought I would make the most of it, while I could."

"Good girl, good girl. So, this Yaya we were talking about, she is Sudanese, she was a practising Muslim when I knew her, but that could have changed. She was very busty, long legs, had short cropped hair. She also had vivid green eyes, which is very unusual for an African woman. She had a dimple in her chin and one other thing, her little toe on her left foot was missing. Have you got all of that?"

"Yes, Dad. Green eyes, dimpled chin, Sudanese, busty and her little toe on her left foot missing."

"Very clever, Belinda, I do not know how you do it, but never mind. I have an account in your name, Belinda Ironi. That will have to suffice for her, you will have to give the contents to her, so she can open her own account."

Michael, for once, speaks softly to his daughter. Whispering the details of her bank account, in her ear. So she is able to withdraw its contents, for this other woman, Yaya.

"OK, Dad."

"One other thing, my dear daughter."

"Yes, Dad, what is that?"

"Yaya will only recognize me as Abshir Dalmar, from the Sunda Kuliah Politik Jeung Hukum."

"Right, Dad, I think I have everything now."

"Oh, yes, before you give her your money, she needs to tell you the name of the village, where the college was."

"Are you sure that is all, Dad?"

"It is, this time around, Belinda."

"In that case I will see you soon, all being well, Dad."

They kiss each other, then go their separate ways. In the car with Lona, Adhiambo tells her who she will be looking for, at the nightclub. Lona then tells her.

"On the Saturday night, I will be at the club as well, looking out for you. So text me once you are in residence, OK?"

"I will, Lona."

They hug and kiss each other warmly, then say goodnight. As Adhiambo walks through the front door, Anjella takes her daughter's dinner out of the oven.

"How is your dad, my little *mondo*?"

"He seems to be surviving mum. I think it is slowly taking its toll, him being in solitary. But it is no more than he deserves, in all fairness."

"Adhiambo, I know he has been a pig all of his life, with no thoughts for anyone else my darling. It seems to have finally caught up with him."

"Not before time, Mum."

The young daughter tidies up, doing the washing up as a matter of course. Then curls up on the sofa, snuggled up close to her mum, to watch a little television. But they do not sit there for very long, due to the garbage being shown on all the freeview channels. They switch it off then both go upstairs to bed, looking for an early night and a good night's sleep. They both got it as well, not rising until just gone eleven.

Anjella goes out to do a little shopping, her daughter tags along with her. Needing to get away from her studies for a little while, giving her brain a rest from it all. While she is out, she attends the bank, where her account is held. She withdraws an amount for herself, so she can buy herself some accessories. Anjella amazed, at the amount of clothes she has acquired, in that one afternoon.

"Have you tried all that on, Adhiambo?"

"I have, Mum, it all touches and fits where it is meant to."

Anjella smiles at her wise *mondo*, pulls her in close, as they go and have lunch out together, getting home early in the evening.

"Tonight, Mum, or rather tomorrow morning, I am not sure what time I will be getting home."

"You be very careful out there, do you hear?"

"I will, I promise, Mum. Lona will be at the club with me, so she will probably bring me home."

"OK but I will be waiting up for you. If anything goes wrong, you text me precious."

"I will, Mum, I promise that as well."

Adhiambo goes up to her bedroom to get ready for her night out. Going through her wardrobe, she has to decide what to wear, what would be suitable for a nightclub performer. She finally decided on wearing her burgundy ruched tie-waist slinky minidress, with a matching half-cup balconette bra and pantie set. Then she puts on her turquoise velvet pull-on high-heel ankle boot. Then, over the top, she wore a heavy pelisse. Checking she had everything she needed, kissing her mother, she locks the door, and goes to the taxi, that was waiting for her. The cab driver parked outside the club in Bedford Square. It was just after 23:30 hours, which was very good timing. Then she got to the door and was stopped by the door attendant. She looked her up and down.

"Are you at the right place, young lady?"

"I am."

"Let me see your identity please."

Adhiambo shows him her ID card, telling him:

"I am here for an audition."

George stops one of the young waitresses, as she passes by,

"Kiara, would you take this young lady to Miss Seuhxs' office, please."

"With the greatest of pleasure, George."

Kiara takes Adhiambo's hand, then escorts her to the owner's office, telling the young girl:

"Just wait here, sweetie."

Kiara goes into Siaba Seuhxs' office. While she does that, Adhiambo takes the chance to text Lona, just to let her know that she is at the club now. She gets an immediate reply, telling her that Lona is sat in the club too. Then Kiara comes back out and sees her into the office before leaving to continue with her duties. Adhiambo stands there in her minidress, as Siabas' eyes light up, on seeing the tantalising, beguiling young lady before her.

"My, you are very special indeed. Take your coat off for me please. What is your name?"

"Adhiambo, madam."

"Please call me Siaba, where are you from, precious?"

"I am from Kenya origionally, but now I live here in London, Siaba."

"Dear me those legs of yours are truly sensational, your hair gleams. Would you take your dress off for me, Adhiambo?"

Adhiambo tugs at the ties of her dress, letting it fall to the ground, revealing her matching lingerie.

"Even more impressive, your whole persona screams at me Adhiambo. Pick up your clothes and come with me, please."

Siaba takes Adhiambo to the changing room, where there is only another girl in attendance.

"Adhiambo this is Yaya, she is on the night shift with you. She will tell and show you what is expected. The girls on the later shift will start arriving at about one a.m."

With that Miss Siaba Seuhx leaves the two girls to get to know each other, as she walks back to her office. Yaya stands up and looks Adhiambo over.

"Adhiambo? Good to know you, you are a real gem. Really alluring, provocative, love the outfit, so saucy."

"Yaya, what a lovely name. I seem to remember my father once knew a Yaya."

"Did he, what was his name, who was your father Adhiambo?"

"Abshir Dalmar, Yaya."

"It could not be him. He has produced a daughter as stunning as you."

"So where did you know him from, Yaya?"

"He was the guru at the Sunda Kuliah Politik Jeung Hukum."

"What village was that in, Yaya?"

"It was just outside a place called Dolo."

As Adhiambo was conversing with Yaya, she looked down at her feet, noticing that the little toe was missing from her left foot.

"I just love your green eyes Yaya, they make you so exotic along with your auburn hair."

"Come on then Adhiambo, just get on the platform as you are and just dance to start with. If someone beckons you, it probably means they want you to dance just for them. For that privilege, they will tuck money into the waistband of your panties. But definitely no touching involved, OK."

"I understand, Yaya."

They go out there and perform out of their skin, Adhimbo enjoying it, apart from the constant attention seeking of the men. They both get beckoned continually, for the whole ninety minutes that they are on stage. With one large party wanting the pair of them to dance on their table, while they dined. Twenty-pound notes were being slotted into the tops of their panties, as they gyrated above the diners. Once a finger just grazed Adhiambo's breast as a fifty-pound note slipped into her panties. Then it was time for Yaya and Adhiambo to relinquish the floor for the next couple of dancers, who had just arrived. Yaya and Adhiambo sit next to each other in the girls' rest room.

"So how did you find it, the experience of dancing for entertainment?"

"Exhilerating, the attention they give you is unbelievable. The money seems to be no object, they tend to just throw it at you."

"Just a warning young lady, do not get involved with any of them. A lot of them are nasty bits of work, outside of this club."

"OK, Yaya, thanks for the advice. I will be seeing my father next week. All being well you will be financed OK."

"Oh, thank you, Adhimabo, when will you know for sure?"

"Next week in all probability. If Siaba takes me on, I will see you next Saturday, with all the details."

Yaya kisses the young girl on her lips, as a sign of acceptance and appreciation. Then she takes a fifty-pound note from her panties and tucks it into the waistband of her new-found friend.

"Here, Adhiambo, put your money in my locker, it will be safe there, until we go home. We will be going out one more time, as all six of us cover the last two hours before the club closes."

As the doors close, Adhiambo has a quick shower, gets dressed, puts her coat back on and tucks her money into the inside pocket. She kisses Yaya goodnight just as Siaba comes into the rest room. Sitting down beside the new girl, she says:

"That was an awesome display Adhiambo. You were outstanding in a devilish sort of way. We will see you next Saturday, if you are interested of course?"

"I am Siaba, and you will. What time would you like me to come?"

"Adhiambo, come a little earlier, so you can start at eleven thirty, OK."

"OK, Siaba."

"You all wowed them tonight, get home safely girls."

They all leave, all going their separate ways. Once Adhiambo is left standing alone on the dark street, Lona appears from the shadows, taking hold of Adhiambo's hand.

"Come on my little pearl, let's get you home safely and to bed."

In no time at all, Lona is parked outside Adhiambo's home. Anjella has seen them arrive and opens the door wide, very gladly indeed. Rushing up to her daughter and she clasps her, hugging her to her bosom.

"I am glad to see you in one piece, Adhiambo. Did you get the information your father required?"

"Yes, I did, Mum, come on let us all go inside and get some sleep. Are you coming in Lona, your bed is still there if you want to use it?"

"That is lovely, thank you so much, Anjella."

They all crash out. While they sleep, Mathew Kirai Iteere, the Kenyan Chief Constable has contacted Commander Ball.

"Helen? So good to hear you. I just wanted to say, thank you for your intelligence. Especially the phone number. We have traced it to the suburbs of Nairobi, Kumasi Road in fact, down by the Nairobi river. Now we have that under surveillance. We have been able to close two bank accounts and arrest three activists. So it is all good."

"I am very pleased, Mathew. I am ever so glad that I took the time to speak to you in person."

"Yes, so am I, Helen. I hear you have also spoken to my friend, General Abdihakin Said Dahir Said. Are you helping him as well?"

"Yes, Mathew. It would seem the only way we are going to get rid of this blight is if we work together. Squeeze them into a corner and suffocate them."

"You are right of course, Helen. We will keep in touch."

"OK, Mathew, speak to you soon."

The Sunday afternoon at home, at St Andrew's Road, Lona was up and in the kitchen. It was four o'clock in the afternoon. She was cooking and had decided to introduce Anjella and her daughter to *crin crin* and fishballs, freshly baked cassava bread, along with some foofoo. Both Adhiambo and Anjella rise. Adhiambo rushes into her mother's bedroom.

"Look at the time, Mum, come on, get up, lazy bones."

They both stroll downstairs in pyjamas and dressing gowns. Anjella smiles then looks at the clock on the cooker.

"Dear me is that the right time, Lona?"

"Yes, it is, Anjella, four forty-five in the afternoon. Dinner will be ready soon."

"That smells scrumptious Lona, what is it?"

"Adhiambo it is *crin crin* and fishballs with foofoo. I am also baking fresh cassava bread to go with it. It is a dish from Sierra Leone."

"I cannot wait my mouth waters at the very thought, Lona."

"About another half an hour, then we can sit down eat, young lády."

Adhiambo goes upstairs and changes out of her night attire, into a fresh, pastel-coloured tracksuit. She counted her tips from the night before, truly astonished at the amount she had accrued. Putting it away and she decided to open a bank account after school, the following day.

"Dinner is ready if you are, Adhiambo."

"I am coming now, Lona."

Anjella and her hungry daughter are already seated, as Lona makes an entrance with the hot food. They all tuck in to the gorgeous meal as Lona asks Adhiambo:

"How does Tuesday sound, young lady?"

"What for, Lona?"

"My apologies, do excuse me, Adhimabo, for you to go and see your father again."

"Tuesday would be good. Lona, will you be at the club again next Saturday?"

"Yes, I will be there, Adhiambo, for your safety always. As long as you are working for us, and you need to work at that club, I will be there every Saturday night keeping an eye on you. So do not worry."

"Oh, I am so pleased, that makes me feel a whole lot safer, Lona."

"Good, it is all part of the service, especially at your tender age."

"Do you have to go back to that club, my darling?"

"Yes, Mother dear, if we are to close Dad and his cohorts down. Surely, you want that as much as I do?"

"Yes, my treasure, it just seems you are taking all the risks."

"Who else is Michael going to trust, the police? It has to be me, or the bombing in Kenya and here will only continue."

"OK, my pearl, I understand, the work you are doing is very important. I just want you to be safe at all times."

"Once this is done, Mum, then we and so many other people will be safe. Like Grandma and Grandpa, back home in Nairobi."

"That reminds me I must phone them, I have not spoken to them all week."

"You need to keep in touch with your family, keep that bond strong. I phone mine at least twice a week."

On Monday after school, Adhiambo made a journey from Plashnet School for Girls to the high street, to a branch of Lloyds Bank. She felt so much better once she had opened the account and deposited her money into it. When she left the bank, she walked down Barking Road in the direction of Plaistow. Quite happily she did some window shopping, then going into one or two of the ladies clothing outlets, buying herself some work clothes for her nightclub activities. Then continuing her walk home, passing Prince Regent Lane, turning into St Andrew's Road, arriving home. Once indoors Adhiambno started to sort out something for dinner. It was all on the table and ready, just as Anjella and Emelia arrive home from work.

"Hiya, Mum, Emelia, so how was work today?"

"It was good, everything goes well with our research. How was your day, my dear daughter?"

"It was a great day in all honesty. Lots of work done at school, so everything glitters, Mum. Only two more exams to do, then my search starts for a summer job."

"That is good news, come on then, sit down Emelia, and you Adhimabo, before all your cooking gets cold."

"Will you cook tomorrow, Mum, I am seeing dad once I finish at school?"

"Yes, my gorgeous *mondo*. I can do that, no problem."

Tuesday flew by, Adhiambo raced home from school, changed then sat in the quiet of the lounge and waited. A knock at the door made her smile as she went to answer it. On opening the door, she threw her arms around Lona's neck, kissing her on both cheeks, not at all embarrassed.

"What a lovely welcome, Adhiambo, have you missed me?"

"I have funnily enough Lona. You are part of my life all of a sudden, I feel so close to you."

"I love your company too young lady, you always make me feel better, especially after a bad day. I feel a special closeness to you as well. So come on, let us go and visit your dad."

Pentonville was very quiet indeed. Belinda sat in the visitors' room waiting. Michael appeared and was smiling, as he sat down.

"Your timekeeping is impeccable Belinda."

"I am pleased that makes you happy, Dad. So I met Yaya at the club, she had all the physical attributes you described, Father."

"Most importantly, did she know where the school was, where I taught her, Belinda?"

"It was just outside a place called Dolo. It was all on its own, she told me. She was sent back to the Sudan, but she was sent to the UK sometime afterwards. She has been over here for two years, came over as a refugee. She came that way, because she was female and no one asked any questions, concerning her personal life, Dad."

"That sounds about right for Yaya, Belinda. She was a flame in a very dark place. She wiped the floor with male students, was top of her class, very clever very learned. A practicing Muslim, back then."

"Not any more, Dad. She told me she cast her dark, devious religion out of her life. She now lives to enjoy life as much as she can. Making up for lost time, as she puts it."

"So her finances, Belinda. There are two accounts I have earmarked for her."

"OK, I am ready to remember the information, Dad."

"Right, the first is 33124463, the bank is the UBA."

"Got it, Dad."

"The second is 0004706621, the bank is the Zenith."

"OK, Dad, that is all fine. But do you know where the local branches for these banks are?"

"Not offhand, I do not have a clue. But both accounts are in your name. So when you find out where the branches are, you will be able to transfer the monies to Yaya."

"OK, Dad. Is there anything else I can do for you, while I have the chance?"

"Yes, my special girl, you can phone this number for me."

"OK, Dad, but before you give me any more information, let me sort out Yaya first, on Saturday. Then I will come back on Monday, to gather or retrieve anything else you want me to do then."

"OK, Belinda, are you busy then?"

"Yes, I have two more exams at the end of the week. Then I have to go and see the headmistress Miss McGowan, in the morning. So I have to concentrate on my studies for a little while longer. So it will be a lot easier next week, Dad."

"So you will come to see me next week?"

"Yes, I will, Father."

"You will be going back to the club on Saturday night, to meet up again with Yaya?"

"I will be going to give her the account numbers and, which banks they are at, Father."

"Good girl, take care."

"I will, Dad."

The week flies by, Saturday soon comes round again. Adhiambo is now finished with all her exams. So she decides to take a nice long lay-in, so she is well rested and ready for her performance at the club later. When the young woman finally decides to get up, she goes through her wardrobe slowly, trying to decide what to wear, to make herself look alluring and provocative, at the 1117 Côte d'Ivoire. She finds a skirt from a couple of years ago. It still fits like her a glove, her legs are a lot longer, so the skirt seems so much shorter. It would be more of a micro skirt, rather than a mini. But her legs for a sixteen-year-old were incredible, tantalising. She gave herself a twirl, seeing how it sat on her hips, revealing most of her charms. She needed to fit in, after all, not stand out from everyone else. So she had to be adult and convincing, to find the new perpetrators, whether it was just Yaya by herself, or whether she had some backing or not, to continue the assault on London now her father had been jailed. As the evening came, the young lady put on a full-length coat, jumping into the taxi she pre-booked from the Saturday before, with exactly the same driver. In this way she did not attract the wrong sort of attention on her journey to the club. She left her mum waiting for Emelia, with Enya's *Winter's Come*, playing softly in the background

"You keep safe, my sweetheart. When will you be home?"

"About the same time as last week, Mum."

"Is Lona going to be there as well?"

"Yes, Mum she will be there looking after me."

"Then I can sleep easy tonight. Emelia is coming over later and we are off to the cinema."

"You enjoy, Mum."

The taxi ride does not take too long. As Adhiambo gets out, she gives her driver a tip. He smiles very thankfully.

"That is more than generous, young lady, thank you very much."

She walks straight into the club, the doorman recognising her this time and letting her in without stopping her. She passes Nina on her way to the changing room.

"Good evening, Nina, how are you?"

"I am very well, Adhiambo. You look very perky, so how are you?"

"I feel good tonight. I am already to dance the night away, with a change of clothes as well, this time, Nina."

"I think they are all looking forward to you tonight my gorgeous girl, especially after all the comments I am hearing here and now."

"Let us hope it means more cash in your tills as well, Nina."

"It will, a new face always attracts more customers, and the old ones stay longer, Adhiambo."

"The doorman is not very talkative is he, Nina?"

"George is all right, he takes a little getting used to. Once he gets to know you, he will talk. He is a police officer and he likes to concentrate on his job. That is a fact only the girls that work for me and I know, so please keep it to yourself. Come with me Adhiambo."

Nina takes the seemingly coy young woman up to the door and approaches the doorman.

"Good evening, George."

"God evening, Miss Siaba, how are you?"

"I am very good thanks, George. I would like to introduce the new girl to you, if I may. She is Adhiambo, and very good at her job as well."

"It is an absolute pleasure to meet you, Adhiambo."

"She thought she might have upset you for some obscure reason, as you did not talk to her."

George turned around properly to meet the young lady's gaze. He bent down to take her hand, then kissed the back of it, then returned his eyes back to hers, so she could see them.

"No, you have not upset me young lady, I just adore African women. They are so friendly and warm, they dress so inspiringly, with what suits them. Delicious every single one. It is when I am working, I get into the zone, little bubble, just so that I can concentrate on who is coming in to this establishment and if I recognise them. You are a *nyar kingi* amongst women, so never be shy. I will talk to you always from now on."

"Thank you, George, I think you are going to be something special. It is my pleasure to now know you as well."

The young Adhiambo heads off into the direction of the girls only room. George smiles at Miss Siaba, kisses her hand as he encloses it within his. She kisses him and goes back to her office. Adhiambo takes off her coat, putting it in her locker, then sits down and applies a little make-up, not needing much as she looks spectacular without any on at all. Looking stunning, alluring and veritably enticing, just as her friend Yaya comes through the door. She comes over and plants a big kiss on the younger girl's lips.

"Adhiambo! Damn you look hot, sultry, sensual. So what did your dad have to say?"

Yaya removes her coat and starts to get dressed, ready for their first performance. Adhiambo talks to her as she changes.

"He has given me the details of two accounts, both in my name. So that I can transfer the funds to you, Yaya."

"OK, that is good, how are we going to do it, Adhiambo?"

"Yaya do you have a bank account?"

"I do with the Zenith Bank ."

"That will make one of them easy then, Yaya, as it is already in a Zenith account."

"So when can we do that one, Adhiambo?"

"I have to see my Dad on Monday. How about I meet you on Tuesday, at the bank."

"OK, about what time, my treasure?"

"Say, two o'clock or thereabouts."

"That is a good time, we can have a coffee afterwards as well. Come on then, Adhiambo, let's go and shake and dance, for these insatiable men. It looks very busy out there, so you be careful who you mix with."

"I will, Yaya, see you later."

They both go out there onto the central open stage, Adhiambo in her very revealing skirt and peephole bra and boots. Taking hold of the pole, and her young nubile, lithe body against it. Sliding down she grips it between her thighs, doing a somersault and just holding herself there. She was attracting lots of attention, nothing but twenty-pound notes being folded into the waistband of her micro skirt. One chancy customer put a fifty-pound note into her bra, then squeezed her ripe plump teat, giving it a tug as well. She just smiled at him, as she fondled herself in front of him. He stood there mesmerised with her, then smiled back into her deep, sparkling brown eyes. He then tucked another fifty into the waistband of her dinky little skirt. Adhiambo was dancing her socks off, being invited to dance at three full tables, in this her first period of performing. She only caught glimpses and words of supposed unconnected phrases of their conversations. The money was continually tucked into her skirt, as she thought the chatter seemed a little devious, dubious and damaging at best. But she continued to concentrate on her dancing, then it was her and Yaya's turn for a break. Adhiambo changed into her very new outfit. Then took on a couple of flapjacks and a drink, to push up and maintain her energy levels. She sat all ready for her next session, where all the girls were out performing together. She did enjoy the attention along with the atmosphere at the club. She knew parading her body, flaunting it in front of all these men so openly like this, was not good for her. But she was not doing it for her good, or for any sort of self-recognition or job prospects. But Adhiambo knew that in the long run it would finally settle some scores with her father and his terrorist lifestyle and all those involved with him. She remembers quite clearly telling her mother that if she ever got the chance, she would cut her father down and hand him over to the police, as soon as she could.

At the end of the night, Yaya came over to Adhiambo, kissing her on both cheeks.

"I will see you on Tuesday afternoon, my kitten. Can I just tell you about those two men in the corner? Be very wary of them, they are not safe to be with. Please do not get involved."

"OK, Yaya, I will keep them at arm's length."

Adhiambi kissed Yaya on her lips. said goodnight and walked out into the sunrise. There, Lona Vardy waited patiently for her, the young girl rushed over to greet her friend very warmly.

"Everyone seems to love you, young lady, they all want you to dance for them."

"They seem to, it must be my fresh new face and long legs."

"Along with your youth, stamina and vigour as well."

"It was good, a lot busier than last Saturday."

"Come on then, let me take you home to your bed."

They both drive home, not taking too long as the roads are nearly empty, which is not surprising as it is Sunday morning. As Lona drives, Adhiambo tells her that she will be doing the first transfer on Tuesday afternoon, at the Zenith Bank, at two o' clock.

"OK, we will be there, Adhiambo. Will it just be you and Yaya?"

"Yes, just the two of us. You are going to have to arrest me, along with Yaya, Lona."

Then Adhiambo laughs out so loud, nearly crying in the process, unable to stop herself. Then when she settles down, wiping the tears away, she turns to Lona.

"I am so sorry, you must think me so stupid. Here I am trying to tell a Metropolitan police sergeant, how to do her job. I was going to add, I guess you know that already."

Lona was laughing with her, she could help herself.

"Yes, Adhiambo, but only until we get to the Yard. Then you will be able to go. They both creep in very quietly, both saying goodnight to each other, then going to their rooms. They both sleep on through the rest of the morning. Anjella woke up, showering and drying off, just there was a knock at the door. Putting her dressing gown on, she answered to find Emelia standing there. They welcome each other warmly, always at each other's house, these days.

"Come on in Emelia, you can help me with dinner while the other two sleep off their early morning."

"What shall we do, Anjella?"

"How about *tou zaffi* followed by banana peanut cake, Emelia?"

"OK, Anjella, you do the *tuo zaffi* and I will make a start on the banana peanut cake."

When all is ready, Anjella shouts up the stairs,

"Come on, you sleepy heads, your dinner is ready and getting cold."

Adhiambo shouts back down:

"On my way, Mum!"

"Coming Anjella, Emelia."

They were all sat around the table, enjoying one of Emelia's national dishes, done to perfection of course looks directly at Anjella with a warm smile.

"I must tell you now, Anjella, Emelia, that on Tuesday night, Adhiambo here, might not be here, when you get home."

"Why is that, Lona?"

"We hope to be making an arrest and, so that Adhiambo's cover is not revealed, we will have to arrest her as well."

"But she will be home on Tuesday at some time, right, Lona?"

"Yes, I promise Anjella."

"Good, how is it all going?"

"Very well Anjella, we have even helped the Kenyan police, due to your daughter's information."

"That is a great thing to have accomplished, so soon as well."

Emelia jumps in to ask:

"Anyone for a slice of the banana peanut cake?"

They all take an unhealthy wedge of the large cake, along with a glass of the *poyo*, that Lona left in the fridge, from the last barbeque, she attended.

"That was lovely Emelia, Anjella thank you so very much."

Monday was all free study for Adhioambo. At lunchtime the young lady walked round to her bank, to pay in some of her earnings from Saturday night. Then at about four o'clock, Miss Rachel McGowan was just about to leave her office. Truly she was an inspiration to all her tutors and pupils. Ahe was always staying late, just in case anyone needed to talk to her. She just loved her job, it was never too early nor too late to spend time with her pupils, or teachers, in whatever capacity they wanted to talk to her. When Adhiambo knocked on her door, Rachel sat down again calling,

"Come in, please."

"Miss McGowan, good afternoon."

"Adhiambo, my prize pupil, what an absolute delight to see you."

"Thank you, Miss McGowan."

"So how can I be of service to you today, young lady?"

"I need to leave early tomorrow, at about midday. Would that be at all possible?"

"Have you completed all your exams, Miss Ogwayo?"

"Yes, Miss, I finished my last one on Friday."

"I know you were taking quite a few, Adhiambo, how many was it?"

"It was eleven subjects altogether, Miss McGowan."

"You are one special young lady. I will tell you what, as you have come in yourself, take the whole day off. I will see your form teacher and we will see you again on Wednesday."

"You are so kind, Miss McGowan. Thank you very much."

They both smile at each other.

"While you are here, Miss Ogwayo, what are your plans for next year?"

"I would like to continue my studies, if I could. That is my plan anyway."

"That is a good plan, if I may say so. Do you have any final objective in sight though?"

"I would like to fight crime, in all its forms, especially terrorism. Mainly because it does help the poor or the uneducated, in any form whatsoever. It just gives rise to so many more dictators, despots and tyrants upon this planet. We have enough of those already, also to further enable women to stretch their imagination, tolerance and perseverance. To better prepare them for the real world. To help fulfil their dreams, objectives and desires, without men telling them that they cannot compete with them in the marketplace. For women to stand and take their place, to show their true worth, without being exploited, or sold as worthless chattels, without having a say in the matter."

"Oh, my dear young lady, that is one massive horizon you want to cover. I think, before we break up, I need to talk to you properly and see what we can do, to fulfil your ambition and work prospectus."

"That would be lovely, Miss. I would love some direction and talk woman to woman with you."

"OK, Adhiambo, I will see you on Wednesday, and we will see what we come up with."

"I look forward to that immensely. To talking to you, I have always loved your help and guidance, since I came her to study."

"That is lovely of you to say so. I said you were special a one-off, off you go then and, keep safe."

"I will, Miss, thank you for your precious time."

Adhiambo walked home with five of her closest friends that waited for her, in the changing room. Then each one said their goodbyes as they tail off to their own homes. Finally, Adhiambo is left to walk the final short distance alone. Reaching St Andrew's Road and she sees that Lona is already there waiting for her. Lona winds down the car window, shouting out to her:

"Come on, honey bun, jump in and we will go straight there."

At Pentonville her father is already waiting for her. He smiles at her, standing up for his daughter. They then sit down together.

"So how did it go, Belinda?"

"I saw Yaya on Saturday."

"Do you know her family name?"

"No, she has not told me yet, Dad."

"It is Yaya Artoli, OK Belinda."

"OK, Dad, on Friday you were going to give me, or at least mention some phone numbers or was it just numbers, that you thought might be relevant to me."

"Belinda, they should be helpful, should anything happen to Yaya. The first one is in Somalia, it is for the map grid of the school I had there. Which still has a lot of bomb-making equipment there. It is hidden in the cellar and, will at sometime, need clearing out. 2521169446, that is the phone number. The map grid reference of the school is 1753, outside Dolo. The phone number I gave you, using the name, Abshir Dalmar, that is all, then they will come and retrieve it."

"OK, Dad. Is there anything else?"

"A Ugandan number for the cell working there. They will have to finance themselves until further notice. 25633417755, there is three in that cell."

"OK, Dad, got it."

"Are you sure, Belinda?"

"Yes, Dad."

"In that case repeat it all back to me, my dear daughter."

"Yaya Artoli, the grid of the school in Somalia is 1753, just outside Dolo. Then a number for me, if Yaya fails to make the grade, 2521169446. Also, I need to contact a cell of three, in Uganda on 25633417755, to tell them that they will have to finance themselves, for the time being."

"That is perfectly remembered, Belinda."

"I know, Dad, I guess I must have some form of photographic ability, along with the sequence I receive the information."

"Ah well, I will not question your ability ever again."

"No problem, Dad, I still surprise myself sometimes."

"OK, so when will I see you again, Belinda?"

"Probably the end of the week, Dad."

"You take care in the meantime then, my dear daughter."

"I will, Dad, goodbye and see you soon."

Lona drives Adhiambo home, they both settle in the lounge as they face each other on the sofa, the young girl turns to the sergeant.

"Lona, there are a few things I need to tell you."

"OK, Adhiambo."

"Yaya's family name is Artoli. The map gridwhere my father had his bomb-making school, just outside Dolo is 1753. A contact number I can use, in case Yaya fails to come up to standard is 2521169446. Also there is a cell of three in Uganda, who will have to finance themselves until further notice. Their number is 25633417755."

Sergeant Vardy is on her mobile immediately to Commander Hall.

"Ma'am I have more information regarding Adhiambo's father.

"OK, Lona, give me all the information you have."

"First, the girl's family name is Artoli, Helen."

"OK, Lona, that will make it so much easier for tomorrow when we arrest her, next?"

"Helen, the map reference of Ironi's bomb-making school in Somalia. It is 1753 just outside Dolo. A contact number if Yaya fails in her objective 2521169446, the first two words need to be, Abshir Dalmar."

"Do you have anything else of any note, Lona?"

"Yes Helen, a mobile number for a cell of three in Uganda, who need to finance themselves until further notice. You can guess what that would entail."

"I can indeed. All sorts of bedlam, mayhem and destruction Lona."

"Well Helen, the number is 25633417755."

"Tell our young beauty, nice work, well done. Does she realize what will happen tomorrow Lona?"

"Yes Helen, she has guessed already and understands the procedure."

"Good, then take care, keep safe until tomorrow, Lona."

As soon as the call is cut, Helen Ball is on the case, doing some networking straight away. She first phones the chief of the Somali police, General Addihakin Said Dahir Said.

"Good evening, Addihakin."

"Good evening, Helen, this is a glorious surprise, it is not often I get the chance to converse, how may we be of assistance to the Metropolitain Police?"

"Well, Addihakin, I am hoping that we will be of some assistance to you."

"How so Helen?"

"We have some intelligence, first the grid of what used to be the Sunda Kuliah Politik Jeung Hukum. In fact, it was a bomb-making school, set up by the Light of Africa. It will need clearing, Addihakin, it is just outside Dolo at 1753. A contact number as well, 2521169446. Use the name Abshir Dalmar, as a reference."

"That is fantastic information, Helen, thank you so much."

"It is always my pleasure, Addihakin."

When the connection goes dead, Commander Ball dials another number in East Africa, Uganda this time. Trying to connect with the Assistant Inspector of Police, Doctor Kashma Steven answered.

"Kashma, how the Devil are you?"

"Helen, I am good, how about you?"

"Great, thanks, Kashma."

"So what do I owe this pleasure, of a direct call from the British Counter Terrorism Unit?"

"I have some intelligence for you, something you may be able to use, Kashma."

"Regarding what, exactly, Helen?"

"Terrorism, Kashma. The Light of Africa is the unit we are discussing."

"Now they are a bad lot Helen. What have you got for me?"

"A cell of three somewhere in Uganda, who are operating alongside the Light of Africa. All I have is a mobile number, which hopefully you can trace."

"OK, Helen, give it to me and we will see what we can do with it."

"Kashma it is 25633417755."

"That is lovely of you, it will be a great help if we make contact with them Helen."

"You take great care, Kashma."

So the line to Uganda was disconnected. Now the commander along with Lewson and Tuley, were taking great pains to make sure everything was in place for the small job tomorrow.

About midday, Adhiambo was going through her ever-growing wardrobe, searching for something to wear that was appropriate to meet Yaya, in the bank. She finally decided on the shocking red side-buttoned crepe midi skirt. A tight tailored long amber low-cut blouse and, pale pink high heel sandals with three buckles. She then made her way to the

Zenith Bank, that was in Berkley Square. She waited outside for Yaya, then there she was shouting and waving.

"ADHIAMBO, ADHIAMBO so good to see you."

"Yaya you look sensational, but then you always do."

They hug each other, then kiss as old friends do.

"Come on then sexy, let us go in and sort your money out, Yaya."

"Adhiambo, my kitten, I am with you."

Going into the bank together, they join one of the queues. As their turn came and they were talking to the cashier and, just as they were about to finalise the transfer, one hand fell on Yaya, another fell on the shoulder of Adhiambo. The inspector had both of them in his grasp as he told them:

"Yaya Artoli, Adhimabo Abshir, we are arresting you both, in connection with terrorism, stolen money, also trying to use monies in connection with acts of terrorism. Come with us, please."

They are both put in the back of the waiting police van, left together to sweat and talk in each other's company. Yaya turned to look deep into Adhiambo's burning brown eyes,

"SO, WHO LET THEM IN ON THE GAME, KITTEN?"

"Yaya, you need to settle, they want us to fall out with each other. I have no idea who let them know. I do not know enough to be worth anything to anybody, as far as I know, my father does not see anyone but me. How about your contacts?"

"Ah now, Adhiambo, I have only known them for about two months, they both frequent the 1117 Côte d'Ivoire. They do not talk to me much, because I am a woman and give me no respect, because of that fact. They normally sit hidden on the right in the dark, by the main entrance."

"I will remember that, if I ever need them. But we do not know if they are trustworthy anyway, Yaya."

"No, I see your reasoning, they could be plants and out to sabotage our plans in an instant, kitten."

"So they need to be left alone for as long as possible, Yaya."

"I agree, but if you need any help, at any time, I have two numbers you can use. But will you remember them, Adhiambo?"

"Yes, I will. Do not worry, I do not need to write them down, Yaya."

"OK, so I have a number for Tanzania, as well as the Sudan. Are you ready to absorb them, or whatever it is you do, my kitten?"

"Yes, quite ready, sexy."

"So the Tanzanian contact is on the number 2558879555 Adhiambo. The Sudan number is 24955112347. The key word is Artoli17, for both of the numbers."

The wagon comes to a stop, then both Yaya and Adhiambo are both escorted indoors and then put into holding cells at the Yard. All the paperwork that it entails, ends up on Helen's desk.

As the two young women await their destiny, Anjella is calling her friend, Miss Suzie Wokabi of Suzie Beauty, back in Kenya, to see if she will come over to England and perform her magic on them all, for her Adhiambo's birthday. Suzie is thrilled with idea.

"When would you like me to come over, Anjella?"

"Whenever you are ready, Suzie, why not make it a holiday and come and stay with me? I would love that to happen."

"OK, Anjella, as soon as I know when I am coming, I will let you know."

"When you know, Suzie, give me the flight details and Emelia and I, will come and pick you up from Heathrow."

"OK, Anjella, I will look forward to that. Love you and see you soon *mondo*."

"*Aheri*, Suzie, take care."

The commander is in her office, with Inspector Lewson and Constable Tuley, talking to them both.

"I need to freeze both of those accounts Inspector. Here you are, all the information you need, take Tuley with you. If the bank will not cooperate with you, then call me back and I will have the total assets of the Zenith Bank frozen. Do you both understand me?"

"We do ma'am."

"I will go and see this Yaya Artoli. Lona, you go and see Adhimabo, to see if she has got anything new."

"OK, ma'am will do."

Adhiambo is dragged out still cuffed, into an interview room where Sergeant Vardy awaits her presence.

"So, my little diamond, did Yaya talk at all, about anything in the back of the van?"

"Yes, she did, Lona, she has contacts in Tanzania and the Sudan."

"Did she part with anything else, Adhiambo?"

"Yes, she gave two numbers. One for the contact in Tanzania and one for the contact in the Sudan Lona."

"OK, ready when you are, Adhiambo."

"The first one is in Tanzania, 2558879555. The one in the Sudan is 24955112347. They both need the key word Artoli17 mentioned before anything else is said, Lona."

"That is fabulous, anything else, precious?"

"Yes, she has two contacts in the club, whom she feels are untrustworthy. She has known them for about two months, she thinks they tend to ignore her, because she is a woman. So they only talk to her when it is really necessary. They sit on the right in a darkened corner, by the main entrance Lona."

"I think we might have to work a strategy to bring them both out of hiding. What do you say, Adhiambo?"

Lona then phones Helen.

"Yes, Lona, what do you have for me?"

"We might possibly have two more leads, one in Tanzania along with one in the Sudan, Helen."

"OK, I am all ears, Lona."

"Helen, with both of these the key word is Artoli17."

"Got it Lona."

"Commander, the Tanzania one is, 2558879555."

"Nice one. Thank Adhiambo for me, Lona."

"With the Sudan number, we are not sure if it just refers to the Sudan, or if it includes the South Sudan, Helen. Anyway, the number is 24955112347."

"OK, I will inform both countries. Thank you both, for all this work, Lona."

Commander Ball put her intellegence head on once again, phoning Tanzania and getting her friend Omar Mahiita, in an instant.

"Good morning, is that the bewitching Helen from the UK's Counter Terrorism Unit?"

"Yes, it is, Omar and how are you these days, how is Tanzania?"

"I am good thanks. Tanzania is hot, sweaty and full of thieves, so how can I help you, Helen?"

"I am hoping that we might be able to assist you a little, in counter targeting the terrorist organization the Light of Africa."

"They are a nasty bunch, but then, they all are. What do you have for me, Helen?"

"I am sorry to say it is only a mobile phone number, Omar."

"But that is the start, my dear Helen, from there anything is possible. Perhaps if we can trace it, it may lead to bigger things."

"So Omar, if you use the number the key word is Artoli17. Then the actual number is 2558879555."

"That is very good work Commander, thank you for the information. Also my regards to whoever got it for you."

"You take care Omar."

Commander Ball then made a call to Sudan, asking for the Commissioner General.

"Salam, Emmanuel."

"Salam, Helen and how are you?"

"I am very good, Emmanuel."

"So, to what do I owe this pleasure, Helen?"

"Do you have problems with an outfit called the Light of Africa, within the boundaries of the Sudan, Emmanuel?"

"Most surely, we do, Helen, it is ever present with its core tucked away somewhere inside Kenya. Perhaps you should phone our friend, Mathew Iteere."

"Ah, but the phone number I have, Emmanuel, is for a contact an affiliate to the Light of Africa, somewhere in the Sudan."

"Can you be sure, Helen?"

"It is a Sudanese number, Emmanuel."

"Then if you are willing to share it with me, we will surely investigate it and try to trace it, Helen."

"Emmanuel of course I am going to share it with you, my dear friend. It has a key word which is Artoli17. The number is 24955112347."

"This may be the key we need, thank you so much, Helen. Speak to you again soon."

"Cheerio, for now, Emmanuel."

Finally, Helen Ball's last on-the-spot call is to South Sudan's Inspector General. It rang for a while, but finally the commander gets an answer.

"This is the South Sudanese Police department, how can we be of service to you?"

"Yes, this is Commander Ball, from the Metropolitain Police Counter Terrorism Unit. Could I speak to Inspector General Makur Maroul please."

"Ohh, yes, please accept my apologies, commander, I will just put you through."

Then a change of voice, to one that Helen instantly recognizes.

"Helen, what an absolute pleasure to speak to you. How may we be of service to you?"

"It is a delight to speak with you again, Makur. But I am hoping this time, we might be in a position to help you, with your fight against the Light of Africa."

"That would be beneficial to us all I think."

"I am sorry to say it is only a phone number, Makur"

"But none the less, Helen, a lead that could take us to a whole den of thieves and cut-throats."

"It could indeed, Makur. If you want to make use of the number, it is 24955112347. Also, there is a key word which is Artoli17."

"Thank you for sharing that with us Helen. If we collect any intelligence on the back of this, I will call you back as a priority. Until, then Salaam."

"Salaam, Makur, take care."

Adhiambo and Yaya were back together in the holding cell.

"So what will happen to us now, my kitten?"

"Well Yaya, I guess we will be held here, until they are finished with us. Then take us to Bronzefield."

"What is this Bronzefield, Adhiambo?"

"A prison just for women, Yaya."

"How do you know that, Adhiambo?"

"I asked the police officer. There you get strip-searched, dowsed with cold water, then you are given the awful Bronzefield uniform, Yaya."

"That does not sound very friendly Adhiambo."

"Yaya, it is a prison for women that commit crimes. If you want to put up with the big boys, you have to suffer the punishment if you are caught."

"Adhiambo, we have been caught."

"Yes, we have, Yaya."

"But those two men I told you about in the club, were planning something. Something that needed the three of us. Now I do not know what they will do, without me in their team, Adhiambo."

"Yaya, the two of them cannot do it alone?"

"Adhiambo, no, they needed a woman, so they told me."

"Was there anyone who could take your place, Yaya?"

"No they did not know anyone else, or trust anyone else Adhiambo."

"Then they will have to call it off, Yaya."

"They said they wanted a houri, Adhiambo."

"What in heaven's name is a houri ,Yaya?"

"It is a nymph, my kitten, a byword for me, So I could become part of their cell, someone they could trust to do a job for them."

"Nothing I need to remember then, Yaya."

"You never know, I did tell them of your affiliation with my school, you being the daughter of the guru, Adhiambo."

"I will remember in that case, to see if they will approach me at any time in the future. I guess we will be going to HMP Bronzefield, at some time or other, Yaya."

"All I can hope is that we are put into the same cell, Adhiambo."

Just then a uniformed constable comes into the holding cell.

"OK, ladies, some more questions for you both, if you would follow me please."

They both step out of the cell, follow the WPC, who leads them both to separate interview rooms. Yaya is confronted by Inspector Lewson and Adhiambo is confronted by her friend and confidante, Sergeant Vardy.

"So, Adhiambo, did Yaya entrust you with any other information?"

"Only that she was going to be involved in some plan, with two of the degenerates from the club, Lona."

"Did she give you any inkling of what it might be Adhiambo?"

"Not really, the two insurgents had told her that they needed a woman, as part of their plan. That is why they allowed her to become part of their cell. But apart from that I have no idea, Lona."

"Were you going to go back to the club, Adhiambo?"

"Lona, it would seem that I have to now, to find out what their plan is."

"I will still be there for you, very close by if you need me, Adhiambo."

"OK, Lona."

"I am going to take you home, OK? I will come and see you on Thursday. Tell your mum I will cook dinner for you all then Adhiambo."

Lona Vardy takes the young Adhiambo home, just as Anjella and Emelia arrive home. They pass each other on the way out and the way in, so Anjella turns to Lona,

"Not stopping tonight, Lona?"

"Sorry, not tonight, Anjella, but I will see you all on Thursday night, if that is OK? I will be doing the cooking."

"That will be a lovely treat for us all, Lona, keep safe in the meantime."

"I will, Anjella."

On Wednesday morning, the headmistress, Miss Rachel McGowan comes into Adhiambo's first period of free study, and sits down beside her, smiling.

"Young lady, would you like to come with me?"

"Of course, Miss McGowan."

Adhiambo follows Rachel into her office, closing the door and offering the young student a chair. There sat in the office was a female chief inspector, from the local police station. She turns to Adhiambo, confronting her with a warm smile.

"So, young lady, you are interested in making a difference. Empowering women on as many levels as possible?"

"I am, for all women in general, to inspire and to create the belief that they can do whatever they want, when they want, how they want."

"That really is a grand idea. We all need role models, so how would you like to spend a day at the station then come out with me in my car?"

"I would love to, Chief Inspector."

"So, Adhiambo, when would you like to come to the station?"

"Would Monday morning be all right, Chief Inspector, Miss McGowan?"

"That would be perfect, you have completed all your exams, so your time is your own now Adhiambo."

"It is good for me, I will see you first thing then, about nine?"

"Yes, Chief Inspector, I will be spending the day with you?"

"You will indeed. If for some reason I am not there, get the desk sergeant to call for, Chief Inspector Volante."

"I will Chief Inspector and can I just say I am really looking forward to Monday."

"Thank you, Adhiambo."

"Thank you for your time, Miss McGowan."

"That is quite all right, Adhiambo."

Adhiambo leaves the office going back to her free study session. Having looked through various vocations, college courses, university study objectives, she still felt unable to decide what she wanted to do with the rest of her life. Perhaps now being given the chance to spend time with a fully blown police chief inspector, might help her with these criteria. The rest of the week rolled on by, Thursday came and Lona came calling on the young lady of the house, Adhiambo. Smiling as always, she put a large cup of mocha in front of her, with a brace of freshly made *maandazi*.

"They look divine, Lona, I have not had one for ages."

Adhiambo dips into the bag, taking one and biting into it, licking her lips as she chews, licking away the sugar from around her mouth.

"They are gorgeous, Lona, where did you buy these?"

"No, no, Adhiambo, I looked up the recipe and made them from scratch, this morning."

"You know how to spoil a girl, Lona."

"I do not go to all this trouble for everyone, Adhimabo. So when is your birthday?"

"In August, Lona."

"Have you made any sort of plan, Adhiambo?"

"I know I have not, Lona. But I do not know whether my mother has."

"OK, we will ask her this evening, Adhiambo."

"Why Lona?"

"You never seem to have any friends around. I thought you could invite them around, we would do a barbeque, with a selection of dishes from Kenya, Ghana and Sierra Leone."

"Lona, that would be amazing. My friends would be lost for words, astounded at such food."

"OK, just make sure your mum and Emelia have not arranged anything."

They then decided to go to the cinema on the spur of the moment. When they came home, they both went to the kitchen and started to make dinner for the four of them. When Anjella and her friend Emelia came home they all sat down to eat, they discovered that her mum had not arranged anything for her daughter's birthday. Anjella was more than happy to do a barbeque, for all her darling daughter's friends. It would be their first large gathering in their garden since they had moved in. Lona spent the night in the spare bedroom. Saturday now sat before them, a day Anjella had off, so she, Emelia and Adhiambo all went out shopping together, incorporating lunch into the day as well. Finally, getting home in the very late afternoon, they all sat down to a cup of tea, with the fabulous choice of banana Ghana or the *kelewele* to go with it. Adhiambo, finally got up, then looking at her mum and Emelia.

"I am working tonight, Mum, so if you and Emelia have made plans, you both go for it. I am just going upstairs to get ready."

"OK, my dear, we are going to the cinema."

"You enjoy, Mum."

"We will and you keep safe, my pearl."

"I will, and I will come home in one piece, I promise."

"Make sure you do, Adhiambo."

"OK, Emelia."

Adhiambo opens up her wardrobe, slowly going through her lingerie drawer, finding a pair of lime green tanga briefs, with a matching underwired demi-cup bra. Then putting on an amber shimmer short lace bateau cocktail dress. Then finishing her outfit off with a pair of amber velvet fur pompom high-heel shoes. Putting on a heavy overcoat, she takes her regular cab, who now knows where to drop her off without asking. Adhiambo enters the club,

"Good evening, George."

"Good evening, Miss Adhiambo, how are you tonight?"

"I am fine, George."

Adhiambo then undoes her coat revealing herself to the doorman, smiling.

"What do you think of me tonight, George?"

He glances her up then down smiles then laughs, holding his two great arms out towards her.

"Exceptional, spectacular Adhiambo, stunning. You will knock them dead tonight, young lady."

"Thank you so much, George, well that is a worthy vote of confidence I must say."

Adhiambo smiles, nods to him in acknowledgement of his sincere appreciation of how stunning she looked. She goes to the performers' changing room, where she sits down to remove her coat. Then limbering and loosening up, just as Nina comes in.

"Have you seen Yaya, Adhiambo? She is normally the first one in, this is very late for her."

"No, sorry, Nina, I have not even had a text."

"In that case, will you be all right to start the show on your own, young lady?"

"I will be fine, Nina."

"So, you go and knock them out, Adhiambo, by the way you look fabulous in that amber outfit."

"Thank you, Nina."

Nina kisses Adhiambo on both of her cheeks, then the young performer goes out onto the stage. She is the central attraction on the pole. She notices that the two gentlemen that were sitting by the main entrance, in the shadows, had not arrived as yet. But the attractive Adhiambo got into the groove right away, dancing and grinding up and down her pole. Getting everyone interested in all her moves, as she was the only dancer out there, she got all the tips too, the gentlemen tucked them into the red belt buckled around her waist. They were all enjoying her work, the gyrations, twists, turns and slithers across the floor. Then finally Yaya's two accomplices arrive together, both seemingly looking for their missing houri. She beckons one of them over to her, before he sits down. She whispers into his ear:

"Your houri will not be in tonight, I am sorry."

He smiles at her, then goes to sit down with his rather wary mate. They both chat together, then look up at Adhiambo as she continues to perform. She stops her pole dance, now all slinky and seductive as he removes her cocktail dress. Now she looks even more alluring in her lime green lingerie. She was at once overpowering, angelic and provocative as she continued to dance freestyle and with the pole. The two gentlemen from the darkened corner came across to her, putting two fifty-pound notes into her bra, asking her:

"How do you know where our houri is?"

"Because I do, we are close like sisters. She was taken by the police at the Zenith Bank on Tuesday. I have not seen or heard from her since."

"Thank you."

He tips her again with another brace of fifties just as her first stint on the stage comes to an end. As Adhiambo goes to leave the stage, the gentleman flashes a bunch of notes in her direction, She goes over to him and he asks her:

"Who are you?"

"I am just a friend of Yaya's."

"Ah but it is much more than that, yes?"

"Yes Yaya knew my father, he was the one who taught all about her politics."

"Where did he teach her?"

"In Dolo, in the far reaches of Somalia."

"Are you sure young lady?"

"Yes, it was at the Sunda Kuliah Politik Jeung Hukum."

"If that is the case, who was the Kapla Jeung Guru?"

"Abshir Dalmar, who just happens to be my father."

"Where is he now then?"

"Here in England."

"Whereabouts in England is he now?"

"He is spending his spare time at Pentonville prison."

"Then it our pleasure to meet you Miss Dalmar. Could we talk to you again in the near future?"

"Of course, you can."

"Later we will ask for you to come to our cubicle."

"OK, I will wait for your call."

He puts the fistful of notes into her waistband, then goes to sit back hidden away in his corner. Adhiambo goes to the changing room, putting all her monies into her locker. Then taking something to eat and drink, she takes time to calm and relax herself. Once again she replenishes her lost body fluids, topping up her energy levels and reserves. She gives herself a good wiping down as she strips off the green lingerie. Once she feels ready, she slips into a peach lace-up mesh and fishnet open-cup mini dress. Along with a pair of orange seducer patent high-heel Oxford-style lace-up shoes. Then she is out and back onto the stage, with the rest of the girls performing, all very artistically with her nimble body. The very attentive male customers are very appreciative of all the hard work the girls put into their work, by putting all their paper money in between the double layers of mesh which formed the lower part of Adhiambo's dress. She saw the two compatriots of Yaya eventually move from their table for two, to one of the private cubicles further back within the club. Then Nina came forward to see Adhiambo.

"My dear young lady, there are two young gentlemen, who would love you to dance for them, in cubicle four."

"OK, Nina, I will got to them now."

So the attractive Adhiambo disappears into cubicle four, she shimmies, shakes and slithers on the table in front of her audience, rubbing and caressing herself as they both watch her. Then one asks:

"Would you be willing to take Yaya's place in blowing up Bow Street Magistrates Court?"

"If I can be of service to you in any way, I will do all that I can to help you achieve your goal. What would you want me to do?"

"We would want you to be our bomber, the centre of attention."

"OK, but I know nothing of bombs, I would need lots of guidance."

"That is OK, we will show you what you need to know."

"OK so you will let me know, if and when you would want my services?"

"We will, are you going to be here next week?"

"I will be, must I wait for you then?"

"Yes then we will talk to you again then, you may go."

Adhiambo leaves after he has tipped yet again. She reappears back on the stage along with all the other dancers. She gives it all the energy she has at her disposal. The tips once again come thick and fast, as all her African eloquence and enchantment of her dance routines dazzle just about everyone there watching. Adhiambo is a robust, provocative young woman, but dancing non-stop for about five hours takes it out of her. Finally, it is time to go home, she puts her coat on taking all her tips with her. She goes around the corner making sure she is not followed by anyone. Then she crosses the road and disappears into a waiting car. As she gets in Lona asks her, straight away:

"Where did you get to earlier on, Adhiambo?"

"I had to perform for Yaya's two associates, in one of the cubicles, Lona."

"Were they forthcoming with anything we need to know about Adhiambo?"

"Yes they were very up front, once they knew who I was, Lona."

"What is their plan, young lady?"

"Lona, they are going to bomb Bow Road Magistrates Court."

"Good lord! When is this going to take place? Do you know how, when, Adhiambo?"

"I know how, I am to be their bomber. I find out next Saturday, Lona."

"OK so now you need to be very careful Adhiambo. These are dedicated terrorists you are dealing with."

"I know Lona. But even so we need to put a stop to it all. The only way is to catch them then kill them. Treat them exactly the same way as they treat everyone else, with complete disregard, give them no respect, because they think it is a sign of weakness. There is no room for morals with these pigs, you need to baste them as soon as you catch them. Just so that they do not get the chance to teach or indoctrinate anyone else."

"OK, Adhiambo, I can see you feel strongly about this."

"I do, Lona, I am sorry but this is the fault of my father. Come on, take me home, would you?"

After a long lie-in, Adhiambo gets dressed, goes in and wakes up Lona, who was using the spare room.

"Come on sleepyhead, I am going to take you all out to dinner."

Adhiambo and Lona finally appear in the lounge, then confront her mum and Emelia,

"Mum, Emelia, are you going to come out with us, for dinner?"

"Goodness, what a question on a Sunday evening, are you going to pay my precious *mondo*."

"Of course, Mum, we are off to Kate's."

"Then of course, we would love to come with you."

Anjella and Emelia both freshen up, then the foursome all stroll down to Kate's Restaurant, enjoying a long lazy evening there. Monday morning soon came around, the young Adhiambo was dressed in her freshly pressed school uniform. The she was heading off down the road to the local police station, to see Chief Inspector Thandie Volante. The young schoolgirl swept in through the doors about ten minutes early, so she decided to sit down in the corner and wait. Even with minding her own business, the desk sergeant came over to her, smiling and very cordial.

"Can I be of assistance, young lady?"

"Well, yes, Sergeant, I am a little early. That is why I sat out of the way. I am waiting for Chief Inspector Volante, I am Adhiambo."

"You wait right there, I will go and give her a call, just so that she knows you are early, OK?"

"Thank you so much, Sarge."

He smiles to himself. It actually sounded as if she knew to call him sarge, he was impressed and knowing his rank as well, impressed him even further. He got onto the phone to the chief inspector,

"Ma'am there is a young lady here her name is Adhiambo, she says she is waiting for you."

"OK, Sergeant Stone, I am on my way."

The chief inspector makes a rather quiet entrance, coming straight up to the young schoolgirl.

"Adhiambo, so wonderful to see you again. I am so happy you could make it."

"I would not have missed today for anything, Chief Inspector."

"Call me, Thandie, Adhiambo, I am pleased you wanted to come."

Thandie puts her arm across Adhiambo's shoulder, taking her outside into the back of the yard.

"Come on, Adhiambo, we are going out for a drive and a chat, is that OK with you?"

"That will be lovely, Thandie, better than being stuck in an office."

"My sentiments exactly, Adhiambo."

They start a conversation almost straight away, about what they both want to achieve. Thandie tells Adhiambo that hard work always pays off. That she herself had passed her Superintendent's Board. Now it is just a waiting game, until the next vacancy becomes available, anywhere within the metropolitan area. Thandie said she cannot wait to exchange her three pips for that impressive crown on her shoulder.

Then Adhiambo speaks up, telling Thandie of her expectations and hopes. Looking at the chief inspector in earnest and eye to eye, "Thandie, I think over here in the United Kingdom, you treat the terrorists too softly. You should treat them like the immoral scum that they are. You should put them down, as soon as you get the chance. Pigs that they are."

"You really do detest them, Adhiambo. It sounds as though you have had some personal experience in that direction."

"I have, Thandie, and I do. They are the ruination of most things these days. Their creed along with a world full of despots, dictators and tyrants, especially in Africa. They milk everything that is of any value. Leaving the normal person with nothing, not even their pride or self-determination Thandie."

"I guess then, Africa is not a very sociable or happy place Adhiambo."

"No, it is not Thandie, being a woman is extremely hard work, a third-class citizen at best. With no rights, that is wrong surely in anyone's book."

"It is wrong being downtrodden and not being able to determine your own life Adhiambo."

"They need to rise up together, throw off their chains, fight for what is theirs. Take it by force if necessary, show these tyrants what women are really made of, Thandie."

"Yes, you would only need one or two to lead the way, then hopefully all the others would follow them to the end Adhiambo."

"You are right Chief Inspector, but I do not think there are women strong enough to take the banner forward. They would need to hold it high, so the whole of the African womanhood could see it, follow it. March together to the citadel and take it over."

"But I am sure your day will come and, when it does, mankind better beware of you all, hey?"

"They will need to be, Thandie, damn, but it is good talking to you."

"Would you like some dinner, young lady?"

"That would be lovely, Thandie."

"What do you fancy then, Adhiambo?"

"Chinese would be nice Thandie."

The Chief Inspector stops outside The Songs of the Silk Road, her favourite Chinese restaurant. They both go in, Thandie instantly recognised. They get shown to a quiet corner, where Adhiambo orders the kung-pao chicken with the special fried rice. Thandie orders the beef in black bean sauce with the egg fried rice, along with two pancake rolls. During the course of their conversation, Adhiambo asks Thandie if she would like to come to her to her birthday party. The chief inspector says she would love to. Now having shared the day together, Thandie returns the young lady home.

"Adhiambo once I can get another free day, I will come and pick you up and I will show you another part of my patch. You keep safe."

"That will be fantastic Thandie, thank you for today and will see you soon."

Adhiambo goes indoors contemplating the idea of being a policewoman. She can get all the experience she needs here in England. Then perhaps go back to Kenya, to join the Kenyan police force. She could become the standard bearer herself; the one that leads the women's rebellion there in East Africa. She could find a way to infiltrate all the dark corners of that continent, to be able to shed light into every nook and cranny. To make sure not a single female was hidden from sight, or chained to a wall, in the dark desolation of loneliness and despair. Would she have the stomach for it? Only time would tell. But for now, she was in the process of helping her very dear friend Lona to sort out this terrorist disease that was here.

So now it was time to make dinner, so that it would be ready for when her mum and Emelia came home from work. Soon she was roasting a small brisket, roasting potatoes, broad beans, peas and braising a large white onion. She was keeping it all hot as she laid the table. Adhiambo took her mother's and Emelia's coats and hung them both up. then they both helped Adhiambo put the dinner on the table, then they all seated themselves close together. Anjella turned to her daughter with a smile:

"This is absolutely lovely, Adhiambo."

"Thank you, Mum."

So the week rolled on by again, with Saturday being the main day of the week yet again. Adhiambo was upstairs deciding what to wear once again and what to take as a change. So into the holdall went an ice diamond net sparkle minidress, along with a pair of pink glitter pointed ankle-strap high heels. Adhiambo then decided to put on a violet leather pleated micro skirt, along with a matching half-cup silk and lace corselette.

Then she adorned her feet with a pair of Victorian champagne satin ankle boots, with lace overlay and dark red ribbon laces. Then she flung on a very heavy coat, which concealed her whole outfit.

"Well, Mum, Emelia, you enjoy the theatre tonight, I will see you in the morning at some time."

"OK, my sweetheart, you keep safe and come home in one piece."

The cab driver sounded his horn, so Adhiambo rushed out and jumped into her cab. She got driven to the front door of the 1117 Côte d'Ivoire. She got out, undoing her coat and stood provocatively and with some intent, in front of her favourite doorman smiling.

"George, good evening to you. So how are you tonight?"

"I am very well and how are you, Miss?"

"I feel great, as always."

"May I say, you look splendid, you sparkle. There would seem to be a little bit of vixen in you tonight Adhiambo."

"I take it you like the way I am dressed tonight, George? Do I arouse you in anyway at all?"

"Miss Adhiambo, you are dressed like a real temptress, a real charm tonight. Yes, you do arouse me, in so many ways."

"That is a good sign, then I should be able to enchant and arouse all the other customers tonight, George."

"I am sure you will young lady, you will have them at your feet, begging for more."

Adhiambo makes her way to the dancers' changing room, putting her coat and holdall into her locker. Then she sits and relaxes for a minute, then she is out onto the stage, getting into the groove straight away. Using the pole to her own ends, she entices the young men to come close and watch her. She also spots that her two compatriots are sat in their usual corner, in the shadows. They both smile in her direction, she pouts her shocking pink lips blowing them both a kiss. She comes closer to the edge of the performers' platform, collecting so many tips in the process. But the move was primarily so that one of her friends could get close to her, he whispers:

"We will see you after your break, please."

"OK, I will see you both then."

Adhiambo carries on dancing, exerting her nimble body in so many directions, thoroughly enjoying all the attention she is receiving. All her contortions receive very admiring glances, with the tips coming thick and fast, all being tucked into her waistband of her very revealing skirt. Adhiambo strobes, caresses her long lithe limbs with both hands, as a finale to her first bout on the stage. She goes off to recharge, have a quick shower and change. She changes from her micro skirt, into the dazzling ice diamond net sparkle minidress, along with the pair of pink glitter pointed ankle-strap high heels, along with a shade of ice-blue lipstick. Then she is back onto the stage, just about to perform, when Nina approaches her.

"Adhiambo, your two fans are in cubicle four, waiting for you now."

"OK, Nina, I am on my way there for them."

Adhiambo goes over to the cubicle where her two supposed friends wait for her patiently. She stops before them, smiling,

"Good evening, gentlemen, good to see you. How are you both?"

"We are very good thank you. You look absolutely delightful young woman, so ripe for plucking and tasting your sweet virgin fruit."

"I enjoy the work but just for one night a week, gentlemen."

"So, we have decided that we are going to do this job on Friday, at 09:00 hours. That is when the court opens its doors, we want you there taking all of the attention and pressure off us, young lady."

"OK, so when am I to prepare for this, gentlemen?"

"We would like to see you at our lodgings, very early on Friday, young lady."

"How early is early, please, gentlemen?"

"At 05:45 hours, so we can get you ready for your appearance young lady."

"Where do you lodge, gentlemen?"

"In Tomlins Grove in Bow, young lady."

"OK, I will be there gentlemen."

"We want you to be modestly dressed, young lady."

"That will be a pleasure, gentlemen, I assure you."

They both approach her, both stroking her long legs all the way up, then licking the topside of her breasts. They both smile as they enjoy themselves, making the young Adhiambo feel very uncomfortable. But she was unwilling to shout out, because she did not want to draw attention to her predicament. Finally, they finished touching her, they both filled her dress pockets with twenty-pound notes, then dismissed her from their cubicle. Adhiambo then goes back to performing on the stage, with all the other girls. Finally, it is time to finish and leave the club. All the girls say good morning to Nina, Adhiambo walks over to Lona who waits for her patiently in the car. She tells the police sergeant that the two insurgents want her to be at Tomlins Grove, at 06:00 hours on Friday morning. Then their plan is to attack the Magistrates court, on Friday morning at 09:00 hours when it opens.

Lona asks Adhiambo, "Why should they want you so early on the day of the bombing, young lady?"

"I do not know, Lona, perhaps for a practice run through, to show me my part in all this, before the big day?"

"I am not sure. I will inform Helen, then find out what we are to do. OK, Adhiambo?"

"That is fine by me, Lona."

So they both wend their way home and go to bed. On the Thursday night Adhiambo's two accomplices head out to the court via Arnold Road, to the rear entrance. First, they place an EOD in a bin, in the officers and officials' car park. Then two IEDs are laid, one at the rear fire exit, then one as close as they could, to the private entrance, set aside for the prisoners and magistrates. They were all set remotely with a minute's delay between all three devices. The two terrorists then went back and, enjoyed a good night's slumber. At 05:00 hours, Adhiambo was up and dressed, in a charise bardot lace off-the-shoulder, long-sleeved midi dress. With a pair of wine vindola high ankle shoes. Getting on the underground at Plaistow, she disembarked at Bow Road. Then, walking to Tomlins Grove, as she approached the dwelling the two insurgents saw her and waved her inside, quickly. Then locking the door behind her, they took her straight away down into their basement. Here they had made a bomb, having adapted it to a bulletproof vest. Then they both turned to the young lady.

"Please take a seat and we will show you what we require you to do on the day."

Adhiambo sat down completely at ease. Then one of the terrorists took hold of both her arms, while the other put the loaded bulletproof vest over her head. He secured it with laces tied at the back. Then he wired it up, so that it was now a live bomb.

"I thought I was going to be the bomber gentlemen?"

"Young lady we had a change of mind. In fact, you are now the bomb. You are live, ready for detonation at our time of choosing."

The other terrorist then told her:

"It will be such a shame to waste such a beautiful young girl. But you need to be sacrificed for the god of Islam, Africa and Ar-Razzaq."

"This has nothing to do with religion, it is your own greed and dissatisfaction with the rest of the world, that is the problem. But kill me it will not change a single thing."

"But it will come with us and you will see what difference you make to our fight."

They take Adhiambo out to their old grey van that had just pulled up outside. They lift her into the back, throw her into the darkness, where she ends up alongside another very young girl. Dressed the same as herself, aged possibly six or seven. She has such big eyes, red and watered with tears. She looks so full of fear, dread and drained of concern, devoid of any interest or interaction with the girl that was now beside her. Unbeknown to either girl, the Luo Lake goddess now travelled with them. The goddess drew both young girls to her breast, gently blowing into their ears. Casting herself onto their parietal lobe. The Luo Lake goddess sits there, enthroned. Adhiambo recognises her *nyamin* in an instant. The goddess states quite clearly to them both:

"If anything endangers either of your lives today, I will be here either to protect you or take you back to my home, to live with me for eternity."

The young girl gives Adhiambo a quizzical look, with a very puzzled face.

"It is all right, my sister, you are in safe hands. You are not alone. My blood-sister will care for you, whatever happens."

The young girl, took hold of Adhiambo's hands, gripping them extremely tightly. This very short journey to the courthouse was uninterrupted. They parked in the public car park, unaware that the Counter Terrorism Unit was already there. They had been searching from the very early hours, they had discovered the EOD along with one of the IEDs. The time tended to tick by, very slowly, it was 08:50 hours. The squad was all in plain clothes, mingling in with the public. A single dog was still searching just in case anything had been missed. Finally, they found the third device, hidden down by the fire exit. So by the time the court had opened at 09:00 hours, all is supposedly safe. But security is still very tight, everyone is checked on the way in.

So for the terrorists getting out of the van with Adhiambo in front of them, all wired up. The little girl left in the van, wired up into the mercury tilt bomb that was making the whole van an explosive device. She was left all on her own, no one the slightest bit interested in her. The driver parked as close as he could to the main fire exit, then just waited for further commands. The two main operatives walk around the van, pushing the now scared Adhiambo, into the main entrance. Where she stumbles, unable to keep her balance she falls onto her back, lying there sprawled out on the floor, in front of the amassed crowds. The main insurgent comes forward shouting as loud as he can, to gain the most attention.

"WE ARE HERE TO COLLECT YAYA ARTOLI, WHO DO WE NEED TO TALK TO?"

"You need to talk to me, I am the Clerk of the Court."

"WE WANT HER, NOW."

"Who might you be, sir?"

"THE LIGHT OF AFRICA. A CURSE THAT WILL TORMENT YOU FOR SOMETIME TO COME."

"Who is the Yaya Artoli?"

"SHE IS ONE OF US, LIKE THIS ON THE ON THE FLOOR, A WORTHLESS FEMALE WHO IS WILLING TO DIE FOR OUR CAUSE."

"Do you know where she is being kept?"

"YES, BRONZEFIELD IN MIDDLESEX."

"Then let me make a call."

"YOU GO VERY CAREFULLY, THIS ONE IN FRONT OF ME IS A BOMB, COMPLETELY UNDER MY CONTROL."

"Then send one of your men with me, the office is only over here."

The silent one goes with the Clerk of the Court. He opens the door so that the clerk can enter, then he is followed in by the guardian terrorist. He walks in surprised by the SO11 operative inside the office, who with a single shot takes him down. From then on in Commander Ball gives the go-head to nullify the other terrorists, if at all possible. Sergeant Vardy starts shepherding all the public away from the danger area, showing them the way out via the staff fire exit. Chief Inspector Volance avoids a severe trampling, as there is a rush in all directions to get out of the building. The terrorists are now unsure of what precisely to do. The top insurgent starts shooting haphazardly at the main entrance, the one to his left pressing the button on his remote, setting off the van outside. It destroys all in its path, along with the driver and the young girl who had been used as the detonator fro the van. Then the terrorist to the right depressing his remote go button, but it short circuited, setting his coat on fire. The Luo Lake goddess was again intervening with the cold water from her Lake Victoria. Making sure the whole bomb was waterlogged, drenching the bulletproof vest, she disrupted all its volatile capabilities. The goddess tousles Adhiambo's hair, kissing both her cheeks and whispering gently in her ear,

"As I told you so long ago, I am your *nyamin*, I will look after you constantly. I also have your young friend here, with me. Such a shame, but I will take care of her, you will see her again. Would you like to say your goodbyes, Adhiambo?"

The two girls grip hands, kissing as an older and younger sister would. The younger sister now understanding that at least two people had cared about her.

Then the goddess evaporated and returned to her home. As Adhiambo lay there, as amongst all the panic the four insurgents were taken down together. Four shots with one subtle result, they all lay on the floor grounded, disabled and ineffectual to any other outbursts of panic. Commander Ball came out of the court office, hauling the fourth terrorist with her.

"Inspector Lewson take the four of them away please, this is now a crime scene."

Helen bends down to Adhiambo, just checking her over,

"You did a great job young lady. We are very thankful to you indeed."

"It was a little disconcerting, Helen, also with the explosion outside. There were two people in the van, the driver along with a very young girl, about six or seven, who was part of the bomb. She was all trussed up like me, I feel so sorry for her."

"OK, Adhiambo, the expert will be along in a minute, to make sure you are safe, that we can remove the bomb from you."

Commander Ball went outside to view the damage, destruction and carnage. It was prolific, it would be hard to resolve. But all being well with the four insurgents still intact, so they should between them be able to glean some information from them. Adhiambo was finally approved as being safe and freed from her constraining device. Lona along with the commander came up to speak to her. First Helen asked:

"Adhiambo do you still think Yaya still considers you a friend?"

"I do not see why not, Helen. We were still talking to each other, until we were separated at the Yard."

Lona looks at her, taking her hand.

"Adhiambo, you have done so much for us already, but we would like you to go to HMP Bronzeshield, to see if you can get any other intelligence from her. Just in case these four do not reveal anything."

"When would you like me to go, Lona, Helen?"

"Now would be good, as part of this explosion going down, just in case you need a cover."

"OK, if you think it will help our investigation, Helen."

"I am sure anything you find out, will help us now or at a later date Adhiambo."

So Adhiambo is put into the back of a police car, taken to the Bronzeshield, where she finds herself in a cell with her friend Yaya. Helen in the meantime has phoned the governor of the women's prison, Charlotte Pattison, informing her of the reasoning behind getting Yaya Artoli in the same cell as Adhiambo Ogwayo. When Adhiambo is put into the cell with Yaya, Miss Artoli rushes up to her friend hugging her close, kissing her cheeks.

"It has been a long time, my sister. Why are you here now?"

"Yaya, four of your friends and myself tried to get you free, but it did not work out too well."

"How come you got involved, Adhiambo?"

"I was approached by your men friends in the club and they asked me to take your place, Yaya."

"Where did you try to get me freed, Adhiambo?"

"From Bow Street courthouse. But we got caught and taken down, my bomb did not go off, so I was caught as well."

"Your bomb, that was a risk sister."

"Yes, Yaya, I was the bomb, I was meant to explode inside the court."

"Was anyone injured in this attack my sister?"

"Only our four comrades, Yaya."

"But I only knew of two locally, Adhiambo."

"But there was a driver and young girl involved as well, Yaya."

"A driver and young girl were there too, were they killed, my sister?"

"Oh, yes, without a doubt, the driver was still in the van, the young girl was used as a detonator for the van, which was a very big EOD, Yaya."

"How old was the young girl, Adhiambo?"

"I would say about six or seven, Yaya. I was at in the back with her. I do not actually think she knew what was going on around her."

"Please, Allah, no, I think that may have been my younger sister, they used her as a bomb, Adhiambo?"

"Yes, when we got out, Yaya, she was plugged into the network of wiring, at the headboard of the van. The driver was told to stay where he was, until he was needed."

"Adhiambo, they have been trying to get my brother to join their cause for such a long time, he always told them no."

"Yaya perhaps telling him that you would be freed, made a difference to him."

"Or they used my little sister to get to him."

"Maybe, Yaya."

"Now I have no family at all, my sister, what have I done to deserve this, what am I to do?"

"Perhaps our lives, Yaya, our line of work compels us to lose all that we love, eventually."

"Perhaps, Adhiambo, it does rather leave us on our own, alone, with nothing or no one to care for. With no one caring for us in return. Exiles in our own country, along with whereever else we try to force our opinions on other people."

"Yaya they do not like having it forced upon them, they lose no love when they see us dead, or hanged for our crimes against them."

"Should they care about those left behind Adhiambo?"

"No, they should not, Yaya, care about us, when we do not even care about ourselves."

"You are right, my enlightened sister, we become fanatics and turn everyone against us with our false aspirations and ideal dreams. We become isolationists, whores without any scruples. Then we cry out when no one wants to befriend us."

"So what should we do about it, Yaya?"

"I do not know Adhiambo, should we admit to our failings and try to redeem our lost souls?"

"If we do that, then we have wasted three years of our lives, Yaya, for nothing."

"Yes, but if I had known I would lose my siblings in this war of attrition, I would not have been a soldier in the first place my wonderful sister."

"So, what will we do, Yaya, whatever we do, we will do it together."

"I will sleep on it and then decide in the morning Adhiambo."

They both go to their bunks and sleep. Yaya is very morose, morbid and mopes in the cell, not talking to her sister, not communicating in any way whatsoever. Then finally Adhiambo manages to sneak a knife out of the kitchen, confronting Yaya eye to eye.

"Yaya, what if you had another sister?"

"Adhiambo, do not be so stupid, who would be my sister now after all this?"

"Me, Yaya, I would be honoured to be your younger sister."

"But how, Adhiambo?"

"Give me your hand Yaya."

Yaya offers up her hand to Adhiambo freely without questioning why. Adhiambo cuts into the palm of her own hand first, then slices into Yaya's. Then they clasp both of their hands together, so that the two flows of blood mingle. As this happens, Adhiambo takes Yaya's face, kisses her on both cheeks, then on her lips. To this, Yaya responds instantly, repeating the ritual on her now younger sister. They both hug, drawing each other close in that instant, as they hug and their blood fuses to become one; the Luo Lake goddess appears, clasping both Adhiambo and Yaya to her bosom, whispering the word consanguineous so that both females could hear her. Then she clasps tightly their hands with hers, anointing their sistership and their kinship with her sacred waters from Lake Victoria. Then kissing them both and once again she leaves them to their own ends.

"I am your sister, Yaya, we are now of each other's blood. Now we are one, I am your family and you are mine forever."

"Are you really my sister, Adhiambo?"

"Yes, Yaya, I and my family are now yours."

"Then Adhiambo there is only one thing to do now."

"Yes, my sister what are we to do? You are my elder sister, what is your plan, Yaya?"

"We tell all that we know, so that you do not have to die, my darling sister."

"You would do that for me, Yaya?"

"Yes, always, Adhiambo, you have given me fresh hope, you have opened the door for me. So I need to do the same for you."

"Then we need to speak to the governor."

First thing on Monday morning, both Yaya and her sister, Adhiambo, were standing in front of Ms Charlotte Pattison, she looked up at the both of them.

"So, ladies, how may I help you today?"

Adhiambo speaks up first to answer the question.

"We need to talk to Commander Helen Ball, of the Counter Terrorism Unit, please, ma'am."

Charlotte picks up the phone immediately, getting instant access to Helen. She gets her attention right away, when Charlotte tells Helen which two prisoners are asking for her presence at the prison.

"OK, Charlotte, I am on my way now."

"Helen, I will keep them both here in my office, for you."

Then Charlotte turns her attention to the two young ladies before her.

"Make yourself comfortable, ladies, Helen is on her way."

All three ladies enjoy a chat with a cup of tea, then there is a knock at Charlotte's door, she looks up.

"Come in, please."

The door opens and Helen appears.

"Good morning, Charlotte, how are you?"

"I am fine Helen, I take it you were expecting this, or at least hoping for something like it?"

"I was Charlotte and now here we are, reaping the rewards hopefully. How have they both been?"

"Very relaxed and patient, enjoying our little chat. If you would sign the paperwork Helen, they are now both in your custody."

"Thank you for your hospitality, Charlotte, take care."

The commander takes them both away, with her back to the Yard. Straight into an interview room, getting Mark Tuley, Inspector Lewson and Sergeant Vardy in on the interview as well.

"So, ladies here we are, to see if you can help us stop any more killings by the Light of Africa."

Yaya speaks up for the first time, shying away a little from the stare of the commander.

"It is me that has all the intelligence. As long as you keep my sister safe, I will tell you all that I know."

"We will keep your sister safe and secure, Yaya, you as well, if you can tell us who these terrorists are?"

"If you have pen and paper, I will give you all the information I have freely. I want nothing for myself, just for my darling sister to be free."

"Adhiambo, what is going on here, what is the problem?"

"Helen, Lona the van that exploded outside the court on Monday, had Yaya's very young sister and older brother inside it. I also managed to create a bond between Yaya and myself, making us blood-sisters. Now she worries about me, in case she loses me as well. She is trying to make everything right, to correct all the mistakes she has made over the past three years."

"Do you think the intelligence she is going to give us is going to be worth the bother, Adhiambo?"

"I am hardly in a position to answer that, Helen. I think it will bear fruit, because of the trauma she has been through. She wants to put everything right as quickly as possible."

"OK, Adhiambo, let us see what she gives us, then who we need to contact."

Yaya breaks down and cries uncontrollably, knowing they are talking about her, even though she is sat there with them. Adhiambo turns to Yaya, taking hold of her in her arms and pulling her in close, kissing her."

"Yaya, you cry all you want, let it all flow out, I am here to protect and love you, no matter what happens to you."

"You will not leave me here alone, Adhiambio, I have no one else to turn to now."

"I will be here for you, Yaya, for as long as you want or need your younger sister."

"I will want you always, Adhiambo, please."

"Then you have me, Yaya. Will you want to work again?"

"Of course, I want to work Adhiambo."

"Then we will sort that out as well, for you, Yaya."

Inspector Lewson reappears with paper and pens, putting them on the table as Adhiambo soothes Yaya, wiping away her big tears, calming the heartache, desperation, loneliness and desolation, that Yaya must feel. Kissing her fingers, Adhiambo tells Yaya:

"When we are finished here, I will take you home to our mother and, then we will have dinner as a family, Yaya."

"Do you promise, Adhiambo?"

"I do, my sister, I promise."

Then Yaya picks up the pen, pulls over some of the sheets of paper, and starts to write all that she knows, all that she can remember. All the intelligence that has been scorched onto her brain since she became an insurgent for the Light of Africa. The two operatives she knew from the Sudan were Omar Elfadil and Aarif Qosi. The commander approaches the two young women,

"Would you both come with me, please? Just to see if you recognize any of the thugs from Monday."

The commander takes them both into the viewing room, where they can see in and the cellmates cannot see out.

"Now, Yaya, I want you to tell me, as the men are brought into view, do see anyone you know." So the first one is filed into their view.

"Yes, yes, I recognize him, that is Omar Elfadil, from the Sudan, he has always been bald."

Then then other three are brought in in slow succession.

"That is Aarif Qosi with his ponytails, from the Sudan just like Omar."

"That is… could you get him to remove his glasses, please?"

The commander buzzes through to the inspector,

"Get him to remove his glasses."

"That is better, that is a Ugandan, Adroa Nakato."

"This one I do not know. But if any of them try to use the name Jalal Artoli, they lie because that is the name of my dead brother, who was killed in the van."

Adhiambo turns to her sister Yaya.

"Yaya, what was your sister's name, who died alongside him in the van?"

"She was the beautiful, Fazilah Artoli."

The two young ladies along with Commander Helen Ball went back to the interview room. Soon all were sitting with a nice fresh hot brew of Earl Grey breakfast tea. Yaya continued to compile her list of known suspects. She now added Adroa Nakato to Omar and Aarif. Then she wrote down, Ateefah Touba from the Sudan as well as Haweeyo Farhan, Ashkiro Gullet from Somalia. Zahra Haroub out of Tanzania and finally Karutunda Juuko from Uganda. They were all the female and male operatives that she knew of, although she was rather unsure of whether they were working here in the UK, or still active in East Africa. She also knew each one of them would have a named account, in each of their home countries. So Omar along with Aarif would have accounts in the Bank of Khartoum. Ateefah's money would be in the National Bank of Sudan. While Adroa would hold his money in the Equity Bank, Karutunda would save with the Tropical Bank.

Haweeyo along with Ashkiro would be with the Amal Bank. Then finally Zahra from Tanzania would be with the Diamond Trust Bank. Whilst the central fund for The Light of Africa, was held in the Equatorial Commercial Bank in Kenya. Yaya finally put her pen down, looking up to Adhiambo,

"That is all I know. I hope that is enough to make my sister safe?"

"It is, Yaya, it will make you very safe as well."

Helen smiled as she parted with that information, for the benefit of both Yaya and Adhiambo. Now that they had the names of three of the culprits for the bombing on Monday. It was easy to apply pressure, especially when the fourth ingrate tried to be Jalal Artoli. Then to be told, in no uncertain terms, that he was not because Jalal had been killed when they had blown up the van, outside the courthouse, along with his sister. Finally, this one relented, as he was on his own. Telling them he was from Kenya and that his name was Kwame Adoyo. Having got the final name and, they still kept them all separated, so they could not converse or corroborate their stories with each other. Yaya also believed as they were over here working, they could also have accounts at Barclays Bank, which was the British bank of choice of the Light of Africa. Helen wasted no time in contacting all her counterparts across East Africa, giving each of them all the intelligence she had just gathered. By now her team was hoping it would result in arrests, along with the possibility of closing down live accounts, thus restricting and even cutting off monetary supplies to this particular terrorist organization. Helen released Adhiambo immediately, then the young woman pleaded with the commander, to release her sister.

"Please, Helen, let Yaya come home with me, even if it just for the one night."

"Commander I will stay with them, and make sure she returns in the morning."

"OK, Lona, Adhiambo, take her, but make sure you bring her back in the morning," said Lona.

"OK, ma'am, as you wish."

The three women drive off, leaving Inspector Lewson, Commander Ball and Constable Tuley to carry on with the serious work of interviewing and breaking down the insurgents they had in their cells. Once home, Adhiambo made a cup of tea for all of them, got out the banana-peanut cake, then sitting down with Lona and her new sister, Yaya, they just wallowed in each other's company. Yaya turned to them both:

"Will I be sleeping here tonight, dearest sister?"

"Yes, Yaya, you will, in a bed just for you."

"That is a lovely thought, will you be here as well Adhiambo?"

"I will be, Yaya, so will Lona and our mother."

"A real mother, will she like me, love me like her own daughter, Adhiambo?"

"Of course, Yaya, your mother will love you, so will her friend."

"Where will I sleep, in the kitchen, my sister?"

"No, you will not sleep in the kitchen. Come, let me show you, your bed."

Adhiambo takes Yaya by the hand as they walk up the stairs. She shows her sister into all the rooms upstairs.

"This, Yaya, is our bedroom, this one with two single beds, where we can sleep close to one another."

"Which one is yours, my dear sister?"

"This one here, Yaya, this new one will be yours, Yaya."

Yaya goes and sits on her bed, bouncing up and down, rubbing her hands all over it.

"It is so soft and comfortable, nothing like the floor I slept on for so long. I will not be alone, as my sister sleeps in the same room as me."

"Yes, so if you have any bad dreams, I can be here for you Yaya."

"Is Lona going to sleep with us, Adhiambo?"

"She will be close by, in the room next door, so do not worry my very dear sister. Shall we make some dinner, Yaya?"

"Oh, yes, ready for when our mother comes home."

All three are very busy in the kitchen, Yaya laughing out aloud, so very happy to be in such company. The happiest she has ever been in her relatively short life. She thought back to her home life, when she was always considered less than the dogs on the street, because she was female and worth nothing in the eyes of her parents. She grew up not knowing any form of love from her mother and father. So even Yaya considered herself worthless, a wasted life, not even emotionally involved with her mum and dad. She wandered the streets uneducated, not wise in the ways of the world. So when she was abducted, she did not expect anyone to come looking for her. It was then that the Light of Africa opened their doors to her. She accepted their invitation to work for them, because she did not know any better. Accepting her destiny was not hers to assume, guide or control. Now she is here with her new family, who have freely taken her into their lives. Her spirit feels reborn, alive and free, a new woman seeing her life as her own, for the very first time, though new eyes.

With dinner almost ready, all three sit on the sofa, with Yaya cuddling up close in the middle. Adhiambo and Lona both wrap their arms around her, so that she does not feel alone, in anyway whatsoever, as they watch the television together. Then all of a sudden, the front door opens, Anjella and Emelia appear in the lounge. Yaya then gets a little nervous, trying to hide behind her sister and Lona. Anjella comes across, kisses her daughter on the lips, then kisses Lona on both cheeks. Then she turns to her daughter:

"Who do we have hiding here, Adhiambo?"

"This is my sister and your daughter, Mum. This is Yaya from The Sudan, she is the most beautiful girl, I have ever met."

"Yaya my stunning daughter, you are like a star in the heavens, you bring so much light into my life. Let me kiss you my darling. Have you cooked dinner for us all?"

Slowly Yaya gains her confidence, then reappears between Lona and Adhiambo. Then Anjella holds her face, kissing away her tears. To this, Yaya responds by putting her arms around Anjella's neck and kissing her back.

"Yaya, this is our very dear friend, Emelia, she loves both of my daughters dearly, come and say hello."

Emelia makes the first move, kissing Yaya on her slightly dry lips.

"Hello, Yaya, it is a pleasure to see you, my darling."

"Hello, Emelia, can I love you too?"

"Of course, you can, Yaya, we all love each other now, so there is no need to be shy."

They all sit at the table, making sure Yaya is in the middle, surrounded by her new instant family.

"Yaya, I told you that our mother would love you and care for us now."

"You did, my sister, now I believe your words. My other mother never cared for me, she went to another country without me. She thought I was nothing."

"Then she was wrong Yaya. You are very valuable to your mother and me, it will always be that way."

"Will you always be here for me, my mother?"

"I will always be here for you, my very dear Yaya. I will be here to love and protect you all my life."

"Then I can call this my home, Mum?"

"This is your home, my dearest daughter, Yaya."

"Thank you, Mum."

"From today, you will need no other, my sister, Yaya."

"The sweetest words from my adorable sister Adhiambo."

The three young women all slept soundly, Adhiambo and Yaya together in the same room, in two single beds, while Lona slept in the room next door. In the morning they all went back to the Yard, taking Yaya back into custody. Then Helen came back out and sat with Lona and Adhiambo.

"So what do you think we should do with our young Yaya, Lona, Adhiambo?"

"Ma'am I think we should release her into the family of Anjella and Adhiambo, so she can live a normal life."

"OK, Lona, how about you, Adhiambo?"

"Well, Helen, we would love to have her in our life. My mother would take her in as her daughter, my sister. I would even give her our name, if that is what she desired most."

"Come on then, let us go and ask her what she would like to do, Adhiambo, Lona."

The three of them go back into the holding cell, where Yaya has been on her own for a little while. Yaya runs up to her sister holding her close, gripping Lona's hand.

"You said you would not leave me ever again, my sisters."

"But we want you to be free forever, my beloved sister."

"So you do not have to come back here, Yaya."

"How can we make that possible my loving sisters?"

"Would you like to change your name to mine, be the same as your sister, Yaya?"

"Of course, I do, sisters should have the same name anyway, Adhiambo."

"Then you would become Yaya Ogwayo, the sister of Adhiambo Ogwayo."

"Yes, yes of course, a lovely name, I am Yaya Ogwayo."

"OK then I will get her released from here as well as HMP Bronzeshield, get her name changed. Yaya, when would you like your birthday to be?"

"I would like my birthday to be the same as my sisters."

"The same as your sisters it is then. How old are you, Adhiambo?"

"Helen, I am seventeen on the twenty-first of August."

"In that case Yaya, your birthday will be the twenty-first of August and, you will be twenty-one. I will go and get the documents sorted out now, for you. I will also inform Charlotte at Bronzeshield, that Yaya will not be coming back."

Adhiambo as well as Yaya kiss Helen very affectionately, paying tribute to all the trouble she has gone to, for the two of them.

"Thank you Helen, my sister Yaya will be of no further trouble to you, we promise."

All the invitations have been sent out for the birthday celebrations, now being treated as a double extravaganza at St Andrew's Road, for the following Sunday. Then the three friends go round to Yaya's digs, at Jude Street, Caning Town, E16. There they recover her meagre belongings. Then on the way to her new home, they stop off at a boutique, to buy her some new clothes. Then Yaya rejoices as she walks into her new home, where she can actually relax and be herself. They all freshen up, taking a well-deserved shower. Then Yaya puts on an ice green high-neck belted tailored slit midi dress, along with a pair of light green kitten heels, prom closed-toe lace strap buckle shoe. Lona decided on and sparkled in a purple velvet wrap lace detail midi dress, her dainty feet encased in a pair of purple suede lace-up open-toe shoe boot. Finally, Adhiambo, as she has already been described as a "Black Beauty".

The three of them head out to the 1117 Côte d'Ivoire club, to tell Sun Nina, the owner, why they were there in the first place. Sun Nina was very sad at the thought of losing two of her most favoured performers. Yet she understood only too readily why they were not going to perform anymore. Nina wished them both a great future. As Adhiambo kissed her goodbye, she invited Sun Nina to their birthday party on the Sunday. Also, they said goodbye to George, the doorman, kissing him and telling him she was going to miss his friendliness. She invited him as well to the shindig. Lona finishes talking to George, then she, Adhiambo and Yaya all wend their way home. Then they all go to bed, ready for the exciting part, the following day.

Then, Anjella, finally makes an appearance, at about half-past midday, going into the room to give them all fair notice.

"Come on you sleeping beauties, time to get up and get ready for your party."

"OK, Mum, we heard you."

"Mum, you are sent from heaven."

Then from the next bedroom Lona shouts:

OK, Anjella! I am making a move."

One at a time they all get showered, all using Adhiambo's selection of perfumes on her dressing table. All three smiling, as they descend the stairs together. All have had their make-up done by Anjella's friend, Suzie, from Suzie Beauty, a stunning young woman herself. Then Jeanette Oromo joined the threesome to make the most alluring female quartet. They are already to receive their guests, first to arrive are all her friends from school. Miss Rachel McGovern turns up shortly afterwards, giving both birthday girls a kiss. Then Chief Inspector Thandie Volance arrives with Inspector Lewson and Constable Tuley. Nina Sun and George arrive together.

Then finally Commander Helen Ball arrives. She has on her person a manilla envelope, which she gives to Yaya.

"This is now your home Yaya, with your sister and your mother. Keep these documents very safe."

Helen cannot conceal her glee as she watches Yaya open the envelope and pull out her birth certificate and three passports. Yaya shouts out to Adhiambo and Anjella:

"MUM, MY DEAREST SISTER, LOOK WHAT I HAVE HERE."

Adhiambo and Anjella both come over to her to see what all the commotion is about, they both look at the documents, then look at Helen.

"What are these, Helen?"

"Obviously you have Yaya's birth certificate. Then you have three passports, which have permanent residence notifications and your work visas for life. I do have one other surprise for you, Adhiambo."

"What in heaven's name could that be, Helen?"

Then out into the garden come Tristina and Ramon, Anjella's mum and dad; Adhiambo's grandmother and grandfather. Both Anjella and her young daughter run up to them, all kissing and cuddling and hugging, as they have not seen each other for such a long time. They then have a family hug, just to consolidate their family bond. The Luo Lake goddess, Adhiambo's and Anjella's *nyamin*, is there also, to share in the celebrations. She also has with her a certain young lady, who cries out on seeing Yaya so happy. Adhiambo gets Yaya, bringing her into the presence of the immortal and her younger sister. They cry, sharing this most intimate moment together. Then, for a few fleeting moments they can actually physically feel each other and speak. The goddess, realising they had not spent enough time together, in their short lives.

Then, Adhiambo turns to all her guests at the party. Thanking Helen, Thandie and Rachel for their great support given to her, she also thanks all her friends and tutors from Plashnet Grove School for making her more assertive, more in control of her life. For improving her self-confidence, self-esteem, self-reliance and self-sufficiency and for making her so streetwise. Then just for a minute or two, she leaves her friends to the party. She would like to talk to you, her readers, if you have the time of course. As young as she is, Adhiambo is adamant that she wants all those savant, sapient girls out there to leave her world with some useful information. This young African girl only wants the best for you and your future.

Her first pearl of wisdom is: never let any outside influences cloud your judgement. Never let anyone deter you from your own self-beliefs or ideals. Your personal growth is down to you, once you believe in something and you know it works for you, that you have in some way felt it steer you away from your problems. Then stick to that belief. Regardless of what other people may try to make, induce and/or enforce upon you according to their way of thinking. Let that be your bible, SELF-BELIEF CAN TAKE YOU BEYOND AND INTO THE NEXT HORIZON.

One other thing that might enrich your life, perhaps more than you can comprehend until you actually commit to this act. My mother taught me this trick, when I was about fourteen. It worked for her against my father, it has worked for me on just a single occasion. If a man tries to interfere with you and you, yes I said you decide you do not want, nor need any unwarranted advances, attentions or any wilful debasing harassments, then your prime objective is to send him on his way, as quickly as possible. With that intention in mind, you need to kick, knee or punch him, as hard as you possibly can in his soft parts. (If you are not sure where that is, they are located in between his legs). Once you have done it, you will always be grateful you did. That you took that moment to make a statement to all possible stalkers and other such vermin, whether in public or private. That you took control and empowered yourself, in that split second. Then two things will happen, as a result of the action you took all by yourself. He will look at you, with a new found respect. Then he will walk away very deflated, knowing he has lost something of great value, especially as a boyfriend, YOU. Of course you, please remember you are a woman and so very priceless.

Second you will realise at that same instant in time, if it does happen to be a boyfriend, he was not the one for you. One last thing, if while on the floor in agony, he swears at you, threatens to do you harm, or even tries to get up to retaliate, ignore the threats. You have just imposed yourself on him once. So all you have to do is kick him once again, in front of everyone if there is an audience. Then turn your back on him and just walk away. Knowing full well that you will not be in that position ever again — you kicked balls once, you can now do it whenever you want.

I just want to say before I go back to my birthday party, thank you all for taking the time to read my story. I do hope you enjoyed it, and good luck with the rest of your life. With my love and warmest wishes.

# GLOSSARY

## Luo Tribal Words

| | |
|---|---|
| Adhiambo | Born in The Evening |
| Aheri | Loving You |
| Mondo | Treasure |
| Nyamin | Blood Sister |
| Nyar Kingi | Princess |
| Oriti Jaherana | Fare Thee Well My Love |
| Oriti Osiepna | Fare Thee Well My Friends |

## Other Words

| | |
|---|---|
| Binch | Type of Meal from Sierra Leone |
| Black Beauty | Hybrid Tea Rose |
| Canjeero | Somali Bread |
| Consanguineous | Of the Same Blood |
| Dried Borana | Somali Goat |
| Macsharo Yariis | Rice and Coconut Cakes |
| Mandazi | Kenyan doughnut. Also known as maandazi, ndao, mahamri or mamri in Mombasa. |
| Old Nana | Great Grandmother |
| Red Maasai | Kenyan Sheep |

Kenyan Folk Song: Little Robin Bird

Little Robin bird,
Little Robin bird
Fell with laughter.
I asked him
I asked him
Striped one, where have you been?
I have been at Koiri,
I have been at Koiri
Spreading pebbles around
And I haven't brought home any banana leaves
They fell into the lake
They fell into the lake
Kamerukias grandmother ate ripe bananas.

Heri Katika Siku Yako Ya Kuzaliwa

Good health and happiness
Good health and happiness
Good health and happiness our beloved Adhiambo
Good health and happiness our beloved Adhiambo.

Quality and long life
Quality and long life
Quality and long life our beloved Adhiambo
Quality and long life our beloved Adhiambo.